MAIN ATTRACTION

"So I get to keep this gig for one more week," Aurora tried to joke. Duncan looked up over his mug. His face was serious.

"You're doing a wonderful job," he said.

She bowed her head. "Thank you, kind sir."

"I mean that. You're a natural out there and you get involved. The audience likes that. Tomorrow the first show airs. I'm sure the public will find you just as lovable—" He stopped midsentence. She wondered what he was about to say.

Aurora stood up. She didn't want him to see what was in her eyes. She knew that whenever he looked at her she felt as if the world tilted a fraction. Walking up behind her, he circled her waist and pulled her back against him. She didn't resist, didn't protest.

He turned her around . . . felt the exact moment when Aurora's resistance evaporated. Her head fell back. His mouth touched hers. Her lips parted. His tongue rushed inside as if an abyss had been created and needed filling. He was there to fill it, and he could think of nothing other than the intoxicating aura that surrounded him, that drove him on, over the edge of sanity. If he didn't stop he'd rip her clothes off in this kitchen and give new meaning to the term gourmet meal . . . .

MIRROR IMAGE

Shirley Hailstock

Pinnacle Books
Kensington Publishing Corp.
http://www.arabesquebooks.com

*To the daughters, sons, sisters, and brothers of Alzheimer's
parents or loved ones. You are not alone*
and
To Christopher D. Coles, III, who came up with the title
Mirror Image, *from a brief verbal synopsis.*

PINNACLE BOOKS are published by

Kensington Publishing Corp.
850 Third Avenue
New York, NY 10022

First Printing: June, 1998
10 9 8 7 6 5 4 3 2 1

Printed in the United States of America

Chapter 1

The camera panned across the row of guests. Marilyn Monroe, Elvis, James Dean, former First Ladies Patricia Nixon and Nancy Reagan, Michael Jordan, and talk show hostess Marsha Chambers smiled and made comments to each other while the audience, prompted by the large, illuminated sign directing them, applauded. The look-alikes sat on the stage and waited for the camera lights to go off, indicating the credits had finished rolling.

Aurora Alexander, the Marsha Chambers look-alike, was the first to stand when the red light on the last camera went out.

She didn't mill around like the others—smiling and making polite conversation with the other guests and the real Marsha Chambers. She headed for the Green Room.

This was the last talk show she was ever going to do, she thought, stepping over electrical cables. No matter how much they paid her, she'd never be humiliated like this again.

"Just what would prompt you to have yourself surgically altered to look like me?" Marsha Chambers had asked her. Aurora could hear the underlying negative tone in the question, but the audience had missed it entirely. They loved this woman. Trained as a social worker, Aurora had talked to women in trouble. She'd learned to read people, read their body language, hear the questions that weren't verbalized, and look for the underlying reason behind the words. Whatever the reasons for Marsha Chambers' comments, she didn't care.

Surgically altered! she thought again, her anger rising with every step. She probably thought Aurora had had her teeth fixed, too. If she'd *had* herself changed, it would be so she *didn't* look like Marsha Chambers. Ever since The *Marsha Chambers Show* aired for the first time Aurora hadn't had an identity to call her own. No matter where she went people mistook her for Marsha Chambers, crowding around her, asking for autographs. Even when she explained that she wasn't Marsha, people didn't believe her. They thought she was trying to remain anonymous, when she was telling the truth. At times it got so bad she had to sign the autographs. This made it worse, since more and more people came, forming a crowd. At one place she caused a near riot. Had it not been for her friend, Nicole, she didn't know how she would have escaped.

In the maze of unfamiliar hallways Aurora found the Green Room and snatched her purse and raincoat. Not bothering to put the coat on, she left the room. Getting away from Marsha Chambers was uppermost in her mind. She stepped over cables and around props as she rushed toward the outside. She suddenly needed to breathe fresh air. She'd been playing this look-alike role for three years, making personal appearances, usually at parties or on local programs, sometimes doing photo sessions for tourists, but it was getting old. She wanted to be herself.

The income helped her pay the expenses for the nursing home where her mother resided. She'd have to find another way to support herself and her mother now. She'd get a job, two jobs. She'd work night and day if she had to, but she wouldn't do this again.

"Can I help you, Ms. Chambers?"

She heard the question as she passed a young woman. Aurora stopped but didn't turn around. She took a deep breath and relaxed her shoulders, damping down her anger. When she faced the smiling young woman she was in control.

"What's your name?" she asked.

"Amy. Amy Peterson. I work in the research department."

"Are you new, Amy? Is this your first job?"

The blonde woman smiled and nodded. She looked to be in her early twenties. "Yes," she said. "I graduated from Smith last May." She paused. "And I'm so glad to be part of the show."

Aurora raised her hand, cutting the young woman off. She recognized the enthusiasm and wished she didn't have to burst the woman's bubble.

"I know you're doing a wonderful job, Amy, and I'm sure Marsha Chambers appreciates it, but I'm not Marsha."

The woman opened her mouth to speak, then shut it.

"They did a taping today of people who look like celebrities. I'm one of them."

"I know," she said. "I mean, I knew they were doing the show." The woman scrutinized her features as if she were a dermatologist checking out a complaint of skin cancer. "If you hadn't told me I'd never have guessed," she finally said.

"No problem." Aurora smiled. She actually felt better. "Good afternoon," she said, and turned to walk away.

Outside the sun shone bright. Aurora squinted. The threat of rain that had prompted her to bring her raincoat was nowhere in sight. It was warm for September.

The studio had been dark, artificial, like Marsha Chambers, all show and no substance. Aurora headed for her car. It wasn't far from the studio door. The parking lot was small. The entire complex was small compared to the major network studios, but this one only housed *The Marsha Chambers Show,* and that was a long way from the major networks. The building was a one story square structure that looked like a renovated warehouse. A large red and white antenna seemed to grow out of the flat roof, giving it an alien appearance. The words *The Marsha Chambers Show* reached into the sky in six-foot letters that mirrored the show's logo.

Aurora shifted her raincoat to her left arm and reached inside her purse for her car keys. She had to look down to find them. When she looked up her heart jumped into her throat and she twisted back, avoiding the white van that zoomed in front of her. It came to an abrupt stop. Aurora's anger flared up again, but she cooled it. There was no need to leave in a state of stress. Show business had seen the last of her. She might as well go with a smile.

Aurora waited a moment for the van to move. When it didn't, she started to go around it. She heard the sliding door wrench open and someone get out. Glancing over her shoulder, she thought she'd see who'd been so rude. What she saw was a blur. Someone grabbed her from behind. It was a man. She smelled his aftershave. His hand covered her mouth and his knee dug into her kidneys. Aurora panicked. Without consciously thinking about it she struggled, but he was strong. She felt the muscles in his arms as she tried to pull the hand away from her mouth to scream. She tasted the oily leather of a work glove.

He dragged her backward. He was trying to pull her into the van. She twisted and turned, digging her feet into the ground, fighting against his superior strength. Her heart raced, pounding blood through her system. Who was this? What did he want with her? His gloved hand was in her mouth. She bit down on it hard. The surprise made him yank his hand away, as she'd expected. In the split second before the surprise wore off she balled her hand into a fist, and—concentrating all her strength in one elbow—she delivered a punishing blow into the soft flesh of his stomach.

Twisting away, she yelled for help. He wore a ski mask, and his hair was concealed behind a blue and white knitted cap. Fear ran through her at the alien effect of him. His entire body was dressed in black, as if it were night and he'd wanted to blend into the darkness. He wore tennis shoes. Aurora wished she had hers on. She'd worn a navy blue silk jumpsuit and high heels. It was all part of the impersonation. Marsha Chambers was taller than she was, and the heels gave her more of the image she'd wanted to have today. Now she was sorry.

He came after her, grabbing for her. Aurora screamed, running away. Looking over her shoulder she saw him coming, getting closer and closer. He was going to catch her. She filled her lungs with air and rushed forward, trying to reach the building, trying to get to the door, where there would be help.

Hands closed over her shoulders and she was pushed to the ground. They rolled over and over on the unyielding concrete driveway. Contact with the ground tore through the thin fabric protection of her suit and ripped the skin on her shoulder. Pain shot through her arm. She kicked herself free and tried getting to her feet. One of the heels of her shoes broke, and she couldn't get her balance before he was on her again. Frightened, she fought him, kicking and screaming, using her hands as weapons, but he wouldn't be thwarted.

"Marsha!" she heard someone shout. Instinctively they both looked in the direction of the voice. A man ran toward them. The masked man jumped to his feet. Quickly he looked from her to the van. He was breathing hard. He headed for the vehicle. In the time it took for

the Good Samaritan to reach her the van roared out of
the driveway, spitting gravel in its wake.

Duncan West never thought he'd find himself running to the rescue of Marsha Chambers. He'd heard
the scream and looked through the studio window. He'd
seen the struggle and without thinking rushed through
the door. Someone was trying to abduct her. The man
was gone now and Marsha pulled herself into a tight
ball and rocked back and forth like a frightened child.

"Marsha?" he questioned quietly. Even though he
and the popular hostess didn't quite mesh he knew
trauma when he saw it, and she'd been attacked. He
could almost feel sorry for her. He didn't want to make
any sudden moves.

People came out of the building behind him. "Marsha!" someone screamed. "She's been hurt." Joyce
Conrad, Marsha's secretary, rushed toward him.

Duncan stood up and grabbed her as she flung herself
toward the woman cowering on the ground.

"Stop, Joyce." She strained against him. "Look at
me." Duncan took the woman's chin in his hand and
pulled her attention to him. "Concentrate on me. Marsha's been hurt." He purposely didn't say attacked. "Go
inside and get the doctor. Then call the police."

The woman tried to look at Marsha, but Duncan kept
her attention on his face. Joyce was one of the few
people who seemed to get along with the talk show
hostess. She'd been with Marsha for seven years. The
loyalty they shared baffled him.

"She needs your help, Joyce. Go and get the doctor
and the police."

Joyce looked directly at him. Her expression changed
as she tried to focus. Without hysteria she would follow
his instructions. He let her go and she turned toward
the building. Duncan went back to Marsha, who was

still huddling on the ground. He took a step forward, and the frightened woman scuttled back.

He held his hands out toward her, palms up. "Marsha, it's me, Duncan."

She stared at him, her eyes wide and frightened. "I don't know you," she said, pushing herself farther away.

"You're all right," he said. He went closer. "He's gone." She moved again and Duncan stopped. "Marsha—"

"I'm not Marsha. My name is Aurora. Aurora Alexander."

She *wasn't* Marsha. "You were on the show?" She was one of the look-alikes. The woman nodded.

Dr. Marvin Taylor joined him, and a crowd followed.

"Marv, thank heaven you're here." Duncan glanced at the crowd, then whispered, "Someone was trying to attack her."

"He was trying to force me into a van," she said in a surprisingly strong voice. Obviously she had good ears, too.

"I think she's hurt."

Marv took a step toward her and again she moved away. Blood ran over her arm and onto her suit. Both knees had been grazed. One bled onto the tear in the fabric, while the other was stained. Her hair was disheveled and she was obviously in pain, and she distrusted them all.

Duncan squatted in front of her. "We're only trying to help," he whispered. She looked at him and for a moment he thought he could see something soften deep in her eyes. He held her gaze for a moment, then extended his hand.

The crowd behind them was getting larger. Soon the entire studio would be gawking at her.

"Why don't we go inside?" Marv suggested. "It'll be more private."

Duncan glanced at Aurora. She nodded.

"Can you stand?" he asked.

"I think so."

He offered a hand and she took it. It was slender and delicate, but strong when he pulled her to her feet.

"Ouch," she groaned as her knees began to buckle. Instinctively Duncan put his arm around her waist to support her. "My knees," she said, reaching toward them with a moan.

Marv went to support her other side but Duncan reached down and lifted her off the ground. He turned and nodded for Marv to lead the way. The crowd parted, hushed and quiet, as they passed through en route to the studio infirmary. Like the others, the crowd mistook her for Marsha. Duncan heard voices whispering Marsha's name and asking what had happened.

Dr. Marvin Taylor was usually on site when filming took place, always prepared for the possibility of injuries to the crew. It was rare that any of the guests needed his services.

The small area outside the infirmary examination room was empty except for Duncan. He perched on the arm of a green leather sofa, looking at the other empty chairs and feeling rather helpless. He didn't like what he'd seen. Someone had tried to force her into a van. He knew the show could be liable for such a mishap. Security wasn't that tight, but then, why should it be? The only thing they did here was film Marsha's show.

He clenched his teeth, thinking of Marsha and her insistence that they set up a studio for her here in Princeton, New Jersey. It had forced him to leave Hollywood, where he had friends and connections. It was the place to be if you wanted to make movies. He'd wanted to film the program at the headquarters of Paradine Studios, but she'd insisted she wouldn't leave New Jersey to return to California.

Duncan knew she hadn't wanted to do the show in the first place. She thought she'd ask for the moon and the studio would back out. Her contract terms were outrageous. She'd asked for everything—control of topics, approval of editing, no reruns during season, her own personal researchers, hiring and firing authority over practically everybody from God down to the gardeners. To his dismay the network went for it, everything except hiring and firing. He'd deal with the fallout, but he needed to be sure she wouldn't fire the lot in anger.

It had worked for Marsha, too. Better than she probably thought, and she thought highly. The show soared in the ratings. Even on the East coast she was the hottest property in television. And now they could be in for a lawsuit over one of the look-alike guests.

The door opened and Aurora came in. Her complexion was a bit pale, but otherwise she looked fine.

"Are you all right?" Duncan stood.

"She's fine," Marv answered, joining them in the small room. "She's a little shaky, and her arm and leg are going to be sore for a day or two, but otherwise there are no physical problems. I think we should get someone to take her home."

"I'll see to it," Duncan said. He didn't mean to stare but he couldn't help himself. Aurora Alexander looked enough like Marsha Chambers to be her twin. The height, the color-of-midnight hair, the nail polish Marsha endorsed, even the smirk on her mouth, were all signature Marsha Chambers. She had the exact same kind of widow's peak at the top of her heart-shaped face as Marsha. Her eyes were different, however. Aurora's were dark brown with the slightest almond shape to them, while Marsha's had been described as melting. Photographers constantly asked her to face the light to show them off. Only the eyes and the disheveled hair and torn clothing separated Aurora from the original.

"Hi," said a voice behind them.

Duncan turned, glad to have a distraction. Joyce stood in the doorway.

"Just making sure everything's all right." She came into the center of the room, leaving the door open.

"It is," Aurora said.

"Good." She smiled. "I can't tell you how fast my heart beat when I saw you lying on the ground."

"Thank you for the concern. I'll be all right."

Joyce was such a good person. She had the ability to make anyone feel comfortable. He couldn't fathom how she and Marsha had hooked up together and why Marsha never seemed to steam-roll over her.

"Do you need me to call a car for you?"

Before anyone could answer another voice commanded attention.

"What's going on here?"

Marsha Chambers had arrived—*more like she made an entrance,* Duncan thought. He looked past Joyce. Marsha took a step into the room. Behind her several other people entered, interested in the commotion she invariably caused. Aurora certainly didn't need more attention after she'd been attacked, and Marsha would surely make a circus of her misfortune.

Joyce supplied the answer to her question. "Ms. Alexander had an accident. She's going to be all right."

"Someone tried to kidnap me," Aurora corrected.

"Kidnap!" Marsha seized the word. Her hand went to her throat in a dramatic gesture and she took a step back. Then she glanced around as if looking for someone. Duncan knew she was remembering the last time.

"It was a mistake," Aurora said. "He probably thought I was you."

"Did you see who it was?" Marsha asked in a throaty voice.

"No." Aurora shook her head. "But no one would have any reason to kidnap me."

"Marsha," Duncan broke in. The small room was already full of people and more had gathered outside. The two women obviously didn't like each other, and he didn't need a full scale argument to provide another slanderous story for the tabloids on the checkout count-

ers of grocery stores across the country. "I was about
to see Ms. Alexander home."

He put his hand on her lower back and pushed her
slightly forward. Marsha stood her ground for a
moment, preventing them from passing. Duncan wondered what the situation meant. The two women didn't
know each other. Why was Marsha so hostile, and Aurora
the same? Marsha had asked some unscheduled questions during the taping, but she often did that. The
audience hadn't noticed anything out of line. He knew
that. He checked audience reaction as if he were a
public relations man. He didn't want anything airing
that could damage her image. That, too, was part of
her contract.

"Excuse me," Aurora said. "I didn't mean to cause
such a problem for your show."

Surprisingly, Marsha smiled and moved aside. Duncan knew she felt as if she'd won. He glanced at Aurora.
There hadn't been any malice in her statement. She'd
sounded royal, like a queen who'd learned duty from
childhood, or someone with old money who knew when
it was time to diffuse a situation. He admired her for
it. If she didn't look so much like Marsha Chambers he
might want to get to know this woman, but with her
face he only wanted to get as far away from her as
possible.

Duncan kept his hand pressed against Aurora's waist.
She felt the warmth of his fingers spread through layers
of clothing to her skin, and she didn't mind it at all.
Initially she'd left the room without limping, but when
Duncan rounded a corner out of sight of the crowd,
her knee hurt too much for her to keep up the pretense.

"I'm sorry," he apologized. "I forgot about your leg."

They took it slower as he led her back to his office,
where he gathered his suit coat and keys. It was a large
office with bookshelves covering most of two walls.

Three Emmy Awards sat on one of the shelves. On the other walls were pictures of him with various Hollywood stars and certificates of achievement from several creative associations. His desk was a huge, carved mahogany structure that was covered with papers and scripts. Aurora had never heard of Duncan West before the job offer for the show came along, but obviously Hollywood was well acquainted with him and his achievements.

He pulled his jacket on and turned back to her. "Ready?"

"I thought you were going to call a car." She knew the other look-alikes had been brought in by limousine. She assumed he was going to have a secretary call one for her. She didn't live very far and she'd driven herself to the studio. Her own car was still in the parking lot. "I can drive myself home. I didn't come in a limousine."

"Marv said someone should take you home, and I need to get out of here for a while."

Aurora didn't argue.

Duncan picked up the phone. "I'll arrange to have your car delivered." He spoke quickly and efficiently, lowering the mouthpiece to ask for her keys. Aurora handed them over. Duncan replaced the receiver and led her to his car. It was black, sleek, and fast as she expected it would be. With the touch of a doctor, he helped her inside. His hands no longer felt warm, as they had during their walk to his office. Somewhere between the examination room and his office he'd turned cold.

He drove with the same efficiency he'd used in speaking on the phone. His movements were tight, controlled, and without effort or flare. She remained quiet until they reached her house in Rocky Hill.

"It's the third driveway." She pointed to a two-car driveway flanked by waist-high rows of hedges. The driveway curved in a circle in front of the house, and the hedges gave way to flowers. Chrysanthemums and roses bloomed in colorful profusion, giving a welcome greeting each time someone came out or went into the large, white house with green shutters.

Duncan stopped the car in front of the door. Aurora reached for the handle, but he was already out and coming to her side. He helped her to her feet, then turned toward the house.

"This is a big house," he commented.

She nodded. She'd grown up here, and it was the only house she'd ever lived in. Her parents had lived here before their divorce. She, her sisters, and brother had grown up here, dated, married, and then left to pursue lives of their own. With her mother in a nursing home, the sprawling colonial was now hers alone.

"Would you like to come in for a moment?" she found herself asking. Even though he now seemed cool toward her, she had the feeling he was not looking forward to confronting Marsha Chambers before it was necessary.

Aurora unlocked the door and turned off the security alarm. Duncan closed the door, and she noticed him looking around. The house had a center hall foyer with stairs at the far end. Rooms sat on both sides of it. Aurora dropped her purse on the circular table, which had always held fresh flowers when her mother was in residence. Now it held a large crystal vase with colored marbles and stalks of silk flowers that needed dusting.

"Would you like something to drink?"

"Coffee?"

"Hazelnut?" Aurora smiled.

"Fine."

"Why don't you wait in there while I get it?" She pointed toward the living room. Duncan walked toward it.

In the kitchen she quickly set up the coffeemaker, then hobbled up the back stairs and dumped the ripped, bloodstained clothes for a pair of loose-fitting slacks and a white cotton blouse. The fabric whispered against her sensitive skin, but did not irritate it.

When she joined Duncan carrying a tray, he was looking at the photos of her sisters on the mantlepiece. He didn't mention her change of clothes. She placed the tray on the coffee-table and sat down, stretching her leg out under the table.

"It's good you have an alarm system," he said.

"Why?" she asked. "You don't really think that guy was trying to kidnap me?"

"No, but it's better to be cautious." He sat down in the chair opposite her and took his cup.

"She's been kidnapped before, hasn't she?"

Duncan's head came up and he stared deeply at her. "How did you know that?"

"Her reaction to the word. People who have never been kidnapped would be surprised. Marsha Chambers had fear in her eyes, a horrible fear."

Duncan set his cup on the tray and leaned forward. His tie hung loosely in front of him. "Three years ago, Marsha was kidnapped by two fans. She was leaving her apartment in New York to go to an exercise club. A limousine was sitting by the curb and she got in, as she did every morning. The fans took her for a ride around the city, kept her with them all day, served her a nice dinner of her favorite foods, and returned her unhurt to her apartment. The whole thing was done in less than twenty-four hours."

"That sounds like a publicity stunt." Aurora knew they didn't do those anymore. "Or at least great copy."

Duncan smiled. It was the first time she'd seen him do that, and a small tingle started in her stomach.

"Marsha was livid. She moved out of New York and refused to allow any of it to be publicized. Not even the tabloids got wind of that story."

"What happened to the fans? Marsha doesn't strike me as the kind of person who would forgive and forget."

"You're amazingly perceptive," Duncan said. "I thought the same thing myself, but Marsha said she wanted the incident behind her. No one has mentioned it since. Today, however, it must have all come back to her."

Aurora almost felt sorry for the talk show hostess. She should have been flattered by the attention, yet Aurora had the feeling she wasn't. Something more than she'd let on had happened. She knew that. It had been her job to read between the lines, know the body language, search for telltale signs of lying, and Marsha Chambers had all the signs of a woman keeping a terrible secret. She didn't think Duncan knew it.

She tested him. "Do you think that's all that happened?"

"What do you mean?"

"I don't know," she lied. Aurora's experience in dealing with runaways and distraught women had taught her to see and hear more than appeared as face value. She felt Duncan was telling the truth, but she also felt Marsha was hiding something. "Since the act was so benevolent, I'd have thought she'd want the publicity."

"Marsha doesn't need publicity."

Not now, Aurora thought, *but three years ago she did. Her show was just beginning and she wasn't in the news all the time. Why did that incident go untold?*

Pulling her leg up, she had to use her hand to reposition it. Shifting to a more comfortable seat, Aurora poured more coffee into her cup. Duncan declined when she offered him more. He was quiet for a moment. Aurora felt uncomfortable under his stare.

"What?" she asked when it went on so long.

He hesitated, looking intently at her. "I wonder."

"Wonder what?" Aurora felt as if she had lipstick on her nose, or something. His gaze roved over her face. She saw him checking her hairline.

"Do you and Marsha know each other?"

She frowned. "You mean before we met today?"

He nodded.

Aurora shook her head. "When she was the weather girl for WNJP we happened to be in the same place one afternoon. We were having lunch in the same restaurant. Her table was filled with studio executives and I was across the room with a friend. She never saw me, that I can say. When I left the restaurant, she was still there.''

"The two of you seemed to dislike each other so intensely that I thought you'd met before.''

Aurora dropped her head. The anger threatened to return, but she tempered it. "She assumed I'd had surgery to look like her. I haven't. I don't even know any plastic surgeons.''

She knew plenty of doctors, orthopedists, psychiatrists, psychologists, physical therapists, and dental surgeons, but she'd never come in contact with a plastic surgeon. With the women in abusive relationships, it almost never progressed as far as needing plastic surgery. In the severest cases the progression passed any kind of surgery at all. Usually the abuse went over the edge, and they were killed by the men they professed to love and who professed to love them.

"Her assumption today that I'd physically altered my appearance angered me. Marsha appears insecure, but that's to be expected in her field.''

"You're younger than she is.''

"Only by four years. Not enough for her to feel threatened. I have no intention of being a talk show hostess. If I let logic prevail, I can assume her questions come from jealousy because someone else is reaping the benefits of her hard work. If that's the case, then I owe her a sincere apology. I have no doubt that she worked and sacrificed to get where she is, and I come along with a face that matches hers and get job offers for that reason only.''

Duncan checked his watch. "I have to go now. Do you have someone to help you?'' He stood up.

Aurora thought of her mother. Even if she were here she would be no help.

"I'm fine, Duncan.'' She moved to get up, grimacing

as her knees argued with her decision. Duncan took her hand and helped her to her feet. His face was only inches from hers. She could feel his breath and smell his aftershave. The warmth between them threatened to turn to fire. She didn't dare look into his eyes or he'd see the confusion his touch had thrown her into. "You needn't worry about me," she whispered.

Duncan released her, and to her surprise her knees locked to keep her from falling over.

"You look tired," he said. "I'd feel better if you had someone with you."

Was she dreaming, or had she heard a catch in his voice? He looked directly at her. Was he seeing her or Marsha Chambers? Aurora was still wearing the makeup that highlighted her cheekbones to give them the same shadows Marsha had.

"I live here alone."

"Isn't there someone you can call? What about one of the people in the photos?"

"They're my sisters, and they don't live nearby." She hobbled along with him to the door.

"A neighbor, then." He paused. "You're going to need help getting up those stairs."

Aurora wasn't looking forward to climbing the steps, but she could do it. She'd already gone up and down them once. "If I need anything that I can't do for myself I promise I'll call someone."

Duncan shrugged and opened the door. Three bells sounded, and he looked up.

"It's the alarm system," she explained. "It tells me a door has opened. It will also signal if the windows or the sliding glass doors are opened. So you see, I'm quite all right."

"It can't signal anyone that you're stuck in the bathtub and drowning."

"I don't take baths. I shower." Again the chemistry between them began to burn. She felt as if the air was heavy, that it was pressing on her.

"Today you need a good soak." His voice was hoarse.

"Yes, Doctor."

He left with another of those smiles that made the flutters in her stomach take precedence over the pain in her knee. Aurora closed the door as he pulled around the driveway. She didn't know what to make of Duncan West. He wasn't like any of the men she'd met in the past, especially men in show business. She was leaving show business. So Duncan West was only a small diversion on her way out of the limelight.

Hobbling across the foyer, she thought of his suggestion that she soak her leg and decided that was the best thing for it. Her progress was slower, since her leg had tightened from sitting. She had only reached the bottom step when the doorbell rang. Had he forgotten something? Hope sprang unbidden in her chest as she went slowly back. Pushing the curtain aside, she didn't see Duncan but her neighbor, Megan.

"What are you doing here?" she asked, pulling her door fully open.

"Are you all right?" Megan asked.

"Sure, why?"

"This gorgeous man knocked on my door and told me you'd had an accident. He said I should come over and make sure you don't drown."

Aurora laughed. Megan came in. "I'm fine, Megan. I was mistaken for Marsha Chambers by an enthusiastic fan."

"He wasn't the fan, was he?"

"He's the show's producer." A mental picture of Duncan West flittered through her mind. She'd liked him instantly. After her initial shock at the kidnapping had worn off she'd thought he wasn't the most handsome man she'd ever seen, but there was something about him that made her take notice—something compelling enough to make any woman remember him. She could only describe it as sex appeal. *No,* she corrected, *pure sex.* And he seemed unaware of it.

He had wide, brown eyes and a nose that was a little patrician, but sensual lips that demanded tasting. Hadn't she wanted to turn her face to his and sample that perfect mouth? Cleanshaven, with neatly cut hair, he had wide shoulders, a trim waist, and powerful legs.

Megan brought her back from the sensual dream. "What was that comment about drowning?"

"I'm going to take a bath and he thought I might need help getting in and out of the tub."

"Of course. I'll help you."

"There's no need, Megan. I can do it myself. You know how some men still think we're wilting flowers." Aurora turned toward the stairs. "I do think he's right about the bath."

Megan, the mothering type, insisted on helping Aurora despite her protest. The moment she got the bathtub full of water, Aurora insisted she leave her to take care of everything else. Megan agreed to make tea while Aurora bathed, telling her she would check every few minutes. Aurora smiled, liking the attention. It was like having her mother back for a little while.

As Aurora sank into the heaping bubbles Duncan West came back to her consciousness. What an enigma he proved to be. In her thirty years no one had ever thought of taking care of her except for her parents. With her mother's present condition, Aurora was the caregiver. Now Duncan, a man she hadn't known before today, had come to her rescue and made her feel like a pampered princess.

Chapter 2

Duncan found himself smiling as he drove through the crowded streets of Princeton Borough. He stopped at the light at Witherspoon and Nassau Streets. The main gates of Princeton University faced him. September brought the return of students to the centuries old institution. Normally, their migration about and around the narrow streets filled him with dread. Before today Duncan had considered the students in his way, but at the moment he didn't mind the congestion.

He smiled with open admiration at a pretty coed who crossed in front of his car. The windows were down. The air was fresh and he had a new attitude. Could it have anything to do with meeting Aurora Alexander?

She intrigued him. He couldn't say why. He wanted to know her better, and he hadn't felt like that in years. In her living room, he hadn't wanted to leave. He'd wanted to ask her questions about the pictures on the mantel, about how she'd come to the show, how she felt about playing Marsha, new trends in music, the arts; he wanted to ask her about everything in the world.

He frowned suddenly, remembering Marsha and how

much one woman looked like the other. Strange, he thought, while he talked to Aurora he hadn't thought of Marsha, yet their faces were mirror images. The light turned green and he sailed through it on his way back to the studio.

Marsha was livid when he arrived. He could hear her voice long before he got to his office. Normally she would have been gone, but tonight she was still there. Duncan dropped his jacket in his office and entered the studio.

She attacked him the moment she turned and saw him. "And where have you been? I suppose the little maiden needed mouth-to-mouth resuscitation."

Duncan looked about the room. Joyce was there, and the cameramen. The entire crew was in residence. They all stood in front of Marsha like servants being reprimanded for stealing silver. Marsha knew better than to throw one of her tantrums in front of the full complement of people who supported her.

"Would you all excuse us?" Duncan spoke to the room. His voice was calm, as if a normal staff meeting had ended on an upbeat note. "Your work today was appreciated. We'll see you tomorrow."

"What are you doing?" Marsha screamed.

Duncan raised his hand and quieted her. The room cleared, and when the door closed he turned on her.

"Don't you ever do anything like that again." Gone was the calm. His voice was still quiet but menacingly low. "Those people make it possible for you to go on the air, which you are under contract to do, so don't you take it into your head that you have the right to detain them and prevent them from doing their jobs. Some of them have been with this show since it began, and I will not have you acting like a spoiled child and keeping them here for no reason except selfishness. They have families and lives to get to."

"Is that what they were doing today?" she ranted. "A

kidnapper came practically onto the stage, and nobody seemed to take it seriously."

"We all took it seriously, Marsha." He kept his voice controlled, refusing to let her draw him into one of her shouting matches. The attempt had taken place in the parking lot, nowhere near the stage, but Marsha had rescripted the action in her mind. "Ms. Alexander is fine. The doctor examined her and she'll be back to normal in a few days."

"Why did you personally have to see her home or wherever you took her? You should have been here."

"That you're right about, Marsha," he flung at her. "Had I been here you never would have kept the crew in this room like naughty pupils."

"I needed to find out who was responsible for this. I wanted the whole story." She'd lowered her voice.

"You thought you could get it from them?" He pointed toward the closed door. "Most of them weren't even there."

"What about security, Duncan? Why didn't the guards keep that man off the grounds? How could he possibly get close enough to actually take someone in the lot? And what if it had been me?"

She really didn't want the answer to that question, Duncan thought. He took a deep breath, restraining himself from saying exactly what he felt. It had been a long day and he really needed to get relaxed and unwind. He wasn't in the mood for a fight.

"Marsha, we really don't know the man was here to kidnap you. I know it happened before, but that was harmless. The fans only wanted to meet you and they did nothing to harm you."

He checked her closely, looking for the fear Aurora had mentioned, but Marsha averted her gaze.

"I'll have security increased in the morning," he said, rubbing his eyes wearily. "No one without cause to be here will be able to get on the premises. Will that satisfy you?"

"What about my house?"

His head came up and he stared at her. "You want a guard at your house?"

She hesitated a second. "Yes!" she said. Duncan knew she couldn't, wouldn't, back down.

"If you want a guard, I'll see that you have one tonight." He was too tired to argue anymore. Marsha could have a guard. If it would make her feel better and keep the show running smoothly, he would make sure she had one.

"Thank you," she said with all the vehemence of an unsatisfied child.

Duncan sank into one of the audience chairs. It was red, with plush cushions and a comfortable back. He stared at Marsha, thinking of the other woman. How much they looked alike, yet how different they seemed. He thought of what Aurora had said. Had something more happened to Marsha when she was kidnapped? Was she hiding something?

Duncan knew that if he asked Marsha she wouldn't answer him. They had worked together since this show first aired, and he'd come to know that she only gave as much information about herself as she wanted people to know.

"Marsha—"

"Duncan—"

They both spoke at the same time. Duncan nodded for her to continue.

"I don't really think that man was trying to kidnap me, but it's not a bad idea to have some more security."

Duncan had already agreed to that. He sat forward, loosening his tie and opening the top button of his shirt, wondering where this was going.

"Maybe it would be good to have that girl back."

"What girl?" he asked.

"The one who looked . . . resembled me."

"Her name is Aurora," Duncan supplied, feeling a strange need to defend Aurora Alexander. Marsha waved her hand as if she couldn't care less if the woman had a name. "What would she return for? Are you thinking of another show idea?"

"Not a show." She faced him, taking the seat to his left. "Give her a job. Something not too close to me. Have her on the set and always make sure she's in the audience during the taping."

Duncan frowned, shifting in his chair. "Why?"

"To foil the kidnappers," Marsha said, as if he should know what she meant. The truth was, Duncan didn't have a clue. Luckily, Marsha went on to explain. "I know the last time it was only fans and they didn't hurt me, but I don't have time for that now. And if ... Aurora," she said, emphasizing the middle syllable, "if she were on site it would confuse anyone who tried to get to me."

"Marsha, there are no *real* kidnappers, are there?" Something Aurora had said made him ask. He studied her for any sign of insincerity. There was none, but Marsha Chambers was a good actress. If she *was* hiding something, he was unable to see it.

"Of course not," she answered with the right amount of surprise in her eyes. "It's just that right now I've got this show." She glanced at the raised platform where she sat each day to begin the filming of the syndicated talk show. "I'm also studying for the movie part in a few months. My nerves are on edge, and I don't want to offend any fans if they do manage a kidnapping." She stopped to take a breath, and Duncan had the feeling this speech had been rehearsed. "If we have Aurora on site she can possibly help if anything happens. I'm not expecting anything, mind you, but we should be prepared."

Marsha knew just the right buttons to push and when to push them. Duncan agreed; they needed to be pre-

pared. He felt responsible for the lax security. Every day
he arrived at the studio and nothing was out of order.
Setting the place up as a secure compound hadn't
seemed necessary. In the three years they'd been here
nothing had happened. Had they been in Hollywood,
they would have had to have security. He knew how too
much fan enthusiasm could harm a person. Fans didn't
seem to think of a celebrity as only one person, and
they were a mob. Yet here there had been no mobs, even
when superstars were guests on the show. The crowds
formed, and the guards controlled them. They were
orderly, happy people, hoping to get into the studio to
be part of the show. No incident had ever required
more than a couple of guards to control it.

"I'll ask her, Marsha," Duncan said, "but I'm not
sure she'll return after the way you treated her today."

The expression on Marsha's face was priceless. She
couldn't conceive of anyone not wanting to be on her
show. It was the highest rated daytime talk show, and
she had the Emmys to prove it.

"Barring the kidnap attempt, you weren't especially
courteous with your questions."

"I have no idea what you're talking about."

"I'm talking about the crack you made to her about
having surgery to look like you."

Marsha had the nerve to look as if she'd never made
the comment. Duncan almost laughed. That movie part
she was studying for might garner her an Oscar, but
nothing could rival the performance she was giving for
him.

"I can tell a snip job when I see it, and I'd swear
that's not the nose she was born with."

Duncan stood up. The smile on his face must have
shown all his teeth. "It's a good thing you're only
booked into Atlantic City once a year," Duncan said.
"Because dropping bets like that would lose you more
than that silk blouse you're wearing."

"You seem to have learned an awful lot about Ms. Alexander in the amount of time it took for you to drive her home."

"No, Marsha." He headed toward the back of the studio. "You're making it sound as if I'm interested in Aurora. That's not the case. She's a good person, that I learned. I also learned she doesn't even know a plastic surgeon." He paused and looked her directly in the eyes. "Now, can we say that about you?"

The smell of baking bread wafted through the air. Aurora stood in her kitchen up to her elbows in flour and spices. The counter was full of breads: banana bread, braided challah, cornbread muffins, crescent rolls, cinnamon rolls. She hummed the refrain of "On a Clear Day You Can See Forever." The morning sun shone through her windows and made the room warm and comfortable. She remembered her mother baking breads there while she sat at the table in the breakfast nook eating them warm, butter dripping from the edges.

She'd see her mother this morning, take the bread to the nursing home where she lived. Cassandra Alexander, who'd been called Cass since the third grade, loved warm bread, and Aurora always brought enough for the nurses and a few of her mother's friends. Unfortunately, her mother did not recognize the people in the nursing home from one day to the next. She also didn't recognize her own daughter, but Aurora continued to go and continued to talk to her.

She couldn't say it didn't hurt, and that she didn't hope one day her mother would know her when she walked in, but so far she'd been disappointed every time. Yet she continued to follow the ritual of coming the first of every month. Her sisters and brother couldn't do it. They didn't live close by, and even when they visited they didn't like seeing their mother in that state.

She didn't know them and having her there with no memory was like a deep, cutting wound. Aurora understood, but she made the short trip monthly and hoped each time it would be different.

Aurora opened the oven door. Welcome heat hit her in the face. This batch of rolls had sugar and cinnamon in them and Aurora would smear icing on them, allowing it to drip over the sides. The cinnamon smell made her mouth water. Pulling her oven mittens on she lifted the pan out and set it on a shell trivet on the counter. Checking her watch, she had just enough time to clean up and pack the car.

Racing around the kitchen as much as her sore leg and shoulder would allow, she got everything into the dishwasher and pressed the wash button. Then she cleaned the flour off her arms and pulled her sleeves down. She placed the warm bread and rolls in boxes lined with tinfoil.

As she set the last box in the car and went to turn the alarm system on, the doorbell rang.

"Who is that?" she asked. It was probably Megan checking on her. She didn't have time for anyone if she were going to get to the nursing home while the bread was still warm. The double doors, which her mother had insisted on buying at a time they couldn't afford them, had oval shaped, beveled glass in them. The specially made curtains which her mother had sewn still hung in front of them. Aurora peered through one of them and saw Duncan West.

He was the last person she expected to see, but that didn't keep her heart from fluttering as if it had only then learned how to beat.

Taking a deep breath she opened the door. "Good morning."

"I hope I'm not disturbing you. I'd like to talk to you, if its convenient." His voice was low and dark, even in the daylight.

"I'm sorry," she said. "I'm on my way out and I can't wait."

"I should have called. I'll come back later."

He started to turn away. Aurora saw his car behind him. The same car he'd driven her home in yesterday.

"You could come with me," she heard herself saying. She didn't even recognize her own voice. It was lower than usual, deeper, at least an octave below her normal range, and *sexier*.

He turned back. A smile curved his lips but didn't show any teeth.

"How's your leg?" he asked, stepping into the foyer and following her back to the kitchen.

"It's stiff but I can manage." She tried not to limp, but the pain gave her away.

From the kitchen they went to her car in the garage. Duncan had had it delivered yesterday. She got in and tested her ability to move her leg from the accelerator to the brake. Surprisingly enough, it was less painful to move when she sat down.

"Where are we going?" Duncan asked several minutes later when she'd backed down the driveway.

"To see my mother."

"Where does she live?" He glanced at the boxes covering the back seat. "In a bakery?"

Aurora smiled. "She's in a nursing home and she likes bread. Each time I go I bring fresh bread for her."

"It smells delicious."

"Why don't you open that top box and have some?"

He reached over her shoulder and grabbed the box. A breath of his cologne reached her over the aroma of the bread. It made her stomach flip. Opening the box she smelled the heat and sugar of the rolls, but seeing his expression as he bit into one of the soft buns had her nipples growing hard. The man was sexy even when he wasn't trying.

"God, these are heavenly."

"Thank you." She bowed her head as much as she could while still keeping her eyes on the road.

"You made these? No wonder your mother loves them. Maybe you should open a bakery."

"It's an idea."

Aurora slowed the car as a white rural fence came into view. At an opening in the railing she saw the green and white letters announcing The Skillman Nursing Home. Pulling the car into a space near the door she cut the engine and got out. Duncan opened his door and stood. They stared at each other over the roof of the car. For the first time Aurora thought of what she had done. She'd brought a man to meet her mother. Was he reading anything into this? She hadn't thought of it, but she didn't know Duncan well—barely twenty-fours hours had passed since they met. Yet she felt a chemistry with him. She knew chemistry wasn't enough. She'd let it lead her before. If there wasn't something else to the relationship, it simply would not work.

"Where should I take these?"

He was holding a stack of boxes. She snapped out of her musings and grabbed the remaining boxes. Then she headed for the front entrance. Two nurses met them at the door.

"It's so good to see you again, Ms. Alexander," one of them said as she took the boxes from her arms. "I know your mother will be glad to get these." She walked a short distance and set the boxes on a table. Duncan did the same.

"You're limping," the other nurse said. "What happened?"

"Nothing," Aurora lied. "I fell down and skinned my knee."

"Did you see a doctor? We could get Dr. James to look at it."

"I saw a doctor. I'll be back to my usual self in a few days." The nurse smiled but looked concerned. "Most of these are for the staff," Aurora said as she always did, and the nurse's expressions changed to a show of appreciation. "I'll take a few for Mom and her friends."

Aurora took three boxes, including the one Duncan had eaten from, and turned to him. "There's a waiting room at the end of the hall," she said. "I won't be long."

He grabbed her arm as she moved to go. "I'd like to meet your mother," he said.

Aurora's eyes opened wider. She glanced at the nurse.

"She's in the art room," the woman said with a nod. She left, carrying several of the boxes.

Aurora set her boxes back on the table and faced Duncan. "My mother has Alzheimer's Disease," she told him with a catch in her voice. "She doesn't know me. She doesn't remember her friends, her other children, even my father. We're all strangers to her."

"Do you mind if I meet her?"

"Of course not."

He picked up the boxes. "Then lead."

Cass Alexander stood before a canvas by a closed window at the end of the first floor. Aurora and Duncan entered the room. It had pictures on the walls, and art books graced several shelves, but mostly it had easels standing in various places about the room. Aurora went to her mother and stood there waiting for Cass to turn and see her.

A moment later the woman turned. "Hello," she said with a smile. "Do you paint?"

Aurora shook her head and did not speak.

"I like to paint. This is a picture of that tree over there." Aurora followed the direction of her pointing finger and saw a leafless oak tree in the distance. Staring back at her mother's picture, she saw the likeness was much like one a third grader would do, but she *had* captured the fact that it was a tree.

She wondered if deep inside her mother had returned to being a third grader.

"Do I know you, Dear?" she asked, facing her painting.

"I'm Aurora, Mom. You used to call me Rory."

Her mother stopped painting and looked at her. "You must be mistaken, Dear. There are no children here." She lowered her voice to a whisper. "I don't think they allow them for very long."

Duncan stepped forward and put his hand on Aurora's shoulder. Aurora grasped it and leaned into him. He was solid and strong, and she took his strength.

"Mrs. Alexander, Aurora brought these for you." He offered her a box.

She took it. "It's still warm," she said, and opened it. "Cinnamon rolls. I love cinnamon rolls, and I always heat them."

"She remembers cinnamon rolls," Aurora whispered, "but she has no recollection of her child. It's so unfair."

"Won't you sit down and have some, too?" her mother asked.

They pulled chairs close to the window. Duncan set the unopened boxes on a vacant chair and each of them had a bun.

"Do you know someone here, Dear? I'm sorry, I forgot your name."

"My name is Aurora and my mother is here."

"That's nice, Aurora." She rolled her name over her tongue as if she were trying to remember something. Aurora held her breath, hoping that just this once she would remember.

"I used to know someone named Amanda. She wore white all the time and she would bring me things when I needed them."

"That's the nurse, Mom."

Cass Alexander's eyes opened wide. "You're right. What did you say your name was?"

"Rory." There was desperation in her voice.

"Is this your young man?"

Duncan had been quiet until then. He sat forward in

the chair. "We only met recently, Mrs. Alexander, but I hope we will be great friends."

Somehow Aurora was warmed by his voice. She knew he was humoring her mother and she appreciated it.

"What is your name?"

"Duncan West."

"I think I knew some Wests once. Oh, there were a lot of them. Can't quite recall where we met, but I know there were lots when it came time to eat. Do you paint?" she asked Duncan.

"No. I never learned."

"You don't learn. You just do."

"I see," he said. "When you paint, do you ever do people?"

"People?" She said it as if she'd never thought of painting people.

"You could paint your mother . . . or your daughter."

She stared at Duncan. Actually, she stared through him, looking for something or someone to put an image with.

"I can't remember my mother. She probably looked a lot like me."

"Yes," Duncan agreed. "Mothers and daughters do tend to look alike." Aurora knew what he was doing. She mentally thanked him for his efforts, but she knew they would mean nothing. She had tried for the last three years to get her mother to remember her or one of her sisters or her brother—anyone with whom they had a common bond—but Cass Alexander had retreated into a world only she inhabited. "Maybe when we come again you can show us a portrait of your daughter."

Her mother didn't agree, but she did smile and she didn't deny having a daughter.

When Aurora left the hospital an hour later she felt happier than she ever had since putting her mother there three years ago. She'd tried maintaining her at home with sitters and nurses, even after she no longer remembered any family, but it quickly became overwhelming. She couldn't hold a job. She missed a lot of appointments, and often her mother wandered away, throwing Aurora into a panic. The third time the Rocky Hill policeman rang her doorbell in the middle of the night to return her mother—whom they'd discovered wandering the busy highway nearby—Aurora made the hardest decision of her life. She couldn't take care of her mother any longer. Tearfully, she sought out the nursing home and moved her mother there.

She had Duncan to thank for her mood today. He opened the car door and she got inside. She didn't know when they'd decided he would drive, but she'd handed him the keys and he'd helped her into the passenger seat before going around and getting in.

"I know she won't remember me when I come again, Duncan," she began as he pulled out of the parking lot. "But I'd like to thank you for coming with me."

"How often do you go there?"

Aurora dropped her gaze to her hands. "I used to go every week. Now it's only once a month."

"It must be hard, but there's no need for guilt about what you're doing for her. She appears happy. She has people to take care of her and you know she's safe."

She thought him very perceptive. He'd nearly read her mind. No one else had understood the anguish at having to put her mother in a nursing home. He seemed to know what she had gone through in making the decision, and what she went through each month when her mother failed to recognize her, though she had never brought up the subject.

Duncan completed the drive in silence. He thought about the woman sitting next to him. How different she was from any woman he'd ever met. He was still thinking about her when he turned the car into her driveway and pushed the button of her garage door opener. The door rose and he drove the car into the shaded space.

Getting out, he came around and reached for her hand to help her out.

Standing in the subdued light of the garage, he lifted her hand. It was light and soft, delicate. He'd never thought he'd use a word like delicate for a woman's hand, but it was the perfect description for Aurora's. She had long, slender fingers ending in sculptured nails. A bright red polish shown from them, and the third finger of each hand had a pattern painted on it. Duncan noticed *The Marsha Chambers Show* logo in miniature on her fingers.

"I had it done for the show," she said, offering her hand for closer inspection.

When she pushed her hand toward him, Duncan could still smell the fresh bread and the scent of the soap she used. He'd never been swayed by a woman's perfumed soap, but his mind created all sorts of pictures of her using a bar of hers, and he was there in most of them. He dropped her hand before he did something stupid, like raising it to his mouth and kissing it.

"Very nice," he said inadequately.

She looked at the hand he'd dropped and he saw her expression change. He hadn't meant to insult her, but she had no idea what the closeness was doing to him.

"The show." He cleared his throat. "It's why I came by this morning."

"Why don't we go inside?" She led him into the house. They entered through the kitchen and she stopped before the counter where she'd been when he arrived. Swinging her gaze from the cabinet to the refrigerator, she hobbled to the cabinet and took down two glasses. Then she poured juice into them and started for the living room. Duncan took the glasses. She reached for the wall for support until she reached the room.

He handed her glass back when she sat on the sofa, her leg stretched in front of her. He took the sofa across from her. They'd sat like this the previous evening when

he'd brought her home. Today light filtered in through
the curtains at the oversized windows and made the
room bright and airy. To the right of the facing sofas
was a large fireplace with a huge mantel, of the kind
found only in old houses. This area of New Jersey had
a lot of houses like this one. It also had plenty of develop-
ments springing up like weeds all over the metropolitan
area.

"What about the show?" she asked. He noticed the
difference in her voice. Earlier they had been friends.
Between them a warmth had developed. It had become
too warm for him. He'd destroyed it when he dropped
her hand. Seeing Marsha's logo had brought him back
to reality. It had nothing to do with Aurora.

For a couple of hours he hadn't thought of Marsha
Chambers or the show. Then, seeing her nails, he knew
his purpose in being here.

"We'd like you to come back to the show." He said
it directly, using none of the charm people often told
him he possessed. If she returned it had to be her
decision, not one she made because he manipulated
her into it.

"Back for what?"

"We'd like you to work there for a while." The way
she looked at him made him nervous. He could tell she
was trying to find the meaning in his words. "If you're
available, of course."

"We?" Her eyebrows went up in question.

"It was Marsha's idea. She thought you might be
willing to stay on, and learn something more about the
inner working of television for a while."

Aurora drank her juice slowly. She didn't react with
anger or enthusiasm. Duncan was unsure of what she
was thinking. Finally, she placed the glass on the table
in front of her. "I'm sorry, but I've decided to leave
show business."

"Why?" Duncan asked, surprised. "You come across on camera very well." He'd seen the film of the program, which would air in several weeks. She was one of the best guests of the day, sitting poised and smiling. Her chin wasn't too high or too low and she didn't fidget in the chair or look at the movement of the cameras or stage personnel. Her attention was on Marsha, or the audience. Little, if any, of her footage needed to be edited. He could see her doing other on camera programs in the future.

"I don't like it," she answered. "I'm never going to let anyone make a fool of me in front of millions of people again."

"What are you talking about?" he hedged, although he knew what had happened.

"I'm talking about Marsha Chambers and her questions that are designed to make the audience accept the answer she wants, even if it isn't the one the guest gives. I hated it, and I'm through with it."

"Then maybe you'll be interested in my proposal."

Aurora stared at him. She folded her arms across her chest. Duncan knew that the stance meant she'd closed off, that she wasn't ready to accept whatever he had to say, but he couldn't take his eyes off the swell of her breast under the silk blouse. "I'm listening."

"I'd like to offer you a job." Her position didn't change. "You said you were leaving show business. Mostly you've worked in front of the camera. I thought you might like to work behind the scenes, maybe in film editing."

"I don't know anything about film editing. Isn't this a position that would require some experience? If not in the actual editing, at least in the industry?"

"You've been in the industry for at least three years, if the resumé you submitted for yesterday's show is correct."

"It is." She nodded. "I've impersonated Marsha

Chambers for three years, attending cocktail parties, standing in for photo sessions with tourists, doing routines on a cruise ship, and traveling with several other look-alikes to do talk shows. That hardly qualifies me for film editing.''

"It doesn't, but we often take in interns or apprentices and teach them an aspect of the business.''

"And this is where I fit in?''

Duncan nodded. "If you like, I'll explain intern programs.''

"I know what they are,'' Aurora told him. "I've even placed some of the young women I used to work with in these temporary positions. They gain work experience and it gives them added confidence and a sense of self-worth when they realize they can support themselves.''

"It can't hurt you. You'll learn another aspect of the business that pays extremely well. If you're good and a fast learner, you can find a permanent job in this field.'' He waited a moment for her to think about it. "Will you try it?''

He didn't realize how much he wanted her to agree to this request until she'd waited a long time and said nothing. He'd told himself when he came here that it was to placate Marsha, but it was really because he enjoyed talking to her and wanted to talk more. He wanted to be around her. She was kind and giving, where Marsha was selfish. She was different from most of the show business types, at least for now. After association she might turn out to be the same, but she'd already been in and around show business people for three years and she still remained . . . *normal.*

"What's the catch?'' Aurora asked.

"Catch?''

"You didn't know I'd planned to leave the business. I only told you about that today. So what is really behind this? What does Marsha want?''

He shrugged, hoping to make light of the situation.

"She only said that you might want to be a participant in the audience, for the filmings."

Aurora dropped her arms and leaned closer to him, her eyebrows knitted together. "Which part of this has to do with the kidnapping?"

Chapter 3

The wind pressed against him with giant, cold hands—she whirled about his head, trying to throw him off balance. He took a step back but stood across from the house, visible. He dared them to see him, dared them to recognize him. Pulling the collar of the blue navy jacket closer to his ears and adjusting the baseball cap to conceal his identity, he watched as overcast daylight bathed the house in a stark coldness. Traffic whizzed past him but he was oblivious to it.

He'd learned to concentrate, block everything out except the one purpose for which he lived, for which he'd survived. And there she was, his instrument, within spitting distance. A hundred feet, a little over thirty yards, separated him from his goal. But he would wait. He knew how to wait, how to bide his time and let things come to him.

Both of them in the same place, he thought. He looked at the sky, at the car in the circular driveway, at the neatly cut hedges and the chrysanthemums. Yellow was his favorite color and these flowers soothed him, calmed him enough to make him wait for the right time. He swung his gaze to the hedges, perfect, green, and ready for winter.

She wouldn't make it to winter this year. He hoped she had enjoyed the spring, the summer days in the sun, maybe spent a few hours at the shore. These last few months on earth should be savored like a fine wine, enjoyed with carefree frolics like childhood, a precious string of pearls about to be broken.

Reaching inside his coat he pulled the small, flat box from a hidden pocket. It looked foreign in his big, gloved hand; midnight blue velvet, soft and feminine. It reminded him of her, of that sensual mouth that pouted at all the right times, that looked into the camera and smiled, making every man in America hard as a rock before her low, sexy voice sent them into instant climax.

She wouldn't understand the pearls. She'd think they came from a secret admirer. He *was* an admirer. He loved her, loved the way she talked and laughed, loved the way she could play to the camera, take control of the audience, even that home audience she could neither see nor feel. She'd played her love scenes to him year in and year out, and it was because of her that he'd come here. She was only one of the pearls in the link. But she was the most important one. When she broke, the entire strand would come undone. *The Marsha Chambers Show* would crash and burn. Unlike him, there would be no phoenix rising, no one to pick up the pieces and begin again. It would be gone, over—the fat lady would have sung. The song was long and lovely but it had to end, and the end was in sight.

She was in there. Somewhere behind those shutters she lived. It would be a shame, snuffing out her life, taking her forever away from a world that worshiped her, but it was necessary. He frowned and crossed the street. At the door he set the unadorned box on the step and rang the bell. He waited a moment to hear the chimes begin, then stealthily disappeared.

Her time was coming.

Coming soon.

Duncan repeated his earlier comment. "The kidnapping wasn't real." They now stood in the kitchen. Aurora needed movement when she argued, and despite her leg she'd left the sofa and returned here. Duncan had followed her.

"You mean the man who tried to grab me yesterday and throw me into a van was a hologram, or some virtual reality creature who escaped from the television station?" She shivered at the remembered struggle. The darkly dressed man holding her, pushing her toward the van. The taste of the glove in her mouth and powerful smell of fear that overtook her, panicked her and made her afraid. It blinded her with its intensity.

"He was real, all right."

"You think I should go back there?" She turned away, making herself busy by grabbing the coffee pot and dumping the dregs of this morning's brew, then refilling it with fresh water. "Maybe Marsha sent you to do her dirty work."

Suddenly her arm was yanked hard and she was spun around like a child's top. Her hand had barely released the pot handle before she found herself pressed against his chest and his face so close she could identify the pores on his skin. The pain in her knee was nothing compared to the thumping of her heart.

"Let's get this out of the way at the beginning." The anger in his voice scared her. "I am not Marsha Chambers's errand boy. I came here to make you a valid offer of a job. She was part of the decision. There is nothing strange about that. We often discuss personnel for the show."

Just as suddenly, he released her and stepped back, as if the closeness was were electric.

"I suppose I owe you an apology," she said. "I didn't mean to say—"

"Forget it." He waved his hand in the air as if there were nothing important they should discuss. "The job is still open."

Aurora took a deep breath. Working at the station would mean seeing him regularly. The thought of that disturbed her but didn't make her feel bad. In fact, it made her feel good. He was certainly attractive and he'd had his arms around her, carried her into the infirmary. For a big man he'd been gentle and caring with her, physically and emotionally. She remembered her neighbor, Megan, telling her Duncan had sent her over to make sure Aurora was all right. A moment ago he'd whirled her into his arms and she'd wanted only to hang there for an eternity.

"Aurora?"

She shook her head, trying to snap out of the cocoon that enveloped her, trying to make her heart return to a normal cadence.

"I'm thinking about it," she said. Turning away she prepared them coffee and offered him a cup. He took it, stepping close to her. She looked up, raising the cup to give herself something to do, but she kept her eyes on him while she tasted the hot liquid.

She did need a job. There were bills to be paid and her mother's nursing home stipend. That took a lot out of her budget and was the primary reason she'd exploited her look-alike potential. Before that she'd moved around in social services. She could return there. There was always a need for trained counselors for runaways or abused women. The pay wasn't very good, and it would never cover all of her expenses. In the end she'd have to get a second job.

"If I take this job," she began, sagging back against the sink. "What will I have to do?"

"It's in production—film editing, actually. You'd tch all the takes from the program and edit them in the manner that shows continuity without long instances of applause or long periods of a one-sided conversation. You'd be surprised how often people go on and on."

"I won't have to go before the cameras?"

He shook his head. "The production is all done behind the cameras. Marsha, however, did request that you sit in the audience during the taping."

"I don't want to."

"I'm sure we can work that out. There may be some shows you'll want to view."

Aurora forced herself not to frown. She couldn't think of a reason to be in the same room with Marsha Chambers. Why the woman wanted her to be in the audience was a mystery. She must have some reason she was hiding from Duncan.

Pushing herself upright, Aurora stared directly into Duncan's dark eyes. He was at least a head taller than she, but looking up at him from her position didn't make her feel as if she were turning him down. Shaking her head, she said, "I think it's better if I don't take this job. Marsha doesn't really want me there, and I'm not sure I want to be someplace where people don't want me."

"Marsha isn't the only person on the show," he said. The tone of his voice made hers catch.

"What?"

"There's the entire crew," he pointed out. "Since this is the only show filmed here, we're closer than most crews who have other people they can interact with. When someone is out, there's a missing link. It's a lot like having a family. People care about each other, even if Marsha gave the impression that they don't."

She dropped her chin so he couldn't see her eyes. For a moment she'd thought *he* wanted her to take the job.

"*The Marsha Chambers Show* couldn't go on the air without the hundred or so people writing, directing, editing, doing set design and prop inventory, lighting, audience preparation and control, and special effects. There's a small city of workers who get that show on the air, and I'm asking you to join that team.''

The offer was tempting, but Aurora was already shaking her head. Then he mentioned the salary and her head snapped up.

''You're kidding,'' she said.

Duncan shook his head.

''I could—'' She finished the sentence silently. She could pay her mother's fees and her bills with that much money and she wouldn't have to peddle her face and body for people to ogle at, thinking she was Marsha Chambers.

''Is that a yes?'' Duncan asked.

Aurora bit her bottom lip, something she hadn't done since she was a child. She'd broken herself of that habit in high school, after her first date told her he knew when she was thinking seriously about something because she'd bit her lip. Now the habit was back. She *was* thinking seriously. She knew she could get a job, but could she live on the salary? If she took this one, could she work with Marsha Chambers?

Of course you can do it, she told herself. It was a phrase she'd often used when counseling women with low self-esteem. She could do this. She could work with Marsha Chambers and eliminate the need for a second job to make ends meet.

''Yes,'' she said. Her voice hadn't been strong and sure, but quiet and fearful. Duncan didn't say anything. Then the doorbell rang, startling Aurora.

A shiver ran through her and the thought that someone had stepped on her grave sprang to mind.

Aurora peered through the curtains. ''There's no one here.'' She looked cautiously to the left and right, then reached for the doorknob.

Duncan grabbed her arm and her hand at the same time. "Don't open that," he said.

"Why not?"

"I'm not sure, but we don't want you getting mistaken again."

"I thought you said the kidnapping wasn't real."

"The *first* kidnapping wasn't real," he explained. "Yesterday's attempt could have been harmless, too, but I'm sure we should be cautious."

"Now you're scaring me. I've never been the object of a stalker." She had faced drug addicts and pimps, but never had anyone set out with a systematic plan to destroy her. She'd been in the arms of the man trying to abduct her, and she had felt only hatred and vehemence in his body. He hadn't uttered a word while he'd fought with her, but his purpose was clearly menacing and evil. She shuddered.

Duncan pushed in front of her and checked the area outside the oval door-windows. Then he opened one and stepped outside. He kicked something and they both looked down.

"What is it?" she asked, looking at the blue velvet jewelry box a step away from Duncan's foot. It looked abandoned on the black asphalt drive.

She moved to pass him. His hand came back to keep her behind him. Otherwise he didn't move, didn't reach for the box, but stared around him, looking at the traffic that rushed up and down the road. "Stay here," he told her. Then he went to the side of the house and looked toward the back. After disappearing around the side he reappeared several moments later, from the other direction. Aurora wondered what he was looking for.

"Whoever left this is gone." He rejoined her, reaching down and scooping up the unwrapped velvet package. Inside, he closed the door and lifted the blue lid of the case.

Aurora gasped. "They're beautiful." Laying on a bed of white velvet was a string of matching pearls. She reached for them, pulled them off the bed, and felt them roll over her fingers like cool water and dangle from her arm. "Why would someone leave these in front of my door?"

Duncan wondered that, too. The pearls were obviously expensive. The box, however, had no store name imprinted in the soft satin at the back of the box. Turning it over, he found nothing. He pulled the velvet insides out, looking for anything that might identify the place the pearls had come from, but there was nothing inside the box. Whoever had left them intended them for Aurora and intended them to be hard to trace. Duncan didn't like this. Somewhere in the back of his mind he wondered if this wasn't another case of mistaken identity.

The show often received gifts addressed to Marsha. Costume jewelry, flowers, cakes and other foods, even an occasional diamond ring with a proposal of marriage, but this hadn't been sent to the studio. It had been hand delivered to Aurora's house.

Why? Duncan wondered. Was this a crazed fan who'd mistaken Aurora for Marsha and was now fixated on her? Did Marsha have an enemy who'd seen Aurora and now thought she was Marsha?

What could this person have in mind? Why did he leave pearls at her doorstep with no note and no indication as to what she should do with them or what they represented? Marsha might know, might understand, but would she volunteer anything if Duncan asked her? He doubted it.

Aurora was fastening the string around her neck. Duncan almost ordered her to stop. For some reason he didn't want them touching her. Rationally, he knew they had no mystical power, but in his mind he'd connected the man in the van with the pearls Aurora was trying to fasten.

He took the knotted rope from her fingers and fastened them. When he secured the clasp he didn't with-

draw his hands from her shoulders, but let them rest
there. Looking past her into the mirror he saw their
reflections. Their eyes met in the glass, and reflected
there was a man he'd never seen before, a man who
could feel. After his marriage disintegrated he thought
he'd never feel anything again, and he hadn't met anyone he wanted to see for more than a couple of dates.

Yet yesterday afternoon when he'd swung Aurora into
his arms unfamiliar feelings had surfaced, and now they
threatened to swamp him. This should be his cue to
run, get away while his heart was uninvolved and his
skin still intact, but he found he didn't want to run
away. He'd wanted to protect.

Aurora fingered the pearls around her neck. She'd
worn them on each of the three days she'd worked
for *The Marsha Chambers Show*. She'd been sure Marsha
would recognize them, and yank them from her neck
the first time she saw her, but the woman ignored her
presence. If they passed each other in the hall Marsha
looked through her as if she weren't there. During the
taping, in which Aurora did not want to participate but
did so at Duncan's request, Marsha refused to make eye
contact with her. No matter where Aurora positioned
herself in the audience, Marsha made sure her attention
was someplace else. Certain the woman didn't want the
camera picking up her face, Aurora often smiled at
the extremes Marsha went through to banish her to
obscurity.

Why was that, Aurora wondered? Before Gwen Scott
threw that newspaper clipping in front her and sent
her into the glamourous world of a Marsha Chambers
impersonator, the two of them had worked in social
services. They were best friends and often relied on
each other in some tough situations. What Aurora and
Gwen knew about relationships could keep Marsha
Chambers in programs for the next year. Although

Aurora was no longer part of the world of personal problems, she couldn't help wondering why people did the things they did, made the decisions they made. Why did Marsha Chambers want Aurora on the set? Why wouldn't she look her in the eye when they passed each other in a corridor?

Of course, Marsha *could* have a real fear of being kidnapped. Even if her abductors had been benevolent and kind, Aurora understood she would have felt violated and helpless, at the whim of someone else. Observation was the key. She'd wait and observe Marsha, find out what secret she hid. Aurora was certain there was one.

"Daydreaming?" someone asked from behind her. She'd recognize that sexy voice anywhere—Duncan's. Other than when she was in the audience, she hadn't seen him.

She swung around on her seat in front of the editing machine. He wasn't dressed like most of the people who worked behind the camera. Their uniforms were jeans, sweaters, and various brand name tennis shoes. Duncan looked like a Philadelphia lawyer, with a crisp, white shirt and red suspenders. He was cleanshaven, providing no mustache camouflage for those sensual lips. Aurora noticed that he lowered his gaze to the pearls, then looked back at her face. Instinctively, she touched them.

"I came by to see how you were doing."

"Well, in the last three days I've learned how to fit three hours of film into a fifty minute format, how to insert commercials, make seamless transitions, and splice film together if the need occurs. I've mastered this little computer here." She shifted around to pat the cream-colored box on the worktable, then turned back.

"I'm told you have a real flair for this kind of work."

"Who told you that?" she asked with a smile. Fred Loring ran the film editing department and she'd been able to work with him and his crew. She'd learned a lot but by no means had she mastered the craft. That would take years.

Duncan's gaze went back to the pearls. His hand reached for them. Aurora's breath became shallow as his hand grazed her skin.

"Any word on these yet?"

She opened her mouth to speak but it was dry. She closed it and shook her head.

"They worry me," he said, letting them fall against her skin.

Aurora put her hand where his had been. She could feel her accelerated heartbeat. Taking slow breaths she asked, "Why?"

"These pearls are worth a lot of money," Duncan explained.

They had taken them to a jeweler the same day they found them. The appraisal proved that each separately knotted pearl was the exact same size, eight centimeters. They weren't cultured pearls, farmed in a vat of sand induced oysters, but grown in the sea, very likely the South Pacific or Indian Ocean. This necklace was translucent, with a luster that showed none of the reddish or whitish sheen that characterized lesser quality pearls. Their orient was as perfect as the gems were rounded. They'd been grown in the mother-of-pearl shells of at least forty mollusks. Aurora's fingers ran over the smooth surface. She knew that to find forty perfectly matched pearls would take tons of oysters. The probability of this many pearls having the same size and luster had to be off the charts. For a moment she shook. She must be wearing a million dollars around her neck.

"People don't just leave an expensive gift like this and say nothing. Have you received anything else? A note or call?"

Duncan stabilized her. She stopped shaking at the solid sound his voice.

"No," she whispered.

"Good." He smiled at her. "If anything strange turns up, you'll call me?"

"Strange? What kind of strange?" Her heart began to speed up again. This time it was from fear.

Aurora could hear the command in his request as she continued. "For the last three days I've assumed the necklace was sent by mistake. I felt someone would come to claim it, and that undertone of something sinister which we've been thinking and not saying would prove untrue. Now, however, I'm scared. I think there is something I don't know. I feel as if I'm being followed whenever I'm out, that someone is watching me from a distance. If I do get any information about these pearls, your number will be the first one I dial." She touched them again. She let her mouth grin, although she didn't feel it. "That is, of course, I would if I had your number."

Duncan let out a belly laugh. He didn't know whether to comfort her or kiss her. One minute she was scared and the next she was flirting with him. And he liked it. It had been years since anyone made him take notice. He saw beautiful women every day and they often flirted with him. They wanted to be on *The Marsha Chambers Show* and he was the power that could grant that wish. They were willing to do almost anything to get a chance at the millions of viewers who tuned in each day to hear what Marsha and her guests had to say. Aurora had turned out to be one of the few who didn't want that. Maybe that was part of her attraction. It had to be something. Hardly a day went by when he wasn't thinking of her and looking for her. When she appeared in the audience his attention focused on her several times during the filming. Often she was smiling or intently listening to what was being said.

She interrupted his thoughts. "It's time I went to the set." Duncan checked his watch. It was time they both went. She stood up and he moved back to give her room. He thought of the women flirting with him to

get on the show—even to be a member of the audience
Marsha would choose for thirty seconds of fame—and
the woman before him who had argued against sitting
on the set.

When she stood, neither of them moved. Aurora
looked at him. She expected him to step back farther
so she could turn toward the door, but he didn't. He
took her elbows and stared into her eyes. "I don't want
you to be afraid."

"It's too late." Her hand came up to the pearls, but
it wasn't the gems that had her heart tattooing. His gaze
followed her hand. The necklace formed a white arc
against the dark red sweater she wore under her suit
jacket. He took her hand before he knew what he was
doing or what he'd planned to do. He found himself
pulling her forward, pulling her mouth toward his.
Then, at the last moment, he turned slightly and let his
lips touch her cheek.

She was warm, her cheek soft and sweet smelling
under his mouth. He wanted to turn into her, feel the
full force of his mouth against hers, but something held
him back. Pushing his hands in her hair, he used them
to anchor her to him, to keep her stationed in place so
he wouldn't make a fool of himself, so she couldn't
turn her head and let him find her mouth. He knew
her mouth already. It was sexy, soft, and wet, and would
be heaven under his.

His arms circled her and pressed her into him while
his nose took in the smell of her hair. She was soft
against him and he could feel his insides liquefying as
she burned his resistance to ashes.

With strength born of frustration and need he pushed
her back. Her eyes were closed. They opened slowly
under his gaze, undoing him, making him lean toward
her.

"We'd better go," she murmured.

The words, filled with sex and passion, were enough
to break his ascent. He heard in her tone and knew in

his heart that if he kissed her he wouldn't be able to stop. They had a show to do. He cursed it silently, knowing he wanted only to leave the grounds and take Aurora with him. He wanted her in his bed, breathing hard and unaware that a world existed with people other than the two of them.

"Duncan?" She cleared her throat. "It's time I took a seat and you got in place."

He didn't say a word. He was incapable of speaking and equally incapable of letting her go. He took her arm and led her from the room. At the door to the set he looked at her, squeezed her shoulder, and went to take up his place in the front of the audience. Aurora moved to the top of the gallery and sat down in the aisle seat which had been reserved for her.

Duncan had sent a guard to Marsha's house. Guards stood posted at each of the entrances and at the base of the gallery. Additional security covered the grounds and entrances to the studio. He glanced at Aurora. Maybe he should get a guard for her. One whose specific duties would be to remain present whenever he entered her airspace. He could see that they, if left to their own devices, would cause ordinary air to burst into flame.

Chapter 4

Cooper Dean knew that most violent crimes were solved or major leads were found within twenty-four hours of their commission, yet he'd waited nearly a week and his friend, Duncan West, hadn't called to report a possible crime. Coop had gotten wind of it when Amy Peterson, one of the researchers on the show, mentioned it to her boyfriend, who happened to work the night shift.

It involved *The Marsha Chambers Show,* and everything involving Marsha Chambers was news. Coop had looked for reasons to visit the set, but this week had been extremely busy in Extortion. White-collar crime was alive and well and living in suburbia.

Dropping a file in the out basket he reached for another, just as thick and just as ugly. Coop liked living on the edge. He got a rush from duking it out in an alley with the bad guys or playing the puzzle game, and finally, when the last piece fell securely into place, he could collect his warrant and go pick up the criminal. His criminals weren't living in gutters. His lived behind high walls with security guards and wives dripping in diamonds and furs. His criminals often went in for industrial theft. Computer chips and information had replaced plans for toys and the latest fashion designs. In his field and in this area of New Jersey, kidnappings, even attempted kidnappings, were rare. He had heard about the one at *The Marsha Chambers Show,* yet no one connected with the show had reported a word.

He could say that was show business, but when it overlapped his section of the world he was the one with jurisdiction. It was time to flex his authority. Reaching for the phone he punched in the familiar number. Moments later he'd passed a secretary and heard the ringing of Duncan's phone.

"West," he answered.

"Dean," Coop said, his voice full of authority. "I think it's time you and I had a talk."

Duncan laughed in his ear. "I wondered how long it would take for word to reach you. A week, that must be a record."

"It isn't a record. I've been waiting for a call from the show's producer to fill me in."

Coop had a reputation in the borough. He knew everything, and nothing got past him. "West, we don't have earthquakes in New Jersey, leastwise not on a regular basis, but you're on uncertain ground if you decide to sidestep the law."

"Why don't we meet for dinner tonight and I'll answer all your questions?"

"When and where?" Coop asked.

"My place, nine o'clock." Duncan was still laughing. "Remember, I like my steaks rare, my salads crisp, and my baked potatoes oozing with butter."

"Yeah, and I like my coffee hot, black, and sweet. Nine o'clock." He replaced the receiver without saying good-bye.

Coop spent the rest of the afternoon alternating through files of paperwork and his latest puzzle of extortion. He'd had a report several weeks ago of a missing

executive and a large sum of unexplained money. When
he went to investigate he found a huge stash of jewels.
The two pieces didn't seem to match, and he was trying
to find a link.

At eight o'clock he gave up the struggle, pulled his
jacket from the back of his chair, and headed for his
car. He had time to drive at a leisurely pace to Duncan's
house. He looked forward to seeing his friend again.
Since Duncan and *The Marsha Chambers Show* had moved
to New Jersey three years ago, they saw less of each
other than when they had lived on opposite coasts. They
both had busy jobs and Coop didn't envy Duncan his
need to take care of Marsha Chambers. He'd met the
diva of talk shows and found her rude, self-centered,
and egotistical. He'd often told Duncan all she needed
was someone to put her in her place. Duncan had given
him the job.

Coop would gladly have taken it. He'd seen her several
times at official functions in the area. She often came
and went with equal speed. Always surrounded by a
group of people, she looked cocooned, untouchable,
and lonely. He wondered at times if this was the case
and that was the reason she didn't interact with the
masses. On the other hand, he wondered if she was just
a snob and thought herself too good for the masses.
He decided on the latter.

Weaving through the streets of Princeton, Coop made
his way to the old brick house along Elm Road. It had
stood in the same spot for over a century, been con-
verted from gaslight to electricity, and from oil heat to
natural gas. Several additions had been built onto the
original structure by previous owners—yet today it epit-
omized the Princeton of the twentieth century—stately,
beautiful and monied.

He pulled into the circular driveway and parked his
car under the front portico. This entrance reminded
him of the south entrance to the White House. A huge
light fixture swung over his head as he headed for the

door. Coop had crossed entrances like this several times since joining the local police force. He'd found that money, even old money, had just as many legal foul-ups as the lowlifes in New York City. Crime here was different. People didn't throw bricks to break into stores and rush away with all they could carry. They used electronic toys to get past security systems. They stole paintings and heirlooms.

The door swung in before Coop could ring the bell. Duncan stood there, an apron over his jeans and shirt and a smile covering his face.

"Now why don't my women stand by the door to greet me as I arrive?" Coop asked by way of greeting. He couldn't say how good it felt to see his old friend. The two of them had grown up on the same mean streets in South Chicago and it was a miracle they'd made it this far in life without being killed. He knew so many kids engaged now in the same dangerous pranks as they'd been. It was part of growing up, part of becoming a man. His job often brought him into contact with those who didn't make it.

"You must be doing something wrong, Coop, if they don't. I thought I taught you better."

"Excuse me, but who taught whom?"

Laughing, he entered the house. It was just like Duncan, he thought. Despite the rooms which he knew were crowded with studio cameras and audio equipment, the main part of the house reflected a stable life style. A huge chandelier hung over the foyer of black and white tile that would have made Fred Astaire envious. Beyond that were rooms with comfortable furniture and books.

"I know you're hungry, so the food is ready."

"I swear if you were a woman I'd date you, even marry you."

"Careful. You know where that leads you."

Coop certainly did. He had two ex-wives and a daughter to support. Duncan led them down the familiar hall and they ended in the kitchen. He had a formal dining room but both felt more comfortable in the kitchen.

The meal was robust, exactly the way Coop liked it. He couldn't have ordered a better tasting steak in any New York restaurant. The two old friends lingered over coffee. Duncan offered ice cream but Coop refused, opting for another cup of hazelnut flavored coffee. Duncan had picked up the gourmet coffee bug while living in L.A. and Coop had to admit he liked it too, although around the squad room he drank the brew that seemed to have come from an oil rig.

"That was a great meal, Duncan. I'll have to compliment Mrs. West on how well she taught you when next I see her."

Duncan laughed. "She'll be pleased."

"I can just hear her now. 'You can't expect women to cook for you all your life. You gotta learn for yourself. And if you learn well, you'll get more women with an apron on than any fancy come-hither line you can think of.'"

The two of them threw their heads back in laughter. Coop's imitation of Duncan's mother was near perfect. Coop laughed, but he thanked her every day for the lessons she'd taught them both, cooking being only one. They could each hold their own in contests involving the kitchen or the streets, and Mrs. Kathryn West had had a lot to do with that.

She'd also taught them when to stop socializing and do their homework. Coop knew it was homework time. He took his cup and went to the counter, filling it to the brim. He took no sugar or cream, and sipped the hot liquid from where he stood.

"I guess this is going to take some time," Duncan said. "Let me turn off the equipment in the other room."

Coop followed him to his workroom. It had been the library for some former resident. Floor-to-ceiling bookcases covered the two side walls. The back wall was cut by two enormous French doors which led to the patio and pool beyond. Coop could see the green pool cover in the lighted distance. Inside, the floor space held television cameras, cutting equipment, and a panel board with enough switches to control the electricity in a small city. Duncan had told him what it was, but he no longer remembered—something to do with sound modulation.

When the equipment went silent they headed for the living room. As they took chairs opposite each other Coop felt the butter softness give under his weight. He envied his friend for a moment, wondering when they had made the decisions that brought them to this point. Coop had been on every athletic team he could find, while Duncan had played basketball and soccer. Neither had been bookworms as adolescents, but today each had a huge library of all kinds of literature. Coop still kept up with basketball and played a regular game, while Duncan had added tennis, golf, and skydiving to basketball and soccer.

He probably could make a good script about them being part and parcel of the same cloned gene, Duncan thought. What a concept that would make—two apparently individual men with a genetic trait that forced them to work together to complete a single universal man. Maybe he'd pitch it one day.

Duncan returned from the fantasy world of movies to his friend. Coop wasn't here to have movie ideas bounced off of him. He wanted to know about Marsha.

"I suppose you heard about the kidnap attempt," Duncan stated.

Coop shrugged. Not much went on around the department that he didn't get wind of. "You want to fill me in?"

Duncan stretched in the chair and placed his coffee cup next to a book about making movies which sat on the polished table in front of him. He related the details of the attempted kidnapping in precise language. He left nothing out except his attraction to Aurora.

"You think this kidnapper mistook the look-alike for Marsha Chambers?"

Duncan nodded. "What other explanation could there be?"

"He could have been looking for her, followed her to the studio, waited until she came out, and tried to force her into the van." He paused. "Then you come charging over the hill in true Sir Lancelot fashion and save the day."

"Not quite Lancelot. He would have won."

Coop stared at him as if waiting for more. Duncan recognized that look. He knew they could sit there all night and be stubborn, but it wouldn't prove anything. He could hear his mother saying that.

Coop broke the silence. "Where is Ms. Alexander now?"

"I hired her. She works at the station."

Coop's eyebrows raised.

"It was Marsha's idea," he rushed on. "She thought if it was the fan thing this was a way of confusing them."

"Kidnapping isn't something to turn your back on," Coop informed him. "No matter how well intentioned, it's still against the law."

"Coop, no one was hurt. Nothing really happened."

Coop raised his hands and slumped back in the seat. "All right, Duncan. You're my friend, but kidnapping gets bounced to the feds. No passing go, no getting out of jail. It goes without exception. If anything else happens I'll have to call them."

Duncan knew the truth of the statement. If it hadn't been for Marsha and her insistence they would have called the authorities the moment it happened, but the studio couldn't afford bad publicity, and they knew that copycat kidnappers were a real possibility.

"I understand," Duncan conceded.

"Good." Coop shook his head. "Now tell me about Aurora Alexander."

The tightness that squeezed Duncan's heart at the

mention of her name surprised him. He hoped Coop didn't see any difference in him.

"What do you want to know? She looks like Marsha Chambers and I hired her to work in the film editing department. If you want to talk to her, drop by the studio. But I hope you won't."

Coop didn't react. He waited for further explanation.

"She was shaken by the ordeal. She's fine now, and bringing the incident up again would make her nervous for nothing."

Coop didn't speak for a long moment. "I see," he finally said in a tone that said he was looking straight into Duncan's mind and reading his heart.

Reading faces, assessing character, and recognizing when a person said one thing and meant another were arts that Cooper Dean prided himself on as a master. He'd sat in his friend's living room not an hour ago and listened to him. He knew Duncan hadn't told him everything. Whether he'd actually omitted something or just had a feeling about something, Duncan hadn't been entirely truthful with him.

Coop loved Duncan like the brother he never had. He'd been raised in a house with three sisters, a mother, and a widowed aunt. He and his father were the only males. Duncan's house had only men except for his mom. The two of them had run together since childhood, and Coop knew Duncan better than he'd ever known another man. He knew there was more to the story than Duncan had shared.

He dialed into the police phone system and left a message for a buddy in Investigations who owed him a favor. Coop wanted to know everything there was to know about Aurora Alexander, Marsha Chambers, and—he gritted his teeth—Duncan West.

* * *

Bread day, Aurora thought, packing the last of the boxes in her car. Closing the door, she felt a gust of wind blow at her hair. The air had turned cold. Red and gold leaves swirled about her feet. The shrubs and trees had been tied and covered against the approaching winter. Aurora lifted her head to the sky. It was overcast, grayish in color, perfectly matching her mood and her once a month attempt to reach her mother.

Going back into the house she checked to see that nothing had been forgotten. The smell of sugar and the heat of baking warmed the spacious kitchen. As usual, nothing was wrong. Hooking her shoulder bag over her arm, she left the house. Pulling onto the road she waited for the feeling that someone was following her to descend. It didn't. She smiled, hoping it wouldn't come. Some days she just knew she was being watched, and kept looking over her shoulder. Other times there was no one there. Today was a no one day. Aurora took it as an omen. Something would happen today. Her mother would recognize her.

Cassandra Alexander didn't recognize her daughter. She'd withdrawn even farther inside herself. Aurora couldn't get her to react to anything. The art she'd seemed to enjoy for the past few months meant nothing to her. Music she'd enjoyed all her life got no reaction. Aurora's constant affirmation that she was there only caused tears to fall from her own eyes—her mother didn't react.

The nurses had to take Aurora away and give her time to compose herself. They tried to soothe her and Aurora appreciated their ministrations, but it wasn't happening to them. It was happening to *her*.

Aurora knew the stages of Alzheimer's. Forgetting people and places, inability to recall simple tasks, then loss of bodily functions, and eventually, total withdrawal and death. Knowing didn't make it easier. It was like knowing someone had cancer and was going to die. When the event took place no one was prepared. Those people could grieve and then go on, though. With her mother, a kind of death would occur before her body stopped breathing and her heart stopped beating. The toll on the family was immense.

Staying away helped her sisters and brother. They weren't here in the same state with her. They were thousands of miles away. Aurora was here. She couldn't stand the guilt of not seeing her mother when she knew she was alive. Facing her in this awful state tore her heart nearly out of her chest.

Duncan, she thought. He'd helped her before. He'd been there. When she'd left the nursing home last month, Duncan was there to talk to, to support her. Why hadn't she thought of it before? She was a counselor. Why didn't she recognize the need for counseling in herself?

She got up from the sofa in the waiting area and fixed her makeup. She would go to her mother and kiss her good-bye. Then she'd find Duncan and talk to him. It didn't matter what they talked about, just that she could interact with another human being.

Duncan was alive.

She was alive.

They thought they could keep him out by adding guards. They were fools. He knew more ways to get around security systems than they could think of in a million years. Security had been his business. He'd studied it, learned what to look for, how to circumvent alarm systems, how to outwit police bands, and how human nature worked. He'd had time and he'd been a good pupil. Nothing could keep him away and no one would ever suspect he'd even been there.

He'd watched the patrols, knew when they changed shifts, when they made rounds, which security guards had families, and how far they lived from the studio. He'd watched the deliveries, seen the banter between the gate guard and the truck drivers. For him it would be a cakewalk.

He pulled the squat, silver, hot food truck up to the guard window, making sure it was close enough so that the guard couldn't take more than one step out of the door.

"Hey," he called. "You must be Finch." He extended his hand. "From Smiley's description you couldn't be anyone else." The guard took his hand and shook it. "I'm Ernest. I'll be filling in for Smiley today. His back is out. You know."

"That ole back problem again," the guard acknowledged.

"I told him to see a doctor, but you know Smiley." He looked at him, knowing that by the end of today he would no longer have a job.

The other man, in his fifties with silver hair, wore a white shirt with gold epaulets on the shoulders and a patch on the sleeve denoting the Princeton Security System.

"I told him more times than I can remember to get that back seen to. I know how bad it can be." The guard put his hand on his own back, empathizing.

Reaching next to him he pulled a bag up and extended it toward the guard. "Smiley told me you liked these and I was to make sure you got it."

A smile as wide as Montana split the guard's face as he dove into the bag and found piping hot apple turnovers inside.

"Here, have some coffee, too." He handed him a cup. "I guess I better get on up to the door."

"What's she calling for today?" the guard asked.

He lowered his voice and spoke in a conspiratorial

whisper. "Red beans and rice. She absolutely has to have them."

The guard rubbed his stomach and leaned toward him. "She's as changeable as a chameleon. If you get there and she's changed her mind and doesn't want them, just drop them back by here."

He gave him the thumbs up sign and put the truck in gear. "I'll be sure to do that." He smiled his best grin.

The red and white bar went up and he drove the truck, a modern version of the old chuck wagon, up to the studio door. Before he could get the awnings up, a small crowd gathered. They grabbed cakes, bagels, and sandwiches, and threw money at him as if they hadn't eaten in decades. Only one person asked about Smiley, and he repeated the story he'd told the guard.

Then she came around—Marsha Chambers's secretary. She held a silver tray. Her daily routine called for the tray. She put the packages he gave her on it. He produced the specially prepared meal he had for her.

"It's red beans and rice," he volunteered. "Smiley's wife made it especially."

"Thank you," Joyce said, accepting the covered styrofoam package.

"Here's her vegetable drink and a dessert."

Joyce gathered everything and left. He didn't have to wait long. Hungry people were known to show up immediately and buy what they wanted. He closed down after only twenty minutes and made his exit, stopping only briefly to raise his hands indicating the entire meal had been taken by Marsha Chambers.

Driving through the gate he sneered, looking into the rear-view mirror. *"Bon appetite,"* he said. He hoped she enjoyed her meal.

It would be her last supper.

*   *   *

When Marsha entered her dressing room the smell was heavenly. Unlike the others, she hated eating in the dining room. She also knew they didn't like eating with her. In her room she could be as sloppy or messy as she wanted. She could hold a chicken leg or let the juice from corn on the cob drip down her arm. She could bite into ribs, knowing the sauce would paint her face and there would be no one there to see it. She could do all those things, but she never did. She never ordered that food anymore. Everything she ate seemed to add a pound, and the relentless camera found them as if it were a homing device.

What smelled so good? she wondered. Her usual meal consisted of some kind of salad or a reduced calorie dish that only resembled real food. This heavenly smell could not be from either of those things.

"Damn!" she cursed, opening the silver covered dish. "Joyce knows I can't eat this stuff."

She turned, intent on screaming for her secretary at the top of her lungs, but the smell of the food crowded in on her. She'd taste it, but not eat too much. Maybe Joyce thought a good meal would make her less of an annoyance today. Oh, she knew what the crew thought of her. Since the incident with the kidnap attempt they had steered clear of her, assuming she would fly into another rampage.

She was sorry for that, she thought as she took a seat at the table which had been set up in the dressing room. The tablecloth was white linen, pristine clean and complementing the silver and china settings which adorned it. Marsha scooped out a spoonful of rice and beans and added a slice of ham to her plate. Closing her eyes at the first taste, she savored the delicious food. She hadn't tasted anything this good since the show aired and she'd forced herself into a strict regimen to keep her weight down. Today that regimen could go to the devil. She ate everything and topped it off with the vegetable drink which only Smiley could concoct.

She finished feeling sated, satisfied, and sleepy. She smiled as she stood up. Then she said, "Ohhh," grabbing her head. The room swayed in front of her, and her eyes blurred. "I guess I'm not used to such rich food." A little nap would do her good, she thought. Stumbling to the sofa, she lay down.

"You've been bad." She wagged her finger as if there was a person standing before her. Marsha didn't hear the slur in her voice. "You can't eat food like this. It makes you feel too good." She giggled. "Then you have to pay." She closed her eyes, wondering when she had had food that tasted that good in the past. She couldn't remember.

Chapter 5

Duncan burst into the editing room. "Where's Aurora?"

"She's not here today." Fred Loring's attention was taken by the machine in front of him. He didn't look up at Duncan and couldn't see the concerned expression on his face.

"Is she sick?"

"Don't know. She said she had something personal to do. I didn't pry."

Her mother, Duncan thought, checking the huge calendar over Fred's desk. Today was the first of October. She'd be at the nursing home. She was all right. His heart calmed.

"Thanks, Fred."

Leaving the room he went to his office and found the number of the nursing home. Punching it in he waited for someone to answer.

He was becoming increasingly paranoid about Aurora. Since that day in the edit room when he'd tried to kiss her, he'd maintained a healthy distance. When they found Marsha today he couldn't contain the panic that ran through him at the thought that she, too, might have received tainted food.

The woman in her mother's room was entirely different from the one who had been there when she arrived. The catatonic, gazing creature was gone. In her place was a personality Aurora often met when she arrived. Her mother still didn't know who she was, but she was coherent at times and often said things she understood.

Usually the subjects were safe in her mind. Inanimate objects, cartoons, stories about things Aurora did not remember or that happened before she was born, *if* they happened. Her mother could be making up stories. Aurora couldn't tell. She only knew she preferred this woman to the other.

Aurora jumped when the phone in her mother's room suddenly rang. No one knew she was here and no one called her mother, that she knew of.

"Don't be frightened. It's only the phone," her mother said as if she received calls all the time.

"Do you think I should answer it?"

"It's the only way to know who's calling."

Aurora stared at her mother. That was a purely lucid and logical comment. Why could she be logical about an inanimate phone, yet not know her own child?

"Hello," she tested.

"Aurora? Are you there? It's Duncan. Are you all right?"

"Of course," she said, feeling the stir of apprehension. Something had to be wrong, or he wouldn't call her there. She hadn't told anyone she would be there. Only he knew, from being with her last month. "What's wrong?"

"They just took Marsha to the hospital. We think she's been poisoned."

"What!"

"They're going to test the food, but Doc's pretty sure it's tainted."

"How did this happen?"

"I don't know. Marsha always eats alone in her dressing room. When she didn't appear for the taping someone went to get her. She appeared to be sleeping, but we couldn't wake her up."

"Is she going to be all right?"

"I don't know. She was still unconscious when the ambulance left. I have to get over there. I just wanted to make sure you were all right."

She was fine. Today hadn't been a day she felt followed. She knew she should tell Duncan about that, but this wasn't the time. He had other priorities. She felt good that he'd taken time to call and find out she was all right before running to the hospital.

"I'll be fine," she assured him. "You go to the hospital and let me know if there's anything I can do."

He hung up. Aurora replaced the receiver. Quickly the feelings of warmth left her and she wondered about the person who'd tried to kill Marsha. This was no prankster kidnapping attempt. This was life-threatening.

Aurora turned back, expecting to find someone there. Only her mother was in the room. She sat in the same place she'd been when Aurora arrived—a comfortable wing chair she'd had since she came to live here. It was a soft yellow with small flowers covering it. Cass Alexander stared into distant space. Aurora knew she'd retreated into her own world. There would be no recognition today.

She approached her mother with a sad smile, kissed her lightly on the forehead, and said good-bye. Her mother didn't respond. Her world was now different, and inside it Aurora didn't exist, not even as a stranger.

Princeton Medical Center was the only hospital in Princeton Township and it was in proximity to the studio. Aurora drove straight there when she left her mother. The carmel-colored building was cramped in the college town in a residential area. Aurora parked in the small garage adjoining the hospital and rushed toward the emergency room entrance.

The waiting room was empty except for a small child and her mother. The child was cradled against the mother as she gave information to the nurse.

"Can I help you?" said another nurse.

"I'm looking for Marsha Chambers."

The woman glanced at her, then did a double take. Aurora knew the woman thought she was looking at the famous star.

"Aurora?"

She turned as someone called her name. "Duncan," she called and went toward him. He grabbed her hands as she came forward. She stopped, knowing she would have continued into his arms. "How is she?"

"They pumped her stomach. She's going to be all right."

"Good," Aurora said, letting out a breath.

"She's sleeping now. She won't wake up before morning. Then she'll have to stay for a couple of days."

Duncan looked dead tired. His shoulders were hunched over and his eyes were barely open. "Come on," she said. "I'll drive you home."

As she turned toward the exit a man approached them. He stopped, staring down at her from a towering height. He said nothing. He wore a suit that had to be custom-made. His eyes were as black and piercing as his skin. He had the kind of face that she couldn't put an age to, but the chiseled character lines told her he'd seen a lot of street action. From which side of the law, she couldn't tell. Duncan looked up.

"Aren't there any cops in this town except you?" he asked. There were hints of humor and fatigue in his voice.

"Not that I know," the man said.

"Aurora Alexander." He looked at her, then swung his gaze to the tall man. "I'd like you to meet one of Princeton's finest, Cooper Dean."

Aurora extended her hand and it was swallowed by that of the giant in front of her. He must be at least six-foot-five.

"Six-foot-seven," he said. "It's the first thing people want to know when they see me."

"I understand," she said, not acknowledging that she had been no exception. "The first thing people want to know about me is if I'll give them an autograph."

"You do look amazingly like Marsha Chambers."

She didn't know whether to say thank you or tell him it was a curse, not a compliment.

"Luckily, they didn't mistake you for her today," he went on.

Today. He knew. She was sure of it. Duncan must have told him about the previous attempt. Word around the studio was that it had been just a harmless fan who'd tried to get Marsha's attention. In the past few weeks it had been all but forgotten. She'd thought it was, but this policeman knew.

He addressed Duncan. "I need to ask you some questions."

"Can it wait?" Aurora asked. "I was about to drive him home."

"I'll ride with you. Then you can drop me back here on your way home."

Forty minutes later Aurora was sitting on the sofa in Duncan's living room, holding a cup of coffee, her feet curled under her. Duncan sprawled at the opposite end of the sofa and Cooper Dean presided like a judge in an armchair across from them.

"Tell me about it. You start." He indicated Duncan.

"Apparently, someone delivered a meal to the studio with tainted food in it. Marsha ate it. The doctor said the food had a slow acting poison in it. When she drank the vegetable drink, it set off the poison. Whoever did it didn't realize that putting a sleeping potion in the food would slow the rate of absorption into the system. It probably saved her life."

"See anyone strange at the studio today?"

"I didn't. The guard at the gate said the regular delivery man didn't show up, but the replacement knew everything about him. He assumed it was all right. The truck comes every day."

"Cancel it."

"We've already done that."

"Where were you while this was going on?"

His abrupt change of direction startled Aurora. "I wasn't at the studio today."

"Where were you?"

"Visiting my mother."

"Coop," Duncan said, "Aurora's mother is in a long-term care facility. If she went to visit her dozens of people would know it. She brings warm bread for the nurses and her mother. I've tasted it. They couldn't forget her visit."

"I'll need to verify it, anyway."

"I'll provide you with the address." He angered her. She never thought she'd be a suspect. She was doing Marsha Chambers a favor by staying on this set when her own life could be in danger. Now that some mishap had befallen the star, *she* needed an alibi. Why hadn't he come around when someone had tried to abduct her?

Cooper switched gears again. "Has anyone heard from the usual delivery man?" Aurora wondered who he was trying to throw off track. Or was this just his policeman's style?

"We weren't able to reach him."

"What's his name?"

"I only know him as Smiley, but call Joyce. She knows everybody."

"Does Marsha have any enemies that you know of?"

Aurora couldn't imagine a woman like Marsha not

having enemies. She was rude and unfriendly. Her ascent to the throne of daytime talk shows had been over the heads and on the backs of her predecessors.

"I'm sure she has enemies. Who in this profession doesn't?" Duncan asked. "I only know one, for sure."

"Who might that be?"

"Me."

Aurora pulled the car alongside the parking garage and cut the engine. Immediately the night wind began to sap the heat in the car. The night wasn't cold but sitting for a long time would be uncomfortable. She shifted in her seat and stared at the man, who took up more room than she thought possible in such a small car.

"You haven't said a word since we left Duncan's. I assume you want to ask me something," she said.

"Is there something you want to tell me?"

The question was a trick question, she thought. He'd probably sat in the same psychology classes she had. But she had a degree and would be willing to match wits with him.

"You know who I am, don't you?"

"I know you're the woman who was mistaken for Marsha and almost kidnapped."

"You said yourself the resemblance is amazing." He looked uncomfortable. Aurora wanted to smile, but forced her expression to remain still.

"Do you know the man?"

"I didn't get a look at him. He wore a ski mask, which I'm sure you already know."

"You're right, but I mean was there anything else about him that might be familiar—cologne, feel of his arms, anything?"

"No, Officer Dean. There was no comfort in his arms. I did not recognize his cologne or his manly smell. I'd say the two of us had never met before he tried to force me into the van."

"I apologize, but I have to ask these questions. And the name is Coop."

"You've known Duncan a long time," she stated.

"We grew up together, went to the same schools. He's like a brother to me."

"So you know he wouldn't have anything to do with poisoning Marsha Chambers?"

"I'd be willing to bet my pension he's as innocent as a newborn baby."

"But me, on the other hand—" Her voice was dead serious.

"You," he said. "I know nothing about you except that you also dislike Marsha Chambers. I don't know why."

"Be careful, Coop. You haven't read me my rights."

"Do I need to?"

She stared at him in the half light. His eyes were unreadable. They had been the same way in the cold light of the hospital and in the bathed light of Duncan's living room.

"I did nothing to harm Marsha Chambers," she stated. "I find her actions toward other people rude. I attribute her behavior to survival."

"Survival?"

"She's afraid of everything—of losing her status as the best talk show hostess, losing control over the people who work for her, of the studio. She orders people around just so she can feel better about herself."

"Go on, Dr. Alexander. Tell me more."

Aurora took a deep breath and sat back. "I didn't mean to sound like—"

"Like a doctor of psychology."

"I'm not a doctor—"

"Not yet. You have completed all the course work and need only to write the thesis to complete the program. Three years ago you abandoned work on that degree to impersonate Marsha Chambers. I can only assume the pay was better than working for Social Services."

Aurora hid her surprise. She'd known that sooner or later he would check out her background. She hadn't expected him to do it before they met.

"Did you check out Marsha and Duncan, too?"

She was rewarded by the upward sweep of his eyebrows.

"Did you find out Marsha Chambers bio isn't really true? She didn't grow up in a loving home, but in one where she was battered until she was twelve-years-old."

He sat still, his eyes steady, a technique people use when being given surprising information they have no knowledge of and don't want the bearer of the news to know they are making a revelation.

"Finally the state stepped in," she went on. "They placed her in foster care. She grew up in the system. Her social worker helped her get into college, and the day after graduation she reinvented herself."

"You seem to know a lot about her," Coop interjected.

"Inquiring minds." She smiled. "I like knowing as much as possible about people who dislike me, and Marsha Chambers has placed me at the top her list."

"What did she do to reinvent herself?"

Again Aurora suppressed her smile. "She disappeared. When she emerged she went to Hollywood and worked at bit parts until she got a break. The rest of her bio is accurate."

"How do you know all this about her?"

"I have contacts. The same as you."

"And they told you this?"

She did smile this time. "They're very good at what they do." She paused. "I wondered what it was about me she disliked so much though she wanted me on the set. I made a few calls and found out."

"What have you done with this information?"

"You mean am I going to blackmail her with it?" She stopped. "Marsha doesn't know I'm aware of it. It's my plan to keep it that way."

He looked away from her. The light from the street-lamp highlighted his thoughtful profile.

"There's power in understanding, Coop. If I can understand Marsha, even if she doesn't know it, maybe one day we can be friends."

"You want to be friends with Marsha? If that's true, you're the only person in the world who would want that."

"I'm not sure I want it. Right now she angers me. As days go by I'm less and less angry though. I think she needs friends and understanding. I don't think she ever learned how to reach out and be a friend. She covers her need for companionship and common interests by controlling every situation."

She was quiet for a long moment. He stared through the window. Minutes went by. She could feel the softness in him. He was a big man. He looked tough, acted tough, and had a tough job to back up the facade. Slowly his head swung around and he looked at her.

She might want to analyze Marhsa. Coop wanted something else entirely.

"Damn you!" Marsha ranted. "This is your fault. Why is it every time I turn around something else happens? I thought we had security. I thought they were intelligent people. They let a stranger onto the lot. After the incident with the kidnapping, how could they let a man in who poisoned me? I want that guard fired."

She was back to normal, Duncan thought. He stood at the foot of her bed. Two days in the hospital, and only the drugs had kept her silent. Now that she was due for release she couldn't talk enough.

"Marsha, Greg Finch has been a guard since the first show was aired."

"Then he should know better. I want him off the lot."

"Marsha," Duncan said, holding his temper. "We've had this conversation before. The answer is no. End of discussion."

Marsha pushed herself up in the bed. She was fully made up as if she were about to walk out on the stage. With her white lace nightgown that was certainly not hospital issue, they could be doing a show on the latest styles in lingerie.

"Duncan, you leave me no choice."

"Marsha, before you say anything let me remind you of your contract terms."

"I am aware of them. And as of now, I am on sick leave."

"You're not sick."

"I am mentally distressed and the medical insurance will pay for three months rest in a sanitarium. Until this maniac is caught I will not set myself up as a target."

"You can be sued for a move like that. It's against all the terms of your contract."

"No, Duncan," she sneered. "These are specifically the terms of my contract. I'm giving the police plenty of time to catch this fool."

She was scared. Marsha Chambers was really scared. Duncan didn't think he'd ever seen her like this. Her image made people think of her as a tower of strength. She wasn't strong. She was frightened. The woman in the bed was like a frightened little girl.

"What makes you think he won't find you in a sanitarium? Why is that a safe haven? If he can get onto the lot, where we have strengthened security, then he can certainly find you in a high-class hospital."

"I don't care. Find another host. I won't be back until the police catch the culprit."

Duncan wanted to kick the end of the hospital bed. Even more, he wanted to kick Marsha, but his upbringing forbade him. She had him with the loophole in the contract, and she knew it. She could stay off the set for the next quarter and there was nothing he could do about it.

"All right, Marsha, you win." He headed toward the door.

"Wait a minute. What do you mean by that?"

"It's what you wanted. You're off the show. For the next ninety days we'll show reruns. Ratings will fall. We'll try to run the best shows, but who knows? By the time all of this is over you could be back to doing one night stands in Las Vegas, if you're lucky. If you're not lucky, it'll be Seattle."

"You know you can't do that. According to my contract—"

"Yeah, yeah," he said. "I know the contract says no reruns during the regular season."

"I'll sue you."

"We could argue that this isn't the regular season." He strolled to the window. "We could also mention that the plaintiff who brought the suit is herself ill and confined to a sanitarium. You might not be able to have a say, in your present state of mind."

Duncan picked up his coat and left the room. It did him good to hear Marsha screaming his name over and over as he casually went toward the elevator.

Marsha Chambers will get her release from the Princeton Medical Center tomorrow but her medical problems aren't over. . . .

He listened to the entertainment news. She hadn't died. *Damn,* he thought. What had gone wrong? He'd given her enough sleeping powder to kill her. Then he'd added the poison to her food.

He should have known she was too tough to succumb to mere food poisoning. Well, he had time. She couldn't hide. He'd find her and he'd finish her and then they could all suffer, like he'd done. Then he could look at them, watch careers topple, and no one would ever know he'd had anything to do with it. He'd be sympathetic, even send flowers to the funeral. He laughed. The strong sound came up from his toes. He felt it throughout his body and liked the sound, the feel, the exhilaration and power of life and death.

Cooper Dean, big man on the force, known for solving the most baffling cases, stood outside a hospital room sweating. He'd been there for five minutes, and soon the staff would begin to get suspicious of him. He'd spoken to the guard and produced his identification, and now it was time for him to push the wide door inward and go inside.

He took a deep breath and walked in. The room was semi-dark. Only a lamp on a dresser crowded with flowers illuminated the room. The rest of the available space, including the floor, also held flower arrangements. Coop was glad he wasn't allergic to pollen. The room smelled like a florist's shop the week before Mother's Day.

Marsha looked beautiful in the bed. He hadn't expected that. He thought she'd be pale and disoriented, but her eyes were clear as they focused on him.

As he went toward her she looked up at him.

"Cooper Dean," he said. "Princeton Police Force." He pulled his ID out and flipped it open. This wasn't how he wanted to introduce himself. He had no choice. His visit would look official, but he was here because he was concerned for her.

"I remember you," she said. "You're—" She stopped.

"I'm Duncan's friend."

She frowned and turned away. "Go away."

"I take it Duncan has been here."

"He has."

"And his leaving was not under the best of circumstances?"

"I wanted to wring his neck."

Coop thought this might not be a good time to talk to her.

"What do you want?" she asked.

He pulled a chair up to the bed. Her back faced him. He laid a hand on her shoulder and she rolled over. Her eyes were watery and Coop's heart twisted. He'd been bluffed before, though, and he wasn't sure Marsha wasn't doing it now.

"I want to ask you some questions, but they can wait."

He wanted to cradle her in his arms and tell her everything would be all right. He wasn't sure it would be. He was too used to seeing things that didn't work out to make promises he couldn't keep.

"How do you feel?" he asked. "Is there anything I can get you."

Marsha frowned at him. She raised herself up on her elbows and stared at him. "What is going on here? You didn't come to ask about my health."

"You're wrong. That's exactly why I came. I wanted to make sure you were all right."

"I'm all right. Now go away."

"You're used to people jumping when you say something, aren't you?" Coop almost stood up. It was a reflex action for him to use his height, to tower over someone and make them cower and give him the information he needed. He didn't want to do that to Marsha. He wanted her to trust him. He knew her history, knew that she had a lifetime of not trusting. It was going to take some time for her to learn to trust.

"Yes, I am. So if you have no questions for me that can't wait, go away."

"All right," he told her. "I will go away—in a moment."

She rolled her eyes.

Coop produced a paper from his inside pocket. "In

case you're interested, we found the real driver of the
food truck yesterday afternoon." Her glance didn't
move. "He's bruised, but unhurt. I know you're grateful
to hear that."

Marsha turned her head to face him. Tears shone in
her eyes. "I *am* glad to hear that," she said, and Coop
believed her.

"The guard helped draw this sketch of the man who
drove the truck that delivered the food. Take a look
and tell me if you recognize him."

She took the paper and picked up the hand control
that could summon the nurse. A button turned on the
light over her head. She looked at the sketch for almost
a minute.

"I haven't the slightest idea who this could be. He
reminds me of no one I've ever seen."

Coop took it back. Aurora and Duncan had already
seen it and could not identify the man in question.
Coop had hoped things would be easy, that one of them
could put a name to the likeness, that he'd be able to
begin a search for a specific person. As it was, he was
still at square one.

Chapter 6

Busy. Duncan crossed the fifth name off his list. He couldn't believe every possible person who could host a talk show had another job at the moment. Television and the movies were unemployment havens. Today's hot property could be looking for scripts the next day. If he didn't know better, Duncan would have thought Marsha was intentionally manipulating things so she could have her way.

He'd threatened to put the show into reruns, but he knew better. He was too much a "keep-your-promises" kind of guy. A contract stood, and no matter how much she wanted to bend the terms of it he wouldn't.

So what was he going to do? He couldn't set up reruns and he didn't have a replacement host to put on during her absence. They were already three days behind. He had to do something in a hurry.

The problem was still bothering him two hours and six calls later. Soon word would begin filtering through the industry that *The Marsha Chambers Show* was in trouble. Duncan got up and stretched. He'd been sitting in the same position for hours and he was tired. Adjoining his office was the studio control room. Entering it through the connecting door, he glanced over at the silent equipment. Through the large window he saw workmen repairing broken seats and some of the lights. Opportunity had presented itself and the maintenance group used it to refurbish the set.

He smiled. Marsha would never notice. She only saw things when they were wrong, not when they were right. At that moment Aurora walked across the room. She stopped at the two steps that led up to the platform and said something. Duncan didn't have the sound on, so he couldn't hear her. Her hair swung about her shoulders, reminding him of the hostess he was seeking.

When she lifted her foot to step onto the stage the thought struck him.

Flipping the switch that let his voice be heard in the studio, he called her name.

Aurora jumped at suddenly hearing her name broadcast over the large set. She spun around, looking for the speaker.

"I'd like to speak to you, please."

She looked toward the dark windows across from her. Squinting she saw nothing. Then the lights went on and Duncan stood on the other side of the glass. She went toward the door and he opened it.

"You scared me," she said as she came in.

"I didn't mean to."

"I want you to do me a favor."

"Sure," she agreed readily.

"Sit down."

Aurora took the seat he offered. The control room was small, soundproof and crowded with equipment. She knew that during tapings many people worked the magic buttons on the control panel and backup cameras that ultimately delivered images into the homes of millions of viewers. This was the first time she'd been in it.

Duncan sat on a high stool in front of her. She waited for him to begin. For some reason he looked nervous.

"Is something wrong?" she asked. "Has something else happened to Marsha?"

Duncan linked his fingers together and then leaned forward, elbows on knees. He shook his head.

"You look like you're trying to tell me something I'm not going to like. Is it my work? I'm not coming up to par and you're going to fire me."

He leaned forward and took her hands. "It's nothing like that. I'm not trying to fire you."

"Then what is it?" Her hands suddenly went cold, then just as fast began to burn with heat.

"I do want to move you from the editing department."

"To where?" She eased her hands away from him. They were becoming too warm and she didn't want him to feel the elevated pulse that accompanied his touch.

Duncan didn't look at her but stared through the window over her head. Aurora waited but he said nothing. Finally she turned to see what he was looking at. There was nothing there. The workmen who'd been fixing some of the seats were all gone. The studio was brightly lighted, its royal blue walls curved around a huge conversation area that sported a sofa and armchair in front of a coffee-table holding a plant that nearly covered all its surface. The area seemed to be waiting for the theme music to begin and Marsha Chambers to walk onto the stage to the applause of a waiting audience.

"Duncan, where do you want me to work?"

He nodded toward the window.

She looked again. "I can't work here. It would take me forever to learn what all these buttons do. I like the editing room, and I'm finally beginning to get the hang of how things work."

"Not in here," he said. Again he focused on the area through the window. "Out there."

Aurora swung around and looked at the studio. It took a moment, but she finally realized what he was saying. She knew about Marsha, about him looking for a guest hostess.

"Oh no," she said, getting up. "I told you I wanted nothing to do with going before the camera again."

"Why not? There's nothing to it."

"I told you I was out of show business."

"Aurora, I'm in a bind. You know Marsha refuses to return, and I've been trying to find a replacement all day. Everyone I called is tied up."

She felt sympathy for him but held her ground. "That's not my problem. You're the producer. It's up to you to deal with these kind of glitches."

"I am dealing with it and I'm glad I haven't found anyone."

"Why?"

"Because I finally realized you're perfect for the job."

She took a step forward. "Because I look like Marsha?" Anger made her voice level increase. "I could fool the audience. Not only can I walk like her and talk like her, but I can pull off the best scam in talk show history. And it would be a scam, Duncan. I won't go on as a Marsha Chambers look-alike."

"Hold on," he said. "I'm not proposing that you go on as a look-alike. That would be fraud."

She let her breath out, glad he didn't want her to do anything illegal, but when she looked at him again she could almost see the wheels turning in his head. He was planning something and she wanted to know what.

"I think you should go on as yourself."

"No," she said. "I don't want to go before the camera." She folded her arms over her breasts and stared at him.

"You haven't told me why." He kept his voice quiet.

Aurora sighed. "Because I don't want to become her—overbearing and hated by everyone I come into contact with. I don't want to interview people I detest, smile into a camera when I know I can't wait to get off-stage. Believe me, Duncan, you put me on the stage and you'll find out how awful I can be."

"I saw you on the tape of the look-alike show and you were comfortable with the cameras. You far outshone all the guests that day. The others were not as photogenic, and didn't know how and what to do. I don't believe it's the camera and I don't believe you'll become another Marsha."

"I'd be too nervous. This is not my idea of having a good time."

"What is?" He abruptly changed the subject. Aurora didn't know how to answer.

"What?" she hedged.

"What job is your idea of having fun? What did you do before you became a professional look-alike?"

"I was a social worker."

"You thought that was fun?" She heard the incredulousness in his voice.

"Every day wasn't a barrel of laughs, but there were times . . ." She stopped, refusing to relay her experiences.

"You'd like to go back to it?"

She shook her head. "It doesn't pay well enough, and even if it did I couldn't return."

"Burnout?"

"Something like that," she admitted. She'd seen too much working as a counselor and she couldn't fix any of it. Yes, she'd gotten girls off the streets and returned them to homes where their parents were grateful to find them and the girls were glad to return. She'd also found parents who hated their children and refused to have them come back. She'd found children lost in foster care, and abused children. Those were the hardest to work with and they had been the turning point for her. She'd become too involved and she could no longer function.

When the ad for impersonators had been left on her

desk, it was an escape. A way to salvage her pride by leaving instead of waiting until her performance became inferior.

Duncan broke into her thoughts. "Aurora, I'm asking you to do a few tapings. By then Marsha will probably be ready to return. Despite her ranting, she loves this show. She wants to protect what she's built. I don't think she'll make good on her threat. If she returns soon enough we'll never even have to air the tapes you make."

"And if she finds out I've replaced her, she'll be angry enough to do the job herself."

"I won't deny that I haven't thought of that. In fact, I'm counting on it." He paused. Time passed slowly. "Will you help me?"

Damn. Why did he have to use that voice? That soft, sexy one that undid her? The voice that spoke of a low-playing saxophone in the early morning hours when the heat is high and the previous day is about to give way to the new one. She had to refuse. She should never have let him talk her into coming here. The money she needed to keep her mother safe had forced her hand. But to go before the cameras? To take Marsha Chambers's place and possibly get killed in the process?

Yet he sat there, perched on the stool in his lawyer outfit. His tie hung loosely from the open collar, blue shirt, and his sleeves were rolled halfway up his strong, dark arms. Visions of waves lapping on a moonlit beach and shared kisses with wine-sweet lips filled her mind.

"Aurora—"

"Duncan—"

They spoke at the same time.

"You go first," he said.

"It's the first kidnapping attempt." She forced her mind and body to let go of the images and concentrate on the present. "You convinced me that it was the work of a kind fan, but I'm not so sure anymore." She stopped to glance at her hands before going on. "Now, with this food poisoning, I just know there's more involved than just an enthusiastic fan wanting a nice evening with Marsha Chambers's screen persona.''

"You're right," he agreed. "Believe me, I'm not trying to put you in any danger. The studio will do whatever we can, and Coop is looking into the kidnapping attempt and Marsha's food poisoning. You'll be safe here.''

She doubted it. As long as he stood in her path it was her heart more than her physical being that was anything but safe. She'd wanted to be safe. When she left Social Services she'd wanted to find a place where she wouldn't be called in the middle of the night, where people weren't crying out, needing her to leave her bed, dress quickly, and get to some place where one of her clients—her children—were in trouble. Of course she wasn't supposed to go alone, but she couldn't wait. Minutes counted, seconds counted, when they called her screaming into the phone.

That last time—when she'd gotten between a pimp with a knife and the twelve-year-old he'd forced into prostitution—she was sure her life would end that night. A swift move her brother had taught her and ten years of ballet lessons helped her manage to kick the knife out of his hand before she kneed him in the groin. Hauling the twelve-year-old behind her, she'd run like hellfire was speeding at her heels.

If she did what Duncan asked her she'd be setting herself up for every kook who lusted after Marsha Chambers. She'd had plenty of that already, and she wasn't ready for wholesale adoration.

"I don't think I want to be a part of Marsha's world."

"You're already a part of it," he pointed out.

"It's limited. I can work here in the editing room and not come into contact with any part of the underworld of television.''

Duncan hesitated. She saw his gaze drop from her face to the pearls. "Why do you wear those?"

"What?" she asked, her hand coming up to touch the smooth round surfaces.

"The pearls?" He stood up, making her want to step back. She didn't. "You *want* to be involved in this. Every day you come in here wearing that string. Why?"

She opened her mouth to speak, but he continued.

"The pearls were delivered to your house. I don't know how he knew where you lived. Maybe he followed us from the studio that day. From a distance it is difficult to separate you and Marsha. If he's fixated on Marsha, he's got you in his sights, and you're waving a red flag in front of this bull. We both know they're worth a fortune. Eventually, the sender is going to want to collect. And you're already setting yourself up for him, as surely as if you were wearing a sign."

Aurora wondered about what he'd said. It wasn't often she was on the end of a character study, especially one she didn't like. Could it be true? Did she really want to be part of the action? Had she worn the gems for a reason other than facing Marsha Chambers? The talented hostess had ignored both her and the pearls. Why had she persisted in wearing them?

"We'll get you as much security as you need, Aurora. In the studio, we'll make sure no one gets to you who isn't a bonafide employee."

"He'll come looking for me," she whispered.

"We'll keep you—"

"What about my mother?" Aurora thought, not realizing she'd spoken aloud. "If anything happens to me, she'll—"

"She'll be fine, Aurora. The studio will also get her a guard, or we'll move her to another location."

"No," she said, a little too fast. "She doesn't understand change. It would make her disoriented and afraid."

"All right," Duncan agreed. "First we move you out of that house. Then we're going to get you some protection. I'll talk to Coop immediately."

"Can I think about this? I'll give you my answer in the morning."

Duncan nodded. "I don't think you'll have anything to worry about, but I want you to be sure." He reached out and squeezed her arm. Automatically, Aurora's hand came up and covered his. Realizing her action she wanted to drop it, but it would appear as if she didn't want his touch. The problem was that she wanted it more than she had a right to.

The weather turned decidedly colder. Winter was going to arrive fast and it would be a bad one. Coop could tell by the blowing wind and smell of snow. Coming from Chicago he had an internal barometer which told him when it was going to snow. Sometimes he could even predict how much would fall. He often found himself having solitary conversations with the TV weatherman over winter forecasts. The same couldn't be said for summer or warm weather—maybe because he was too busy to take in the weather, then. Crime rose with the temperature.

The temperature was dropping, along with his ability to pull anything together on this case. He had nothing. Days had passed. The regular driver of the food truck had been found—tied up and with a huge bump on the back of his head, but otherwise fine. He could provide nothing in the way of clues. He hadn't seen who hit him. He'd been hit from behind. The man could offer no reason why the thief had known so much about him and about the people on the Marsha Chambers set.

Coop went over and over the meager details he had to work with. Finally he turned toward the windows. His reflection looked back through the darkness. It got dark earlier these days. Sighing, he decided to end the day. Maybe he'd drop by on his way home and check in with Duncan.

As soon as the outside air hit him he knew something

was wrong. The perception came with being a career cop. It was an instinct, like his sense of smell. He knew something was wrong, but didn't know where. Turning the radio up so he could monitor the calls, he left the parking lot and turned toward the center of town.

The bulb must have blown, Aurora thought as she pulled into the dark garage and closed the door. She had a light on a timer. It was a habit she'd developed while her mother was still living there. Often Cass would get up in the night and wander around the house, not knowing where she was. Once she'd fallen and twisted her ankle. Aurora had put a night-light in her room and a lamp in the living room that stayed on. After her mother went to the care facility she'd removed the night-light but left the living room lamp on the timer switch. Occasionally, the bulb outlived its usefulness and she came home to a dark house.

She didn't like the house dark. It was lonely there. She'd grown up with three sisters and a brother. The house was always full of noise, and lights were always on in practically every room. Now that she was alone, the one light seemed to scare the loneliness away.

Inside the door she flipped on the kitchen light. Immediately, she knew someone had been there. Her heart stopped, and then leapt into her throat, beating hummingbird-fast. She listened. Was he still there? Her senses heightened, making her hearing sharper, her sense of smell more acute. She felt the silence pressing against her as if she were wrapped in a rug. Should she continue or call the police?

Irrationally, she wanted Duncan. She wanted to call him, ask him to come over and hold her, make her feel safe. Pushing her mind back to the house she laid her purse on the counter, keeping her keys in her hand. Tentatively she approached each room, turning on all the lights as she went. At the last room she sighed with relief and fell against the wall for support. She was alone, but someone had definitely been there. He'd taken nothing that she could determine. He'd touched things, moved them around. Her perfume bottles, the sachet packets in her drawers, her clothes in the closet, had all been pushed aside as if he wanted to see behind them.

Catching her reflection in the mirror she saw the pearls and her hand went to them. Duncan's words came back to her. *Eventually, the sender is going to want to collect.* What did he want? And why her? Why didn't he find the real Marsha? If he got her by mistake, would he believe she wasn't the real talk show hostess? What kind of profile could this man have? She didn't have enough information to draw any conclusions, and Marsha hadn't been any help. Everyone insisted her previous kidnapping had been by fans. Aurora didn't think so, and she didn't know if this was the same man or if he was after Marsha again.

Feeling uneasy she went back to the kitchen to put on some water for tea. The doorbell rang as she reached the bottom step. Her feet faltered and she tripped, nearly losing her balance.

Was it him? she wondered. Would he come back? Ring the doorbell? Looking around for a weapon, she grabbed the fireplace poker. Thinking how like someone in a television drama she must look, she inched her way toward the glass doors. Never had she thought of the double doors as being anything but beautiful. Tonight she thought they offered little protection from a possible murderer.

The bell rang a second time and someone called her name. *Duncan!* She dropped the poker and rushed to the door. She saw him as she flung the door open. Later she would tell herself she was just propelled into his arms, that it was the ordeal, the fear she'd felt knowing someone had been in the house, but right now she needed the solid warmth of him to steady her, control her raging emotions, and soothe her terror.

Only after he pushed her back into the room and closed the door did she notice Coop standing in the background.

"What happened?" Coop asked, his eyes glancing at the dropped poker.

"Someone's been here."

"Are you hurt?" Duncan asked. She looked at him. Concern and fear were warring for dominance in his eyes, which she'd always considered melting. Tonight they were hard and brilliant as polished glass.

"I'm fine. He was gone when I got here."

"Thank God." Duncan let out a breath but didn't let go of her. As they faced Coop, Duncan's arm fell from around her shoulders down her arm to link their fingers. Her nerve endings tingled, making her feel protected.

"Is anything missing?" Coop brought her back to the crystalline world of reality.

"Not that I can tell. It's more like the person wanted to get familiar with my taste. The clothes have been moved, sorted through, perfume bottles lifted and examined, then replaced."

"I don't like this," Duncan said.

Coop reserved his opinion. Aurora could tell he didn't like it, either. Whoever was now stalking her had more knowledge of her than any of them had of him. Even the combined comprehension of a trained lawman, a social science doctoral candidate, and a seasoned observer of human nature couldn't put the pieces of the invisible Humpty Dumpty character together enough to profile the individual.

"I'd like to take a look around."

Aurora nodded and Coop left them. The silence was awkward after he left.

"I apologize for running into you."

He stopped her. "Shhh. I'm just glad you're all right."

Aurora smiled tentatively, but she was still a bit over-whelmed by the experience. "I was just about to make some tea."

Duncan followed her into the kitchen, where she filled a kettle and set it on the range. He heard the soft whoosh of connecting gas when the burner lit. She was scared. He could feel it in the tremors which had come through her hand and passed to him. Thank God Coop had suggested they come by here tonight. She would have been alone. He knew she wouldn't call him. She would have weathered the situation alone. Just as she supported her mother alone, lived alone, worked alone, and didn't want to need anyone for anything.

She needed someone tonight. She needed to be held and stroked, told that someone else would bear the burden for the next twenty-four hours, that she could sleep without the world resting on her shoulders.

Coop joined them in the kitchen as Aurora set cups in front of them. "I didn't find anything."

"What were you looking for?"

"A method of entry, broken window, jimmied lock. Everything here seems to be in order. What about the alarm system?"

"It was . . . off." Her voice held wonder. She hadn't thought of it. It was so automatic for her to reach for the alarm that she'd turned it off, even though the red indicator light had not been on and the signal noise had not sounded. "I'm sorry." She glanced at Coop. "I didn't remember it until now."

"Anything else?"

"The lights were off." She pointed toward the dark lamp in the other room. "That one is on a timer. It was off. I assumed the bulb had burned out."

Coop went through to the lamp with his lazy gait and switched it on. Connecting the current to the device—a procedure learned by children around the age of seven—produced light in a lamp. Tonight was no differ-ent. Illumination spilled from the shaded beacon, causing Aurora to react slightly. Only Duncan could see it, since his eyes were focused on her.

Coop returned, drinking his tea in one long gulp. Then he asked more questions for which Aurora didn't have the answers.

"This is a big house," Coop finally said.

"It's my family home."

"From the pictures in the living room, I see you have sisters."

"Four," she told him. "And a brother."

"Where are they?"

"Spread across the U.S. I'm the only one who's still in New Jersey, except for my mother."

Coop didn't ask about her mother. Duncan had already told him about his visit to the nursing home where she suffered from Alzheimer's Disease.

"I'll have patrols increased in this area so we're on the lookout for anything unusual," Coop said. "May I use the phone?"

Aurora indicated the wall phone near the kitchen counter where they sat drinking the tea. He was a Princeton cop and she lived in Rocky Hill. The police cooperated with each other, so he could do what he said.

"In the meantime, the reason Duncan and I came tonight was for the necklace."

Protectively, her hand went to her neck.

"It's the only lead we have. We're going to try to find out where gems as perfect and expensive as those came from, and who bought them."

Aurora reached up and undid the clasp of the necklace. Coop picked up the phone.

"We'd also like the box it came in. It might help."

Sliding off the stool Aurora said, "I'll get it."

She left them alone in the kitchen.

"What did you really find?" Duncan asked the moment she was out of earshot.

"That's just it," he said. "I didn't find anything. The

windows were all locked and the security wires were intact. I could find no door which had been forced. She confirmed that the alarm system had been disabled, but if she was as used to it as she says maybe she never really set it before going out. In all, I found nothing. I can't even tell if anything has been moved or touched."

Duncan felt helpless. He wanted there to be something tangible, something they could face. He hated the invisible, the dark side of life. He'd always believed that when he went into the fantasy business it couldn't touch him. Even when the movies detailed life, they weren't filmed that way. They were done in small segments, in disjointed scenes, and often out of sequence. Only when the whole product was aired was it seen in continuous motion. His knowledge made him view it as entertainment. Tonight was not entertainment.

Aurora appeared at the entrance to the kitchen. Both men turned to look at her. Her eyes were huge and bright. Her face looked pallid, and fear had returned to her body, making it stiff and hard to move.

"It's gone," she said.

Chapter 7

For the space of a lifetime not one of them spoke. Absolute quiet seemed to roar through the kitchen. Duncan and Coop froze like ice figures. Then they all spoke at once.

"Are you sure?" Coop asked.

"Of course I'm sure," she snapped. "I put the case next to my jewelry box, and it's gone." She'd reached for it, knowing exactly where it would be, but it wasn't there. At first she'd refused to believe someone had taken it. Then reality set in and she began to shake. She couldn't scream, couldn't speak. Her heart clogged her throat. Whoever had sent the pearl necklace had returned for it. She hadn't been home and the necklace had lain about her neck, now more like a noose than a decoration. Breathing became difficult and she gasped in the silent kitchen.

"How about anything else?" Coop interrogated. "Other jewelry items?"

"Nothing, nothing!" she shouted. "He knew what he wanted and he came to get it." She stared at Coop as if he were the enemy.

Duncan moved toward her and pulled her into his arms. Aurora wanted to crack, wanted to relax against him, and let him shoulder her worries, but she stiffened, refusing to allow anything to break her. If the tiniest sliver ate into her resolve, she'd shatter.

"It's no longer safe for you to stay here. I think you should find another place until this is over." Aurora heard Coop's voice. It sounded gentler, as if he understood her pain. "Don't worry about the house. We'll keep it under surveillance, and I'd like to post a police-woman here."

"Don't worry about her," Duncan said. "After this I'm taking her to my place."

Aurora didn't know how she could expect sleep to come tonight. First her house, then the necklace case, and now she was imprisoned in a guest bedroom at Duncan's house. She should have insisted he take her to a hotel but she'd been too tired, her nerves too close to the surface to argue with him about where she slept. And she didn't want to be alone.

She tried a bubble bath, then a slick satin gown she rarely wore. Climbing between the sheets in the comfortable, queen-size bed should have made her ready to blot out the world for the next eight hours, but her mind was active and she was wide awake.

Barely a wall away Duncan slept. Images of his bronzed body in various stages of undress seeped into her thoughts and made the pit of her stomach ache. This was the worst mistake she'd made, coming here.

Sitting up in bed she rested her head on her knees and tried to think of something else. *Work*, she thought. Then she remembered her conversation with Duncan earlier today. It seemed years ago now, though it had only been a few hours. Should she replace Marsha? Should she go before the cameras and interview Marsha's guests? Would it be difficult to ask canned questions, look and sound spontaneous?

She knew the answers to those questions. She needed time to get used to interviewing and to giving an audience what they expected, and she knew she'd be nervous. What she didn't know was who would be there. Had the killer come to the studio? Had he been in the audience? Was he an employee with a score to settle? She rejected that one. No one at the studio would ever have mistaken her for Marsha. Unless—she stopped, her head coming up as she stared into the dark room— unless he wasn't at work that day. She rejected the theory. When he returned he would have discovered the truth, then stalked the real hostess. Knowing that the stalker had mistaken her for Marsha and was actively trying to get to her should make her refuse the offer. "But I'm the victim," she said aloud. He was making her the victim of this B movie, and she wouldn't be a victim. She'd seen victims, knew what they lost when they became the objects of someone else's program. Some of them needed therapy afterwards, years of therapy, and there was no guarantee of recovery.

Sliding out of bed she went to the window and looked out on the yard below. Moonlight made it easy to see the rosebushes fringeing the back fence. The decision had been taken from her tonight. She was already involved in the stalking whether she liked it not. If she were going to survive this and remain intact, she would have to admit she was already part of the teleplay. It would be better if she could set the scene and provide some of the dialogue instead of sitting back and letting other people try to keep her alive. She'd do it herself.

Weren't those the same words she'd told the women she counseled? They had to take charge of their own lives and not allow anyone to make them victims. Now it was her turn to prove the truth of her own words. God, she hoped she was right.

* * *

Aurora logged about two hours of sleep the entire night—in fifteen-minute intervals. Her head felt heavy and fuzzy at six A.M., when she dragged herself to the shower and tried to make herself look as if she carried no worries and today was just another work day. She knew it wasn't. She also knew she couldn't stay here another night. The thought of returning home made her shudder with anger. She'd been forced to flee, and returning there—although better than trying to sleep in the same house with Duncan—was not an option. She'd have to find another place.

She had plenty of friends but rejected the idea of calling one of them. It was enough that her own life had been uprooted by a stalker. She didn't feel it fair to possibly endanger someone else. They no longer had the shore house. Her father had received that in the divorce settlement and immediately sold it. It wouldn't have mattered, anyway. The house stood in Cape May and was too far away. Her drive to the studio each day would take hours. Her only option seemed to be a hotel. She couldn't stay there for long. She prayed Coop would find the stalker soon and life would return to normal.

By seven-thirty Aurora was ready. She'd taken care with her personal grooming, then packed everything into her suitcase. Maybe she could find some coffee in the kitchen. By the time Duncan rose she wanted to be ready to defend her reasons for refusing his hospitality without telling him the truth.

She smelled the coffee before reaching the kitchen. It was old coffee, burning. She wrinkled her nose as she took the pot off the burner and dumped it into the sink. Methodically she cleaned the pot and searched for fresh coffee. She found it in the third cabinet she opened and brewed a fresh pot.

As the hot liquid reached her stomach it protested her lack of proper attention. She hoped Duncan wouldn't mind her making some breakfast. Finding his refrigerator stuffed with food, she wondered if he had a housekeeper. Unwilling to wait for anyone to come in and fix her food, she pulled bacon, eggs, and milk out and set them on the counter.

She was busy orchestrating a froth of eggs when Duncan spoke from the doorway.

"Smells good in here."

He smiled, still wearing a bathrobe. His face had a day's growth of beard and his eyes looked tired, but Aurora had never seen a sexier looking man in her life. She was glad she wasn't breaking eggs, or they'd surely be on the floor.

"Would you like some breakfast?"

"Do I have time for a shower first?"

She nodded and turned to pick up a mug. The magnetism between them was strong as hydrogen bonding. Pouring him a cup of coffee she handed it to him, remembering he hadn't taken any sugar or cream the previous time she'd seen him drinking it.

"Twenty minutes," she said as his hand brushed hers.

"Thanks." He turned to leave but turned back when he saw her suitcase. He looked at it, then back to her. Aurora followed his gaze. She'd hoped she'd have more time to think about what she would say, but Duncan had come in before she expected.

"Duncan . . . I . . . I want to thank you for letting me stay here last night. Today I'll have to find someplace else."

She wanted to drop her gaze, not let him see any weakness in her eyes, but she kept her head level.

"Not a problem," he said and left her.

Aurora sat down and let her breath out. Was that all he had to say? Obviously, her presence had no effect on him. She wanted to kick herself for the sleepless night she'd spent, for the hours she'd given in thinking of him only a room away.

Getting up, she beat the eggs into a yellow froth. She

hadn't even asked if he liked his eggs scrambled. As she beat them harder she said, "I don't care. He'll eat them as they are or I'll force them down that velvet-voiced throat."

The shower head spewed cold needles, stinging Duncan's skin. He needed that. His mind went back to Aurora in the kitchen. Did she have to look that good in the morning? Did she have to make him think of sharing breakfast every day, waking up to the same woman, making love throughout the night and feeling like he wanted to do nothing more in the daylight than make love to her again?

How could he have ever thought she reminded him of Marsha Chambers? The two were nothing alike. Aurora did look like her but she had a beauty of her own, and that was what Duncan saw when he looked at her. It was also why he had to get her out of his house.

Duncan had never had problems sleeping. He'd slept through thunderstorms, his college roommate's excessive snoring, and Cooper Dean's personal filibusters on some obscure point of law. Yet last night his script failed him. If he could have fallen asleep he might have passed the night without incident, but he hadn't been able to fall into that dark, warm cavern where day and night met, joined, and exchanged vows.

At two o'clock in the morning he'd swung his feet to the floor and stood up. He'd spent the balance of the night in his office drinking coffee and working while he tried not to fantasize over the woman in his guest room. He'd been unsuccessful. Then he'd heard her moving about the kitchen and nothing could keep his mind on schedules, set preparation, glitches in guest appearances, or any of the hundreds of details he had to deal with daily.

The only thing he'd thought of was getting her out of his house. Then he'd seen her in the domestic setting.

Why that should affect him he hadn't a clue, but it did.
He'd seen her before in her own kitchen, up to her
elbows in flour, but this was his house, and he liked
what he saw. He liked it too much to keep her there.
Staying with him was not an option. He couldn't function with her this close. If she accepted the job as substitute hostess he didn't want anyone implying that his
choice was based on anything other than her talent.

Duncan hadn't decided how he would tell her they'd
have to find another place for her to stay. Then he'd
seen the suitcase. Luckily she'd already made the decision.

Joyce was kind enough to let Aurora use her office
to make some phone calls. Aurora spent most of the
morning there. Every place she thought was decent
proved to be above her price range. Finally she'd called
a friend in the nearby town of Lawrenceville. At least
she had someplace to go when she left the studio
tonight. She'd worry about the rest of it later.

Walking into the film room she took her place at the
editing machine and had switched it on when she saw
the pink message slip. The room was open without
offices or cubicles. It held several stations and afforded
no privacy. The message was from Duncan, asking that
she come to his office. His handwriting was strong and
sure. He'd been here personally leaving it for her, not
calling and having someone else relay the message.

She went to his office and was waved right in by his
secretary.

"Hello," he said. He looked every bit the television
executive, but there was a tenseness about his smile, as
if the secret of them spending the night in the same
house had been broadcast to the staff and the story now
had more flavor to it than the actual truth. She sat down
in the chair he indicated.

"You should know that I've decided to accept the

substitute hostess job.'' She thought she'd get it out as fast as she could. Then this interview would be over and she could leave his office. The space was too small, just as his kitchen had been, and even his huge house. The electricity around them simmered and she was not sure when it might burst into flame.

''I think it's the right decision,'' he added in a businesslike manner. ''You'll find it will probably do wonders for your career.''

The words *I don't want a career* didn't come quite as quickly as they had in the past. She already knew television paid well, and as long as she had her mother to support she'd need the money. Maybe she'd grow to like being a talk show hostess. She wasn't sure she could do the job, but she'd give it a try.

''That's not why I asked to see you,'' Duncan was saying.

''It isn't?''

''I do want you to do the show.'' He sat forward behind the desk. ''Since you've decided that, it does make things easier to explain around here.''

Fear gripped her heart. Had someone discovered she slept at his house?

''On the grounds we have a house which we sometimes use for guests of the show. Not always. Most guests stay at one of the area hotels. They like the amenities hotels offer. However, there are times when glitches happen—we forget to book a room, or there's a change in schedule. During those times we use the guest house. I've made arrangements for you to stay there.''

Aurora sat stunned. ''This is a sort of isolated location.''

''There are twenty-four hour guards. You'll be safe here.''

''Thank you,'' she offered in a tiny voice. She was so thankful that she wanted to hug him but she sat still in the chair. Duncan had saved her from having to stay at her friend's house. She didn't want to bring anyone

else into the mess that comprised her life. Staying at
the studio was the best idea, and it was affordable.

Joyce dropped her at the guest house directly after
lunch. It was more like a guest *mansion*. The grounds
were extensive, with gardens and flower beds that had
been prepared for winter. A few hardy roses still
bloomed in the cold October sunlight.

The house couldn't be seen from the studio. The
studio itself was built on the outskirts of Princeton Township, and Aurora could tell the house had stood for at
least a century. Inside everything was twentieth century.
The kitchen could fill any gourmet chef's wishes. Cop-
per pots she could see her reflection in hung from a
frame against one wall. A butcher block center island
gave plenty of space for laying out ingredients. However,
the room had the feel of being little used. The living
room covered one side of the house. Its furniture was
modern and done in soothing colors. She felt comfortable there. The windows were huge and bowed, providing a curved window seat where she could sit and look
through the old-world system of panes. Aurora imagined
the wooded yard under the cover of snow and smiled.

Upstairs the house had six bedrooms. The master
suite boasted a king-size bed with white lace coverings
and a plethora of rose-colored pillows. The carpet, also
white, sank deeply where she stepped on it. The bathroom seemed the size of a small city, with a shower
that had six heads completely circling the octagonal
structure.

The place was fit for a queen. Not even Marsha Chambers could find fault living here. Aurora unpacked her
meager belongings and returned to the living room.

Duncan had announced to the studio staff that
Aurora would try the hostess spot just before she and
Joyce had come to the house. People congratulated
her. She'd smiled, accepting them, yet she doubted
her ability to pull off the job with the ease of Marsha
Chambers. She'd requested tapes of past programs and

Duncan had sent them over. Her afternoon would be spent reviewing the tapes, watching interview techniques, body language, and generally absorbing the workings of the talk show.

By five o'clock she'd watched four shows and was glad she had a little experience in the film editing department. Slipping the fifth tape into the machine, Aurora listened to the familiar music. Marsha walked through the audience and brought the mike to her mouth. The pad and paper Aurora'd used to write down what she saw lay at her feet. Last night finally caught up with her. Her eyes drooped.

It was the last thing Aurora remembered before the phone rang.

Duncan dropped the phone, already rising from his chair. His watch read seven P.M. Aurora should have been there half an hour ago. He ran through the facility and out the back door. Crossing the compound, he headed for the guest house. His feet echoed on the lighted path. He hadn't seen one guard in his rush to get to the house. Where were they? Had something happened to Aurora, and on the compound grounds?

Banging on the door he shouted her name. Shaking the doorknob, he found it locked. "Aurora!" he shouted, continuing to wrench the door. Aurora opened it and he nearly fell forward.

"What's wrong?" she asked.

"Are you all right? You didn't answer the phone."

"I didn't know where it was," she explained. "I was going toward the sound when it stopped ringing."

Duncan slumped against the doorjamb. He'd thought the worst. "You were supposed to meet me in the studio."

"I'm sorry. I was watching the tapes and I fell asleep."

Duncan wanted to laugh. His heart was returning to normal and he could feel the night air. As he closed the door he'd left open, they faced each other. Then he grabbed her and pulled her against him. He'd tried to fight this feeling. Last night he'd spent the entire night trying to forget how she felt against him when she'd gone into his arms. But now, after the adrenaline had pumped into his system, he was sapped of any restraint. She smelled good, perfumed, and womanly.

He should push her back, he told himself. He promised himself he'd do that in a moment. He'd just hold her for a little longer and then he'd push her back. He wouldn't turn his head and press his lips into her hair, the sweet smelling, heavy mass that framed her face. He wouldn't slide his mouth to her forehead, and down her jawline, and find her mouth. He knew her lips would be soft, wet, and waiting for his possession. He wouldn't squeeze her into him, press her shape against his as if the two of them could merge. He wouldn't do any of that. He held himself back, telling his mind to push, telling his body to stop the rapturous feelings that coursed through his system.

Groaning, he turned his head.

He shouldn't do this.

He couldn't.

Wouldn't.

Did.

Chapter 8

Sitting in Marsha's chair frightened Aurora. She'd looked at the studio from the guest chairs but never from this angle, knowing that her face would be posted on the gigantic screen, going into millions of homes. Fear of failing tinged her consciousness each time she saw the red light on the camera Duncan operated.

Despite him telling her these interviews might never be aired, she knew better. She'd seen the schedule for the next several days. One Hollywood idol had a new movie being released next month. He was coming to plug the movie. Then there was a show on breast cancer, in which several women would tell their personal stories and urge women to perform self examinations and have regular mammograms.

"You're too stiff, Aurora," Duncan said, critiquing her practiced interviewing technique. She'd been trying to run through a mock interview, keep her eyes on the person she was talking to, who was Joyce, and remember the questions Duncan had given her to ask. All this while Duncan recorded her on film.

They'd run through it seven times and she was still

too stiff and too nervous. She wasn't sure her stiffness didn't have something to do with him kissing her earlier. Then she hadn't been stiff at all. Her body had had no more consistency than a bowl of oatmeal. Her legs were rubbery and her heart pummeled against her ribs in an effort to burst through her chest. Her feet had dug into the plush carpet seeking support. Duncan's arms were the only thing which kept her from falling.

She'd been trying to forget that kiss and concentrate on the interview but she couldn't. Each time she looked at him she remembered his mouth on hers and the weakness assaulted her.

"Why don't you tell us how you prepared for the role of—" Her mind went blank. What was he preparing for? "I'm sorry." She looked at Duncan.

Duncan sighed. "Joyce, you'd better go home. I'll stand in."

Joyce smiled and left them.

The studio seemed awfully bright in the places where she sat. She could hardly see the audience seats. She squinted against the harsh lighting.

Duncan took the seat Joyce vacated. "I don't want you to pretend any longer, Aurora."

She relaxed and leaned back in the chair.

"I don't want you to pretend you're Marsha Chambers." He paused and leaned back. "Be Aurora Alexander."

Aurora threw the script he'd given her across the set. It landed on the top step leading to the stage area. Sitting forward in her chair, she realized that looking at tapes of the previous shows had rubbed off on her. She was trying to do what Marsha did, and Duncan had seen it. She wasn't Marsha. Being herself was better than trying to imitate someone else—she would come across as more genuine. She remembered her interviews with battered women and runaway children. They had talked for her because she'd shown she cared about them. Maybe it would be the same here.

Duncan lounged in the chair positioned to her right. His head lay back and she couldn't see his face. His body said he was tired. Aurora saw the light on the camera and knew it was still recording.

"Why did you become a producer?" she asked softly, sincerely.

He didn't raise his head, just began talking. "I didn't start out being a producer. I worked for a small television affiliate in Seattle. It was the kind of place where you did what needed to be done, regardless of your title."

His voice was tired. He spoke from the heart. Aurora could hear it.

"After about a year one of the local news anchors got tapped for a national job. The staff threw him a going away party at a nearby bar. The party broke up and three guys piled into a cab to go home. The cab was involved in an accident and the news producer at the station was killed. The next day I was producing the news."

He'd spoken with such poignancy that Aurora wanted to cry. She reminded herself she was the interviewer.

"How long did you stay there?"

"Three years. Then I went to New York and produced a soap."

Aurora knew he'd worked on *Greenwood*. The show was a fledgling when he took over. It turned around, rose in the charts, and was still one of the top rated daytime dramas.

"*Greenwood* wasn't doing very well rating-wise when you took on the job. Of course, we know where it is today. Why did you leave an Emmy winning news program to play doctor to a soap?"

Duncan lifted his head and looked at her. She wasn't holding any papers and had no planned questions, but she was interviewing him, probing more of his life than he thought she knew. Sitting up straight, he looked at her. Something about the look in her eyes made him want to answer. She looked genuinely interested. He wanted to tell her. It wasn't a secret, but he wasn't used to talking about himself.

"From New York you returned to the West Coast," she stated.

"I went to Los Angeles. I had the idea of working on blockbuster movies, but again I got offered a job in television and I was back to producing." He could have stopped there. Why didn't he? "I worked on a sitcom. The show was plagued by problems from day one. The actors couldn't work together, the set wasn't comfortable, the writers were poor."

"None of this was known to the public. *Lost in Love* went on for several seasons. All the actors are making it big time."

He nodded.

"When it went off the air you signed on to this show."

"It wasn't this show. That came a few months later. But I've been here since."

"Are you ready to move on?"

The question was so perceptive that Duncan wondered if she hadn't heard the rumors.

"Have you been listening at keyholes?" He grinned.

"There is talk that your time here is limited, and that you have at least two very hot irons in the fire in Los Angeles."

He looked at her but didn't say anything.

"Wouldn't you care to comment, dispel the rumors, put the tongue-waggers to rest?"

Somehow he felt he needed to answer her. She was a natural at interviewing. She made him feel that he was sitting in an intimate living room before a roaring fire with a glass of warm brandy, not on the set of a program that went into twenty millions homes each day. He felt that if he answered her only the two of them would know. Duncan knew he'd been right in choosing her to stand in. When Marsha saw these she'd get up from a deathbed to protect her interests.

"The truth is, I *am* working on a Hollywood connection. I don't care to comment on what the projects are. Let's just say they're big."

"And plural," she said grabbing the word. "As in more than one?"

Duncan remained silent. Then Aurora took another tack. She began asking him about his childhood, his parents. He answered all her questions, even the tough ones.

"So you and Cooper Dean ran a gambling operation at the age of twelve?"

"We were both headed for a life of crime."

"You don't look the criminal type. I see more of a Philadelphia lawyer in you. What turned you around?"

Duncan checked his clothes. He didn't go for jeans and T-shirts on the job. He met with many people coming in the studio. Even though it was television, people expected him to dress as a businessman. And he did. He'd pulled his tie loose and discarded his jacket, but the implication of a suit was still present. "Coop took a bullet in the shoulder one night as we ran from gang members who said we were working their turf. We gave it up then and there."

"And they let you?"

Duncan heard the amazement in her voice, watched her eyes widen. He knew how gangs worked. If they wanted you dead, you were dead. "My parents packed us both off to spend the summer on a farm. We were worked so hard there we had no time to do anything like getting in trouble."

"You did have time to talk, however."

God, she was good, he thought. "We talked most nights." He laughed, remembering the dark bedroom he and Coop had slept in. "We talked about what we'd do when we got back, what we would be when we grew up, but mostly we talked about home."

"You were homesick?"

"Not in the way most people are. We talked about our parents. About whether they had made a success of their lives. We were twelve, remember, and your parents are way over the hill when you're twelve.''

Aurora bowed her head and gave him her direct attention. She kept the interview on keel, not allowing him to divert it to another subject. She was going to be wonderful. He was sure of it.

"What did you decide?"

"We decided that Mr. Woodford was a success."

Her eyebrows went up.

"Mr. Woodford owned the farm. He struggled with Mother Nature every day of his life. He took two city boys onto his farm and tried to teach them the meaning of life. It got through. And so he was a success."

Duncan went to see Mr. Woodford every chance he got. He always learned something new, and he enjoyed getting his hands in the earth and coaxing the land to give him what he wanted. "You gotta love the land," Mr. Woodford had told him. He could still hear the rough way his voice sounded when he talked. The more he believed in something the rougher his tone. To this day he still took city boys in for the summer. Duncan couldn't help but believe they left better than they arrived. He wondered how many kids had turned their lives around because of Mr. Woodford. He was a man who quietly taught them that the integrity of doing something and doing it well was the best use of their lives, whether they chose to be garbage men or company presidents.

"And your parents?" Aurora brought him back. "Do you consider them a success?"

Duncan leaned against the soft cushions of the chair. "My father once said, 'I can't protect you from the world. You're going to have to make your own decisions and your own choices. Some of those choices will be the right ones and some won't, but in the entire scheme of things, let's hope you have more right ones than wrong.' " Duncan's throat was tight. "My father was a success."

* * *

Is he out there? Aurora wondered with a shudder. He didn't know Marsha wasn't here. Would he do anything in the studio? He'd tried to kidnap her in broad daylight. Was he bold enough to make another attempt? Aurora's skin tingled, telling her she was scared.

The audience had taken seats. She could hear the excitement created by a room full of people. Her stomach lurched. She swayed between throwing up from fright and the excitement of being on stage. There was as much electricity in the air as was supplying the cameras. Tourists from all over the U.S. were out there. They could return home and tell stories of how they'd seen the show filmed. They were the safe ones. What about the man who was looking for her? *Looking for Marsha,* she corrected. Was he out there? Had he passed through the gates and entered the studio like any other guest?

She heard the associate producer playing crowd pleaser. He told jokes, making the audience laugh. His job was to get them ready for the show, have them in a good frame of mind before she took her seat.

The music began and the audience, prompted by overhead applause signs and the producer's gestures, made a noise as the voice of the announcer introduced *The Marsha Chambers Show.* Then a second voice came over the studio. She recognized it as Duncan's. *Sitting in for the vacationing Marsha Chambers is this week's co-hostess, Rory Alexander.*

Aurora put a hand to her stomach and took a deep breath. She had no choice now but to step into the light. *One more second,* she thought, then entered with a smile. Duncan had called her Rory. It unnerved her to hear the family name over the loudspeaker. Seeing it painted across the large monitor arrested her attention. She smiled, thinking how wonderful it looked in huge purple letters.

The teleprompter rolled in front of her. She swallowed her fear and began to read the memorized greeting. At the end of the first applause segment, she introduced herself.

"You're all probably wondering why I was chosen to take Marsha Chambers's place while she's away. Here's one reason."

She looked at the monitor. From the center of the blank screen Marsha Chambers appeared. The film of the previous show rolled. "And now, my own personal look-alike." The monitor showed Aurora stepping onto the stage to wide applause. The film froze on her face and the engineer in the control room split the screen and placed Marsha's picture next to Aurora's. "See the resemblance?"

The audience applauded. She scanned them, looking for disapproval. She saw none. There were wide smiles and happy grins. Aurora relaxed. They weren't going to stone her. If she interviewed well, everything would be fine. The guest today was a movie star, one of her idols. If she didn't trip over her tongue everything would go fine.

"We're going to get right to our guest today. You all know him." She didn't even get to finish the introduction before the audience went wild. "He's one of my idols, too, and I've only just met him in the green room a moment ago." She was barely able to continue over the noise. Aurora decided to change the programmed intro. "I suppose he needs no further introduction. Ladies and gentlemen, meet the star of such movies as *The Pelican Brief, Philadelphia* and *Glory.*" She waited for the screaming to die down but she didn't think it would. "Denzel Washington!" she screamed over the mayhem.

Aurora knew a lot of the applause would have to be edited out of this interview. When she could speak they both took seats in front of the audience. She asked some of the questions which had been prepared for her and some she wanted to know the answers to, and then they went to the audience. The program took on a whole new aspect when she included audience questions. They were serious, funny, even risqué at points. She was having a good time. She'd completely forgotten that the stalker could be a member of the audience, forgotten how she'd fought against going in front of the cameras, forgotten Marsha Chambers's insults. The only thing she didn't forget was Duncan standing on the fringe of the audience and overseeing everything.

She didn't forget her interview with him. Duncan was leaving soon. He had big projects going on in Hollywood, and he had no ties, nothing to keep him in New Jersey. The world of film was on the coast, and when his plans came together—as they would and should— he'd be part of her past, not her present.

Be careful, she cautioned her heart. *Don't let him get too close. He's a knight, he comes to your rescue, but he's also chasing a dream, one he's had for a lifetime. Keep your head, and your heart won't get hurt.*

This was good, he thought, leaving the studio with the other guests. It's exactly what he would have done. The old confuse-the-villain-plot. He nearly laughed out loud. Marsha Chambers was worth every one of those Emmys she picked up year after year. She was a talented actress. But she was making a mistake. She wasn't dealing with a fool.

She could say her name was Rory. She could even show footage of a previous show and the audience would eat it up. She could use any name she wanted. He knew about television, knew that a good engineer could put anything on the screen and people would believe it.

Well, he didn't believe it, not for one minute. She was Marsha Chambers. He'd bet his right arm on that. And even if she was some look-alike, that was just too bad, because *she'd* get what she deserved for trying to get in his way.

He had plans. Nobody got in his way.

* * *

Aurora was still on an emotional high when the last light in the studio went out. Adrenaline poured into her blood and kept her floating with excitement. She'd only stumbled over a couple of words, and they would be edited out. The audience had been friendly and Denzel had made her feel comfortable. She hoped each show would have this much excitement, this much electricity in the making.

"You look like someone who's just gone to her first ball," Duncan said, coming into the studio.

"I feel like it." She got up and pulled her coat on. They were going to get something to eat. Even with the dream kitchen in the guest house, Duncan said she shouldn't have to cook her own meal on her first night.

As he drove through the streets of Princeton toward the restaurant, she relived the show as if he hadn't been there and she needed to give him the play-by-play.

In the restaurant she was immediately greeted with the usual mistaken identity attention. This time she didn't correct the waiter. She felt too good tonight, and she wouldn't allow anything to spoil the feeling.

"So you liked it?" Duncan said after they were seated and Duncan had ordered champagne cocktails. He said a princess on the night of her first ball needed the bubbly. She didn't disagree.

"I admit you were right. Things went much better than I thought they would." She wondered how Marsha could possibly scorn the fun she'd had today. She didn't bother to ask.

"You know, Cinderella, every show doesn't have a Hollywood celebrity as the guest."

Aurora nodded.

"We try to add variety."

"I know."

"You'll be all right?"

"I'll be fine."

Aurora was sure of it. She had a lot of help on the stage. There was Duncan giving her signals from the side of the studio, the questions she had prepared, and the ones which came up on her own. She was more sure now than she'd been yesterday that next week would go all right.

She brought up the real hostess. "What about Marsha? Do you think she's heard about the taping?"

"I'm not sure. It hasn't been that long. When I spoke to Coop he told me she's been moved to a private location."

Aurora didn't want to think about Coop or what he might have discovered about the stalker. Not tonight. Tonight she wanted only happy thoughts.

Duncan interrupted her thoughts. "I thought you liked doing the show."

"I do. I just thought that Marsha might have changed her mind."

"Marsha can be stubborn," Duncan went on.

The waiter brought their drinks and he toasted her. Warmth poured into her face. She was glad the restaurant was dark, or he might see the rosy glow that changed the tone of her dark brown skin.

Dinner was easy and satisfying. Aurora couldn't think of a time when she'd felt this carefree. Certainly not since she'd come to the studio. Before that she'd had the strain of maintaining her mother in the nursing home. Her sisters and brother were in no position to help her. Claudia, the youngest, worked in Hawaii, living hand-to-mouth. Adrienne, the oldest, had three small children and was married to a high school science teacher. She couldn't afford to support their mother. Their brother, Eric, had only just decided to do something with his life. He'd bummed around doing one odd job after another until he was thirty, then decided to go to law school. He'd graduate next year. And Nora, Eric's twin—Nora the nomad, the family called her— was in Montana living on a ranch. She sent money regularly, but she was the only one. It was a small amount, not nearly enough. The others sent money when they could spare it, but Aurora bore the bulk of the financial burden.

Over dessert and coffee she and Duncan talked easily, and leaving the restaurant she felt like Cinderella getting into her gilded carriage and riding through the streets on her way back to her castle.

Then the fairy tale ended. As Duncan turned onto a deserted road leading back to the studio, something bumped the back of the small car.

"What the—" Duncan looked into the rearview mirror. Behind them was a dark van. He couldn't see anyone inside. Fear kicked in and he knew instinctively that the driver was the same person who'd stalked Aurora. Pushing the accelerator, he moved the speed up a notch. The van kept pace with them.

Princeton streets were small and narrow. In the borough at this later hour, cars were parked on both sides of the street at this late hour. In the township, trees, gullies, or landscape rocks dotted the curbless roadside. Beside him Aurora held her breath and said nothing. She looked over her shoulder constantly at the approaching van.

Duncan swung the car into a sharp right turn, barreling down an unknown alley. The van wasn't as agile. Duncan thought they'd lost it. He came out of the alley at high speed and missed the van by inches. He swerved the car. His position was no better than it had been. The van stood on his tail like a shadow, moving closer and closer. It bumped the car, making them pitch forward.

"Where are the cops?" Aurora asked.

Duncan knew he wasn't going to be able to count on cops. They were in this alone. The van pulled alongside them, inching closer and closer, trying to push the small car off the road. Duncan moved to the right. Ahead he saw a boulder coming up fast. Quickly he hit the brake.

The car left rubber on the dry road as friction created smoke, and an acrid odor penetrated the car. Duncan swung the car around and headed in the opposite direction.

Before the van could execute the same move he swung the car onto a nearby road. He'd hoped for another side road to take so the van wouldn't see the taillights when it made the same turn, but he was out of luck. The road went straight up. He kept ahead of the van, negotiating the sharp twists and turns that area of central Jersey was known for. Then he saw the blinking red light ahead.

The van gained on him. There was no way he could take the turn at the speed he was going. He'd kill them both. Sure that was the goal of the driver behind them, Duncan had to settle for sailing through the light. Trees lined the road on both sides, preventing him from seeing any oncoming traffic.

"Damn," he cursed. There was a car stopping at the light. The car started up. Duncan checked the mirror. The van was practically in his backseat. Aurora held onto the dash in front of her, a position that would surely break her arms if he slammed into the car in front of him.

He had to make a decision. The car was in the intersection. Bright lights flicked up in the direction behind the car. He knew another was approaching. He had no choice but to swerve to miss it. It was going to be tight—if they made it at all.

"Move your arms!" he shouted. At the same time, he pulled the steering wheel into a wide right. The oncoming car braked and swerved. He went into the embankment, across the field, and plowed through a wooden fence.

Aurora screamed.

Two air bags popped out and pushed them back. The car continued its slide across the field, plowing up dirt and creating parallel scars on the black earth. The abrupt stop against a tree made Duncan's head snap back against the headrest.

He tried to call Aurora. His voice was too low. Nothing came out. Looking at her, he wanted to know if she was all right. Pain clouded his eyes. She lay limply against the door. Muffled voices penetrated his brain, people screaming a long way off. In the mirror he saw the van. Then the darkness took him.

Chapter 9

"Hey, Buddy, what happened to all those lessons in defensive driving I taught you?"

Duncan lay on the hospital emergency room bed and tried to smile as Coop came through the curtain. He knew Coop was concerned, and this was as close to admitting it as the six-foot-seven cop would ever get.

"From what I'm told by the witnesses at the scene you did some pretty fancy work getting into that field. You want to give me your version?"

"What about Aurora?" Duncan asked. "Is she all right? She had her hands on the console. I was sure she'd break her arms."

"She's fine. A few cuts and bruises, nothing a little makeup can't fix. Her X-rays and lab tests had just come back and the doctors were releasing her. She had a big smile on her face when I saw her."

Just as Duncan began to wonder about his own tests the doctor came in and released him. "You can dress," he said. "You'll be sore for a few days but over-the-counter pain-killers should be sufficient. I suggest you see your own doctor for a full checkup."

With that he wrote something on a clipboard and left the curtained room. Coop went to find Aurora while Duncan found his pants.

Daylight was four hours away when they left the hospital in Coop's police car. Aurora sat quietly next to Duncan in the backseat. She looked tired and shaken. He slipped his arm around her and pulled her close. She didn't resist. Her head fell on his shoulder and he cradled her there for the drive back to the studio.

Aurora wanted out. She didn't like being chased down streets by some unknown van. She didn't like having to leave her home and have guards patrolling for her safety. She didn't like the fact that she'd agreed to this program and plunged herself into a danger that was too deep to get out of. The killer was fixated on her, now. Marsha Chambers sat comfortably safe in some unknown location while she, Aurora, stood in the forefront of danger.

She snuggled closer to Duncan. His arm tightened around her. For a moment she imagined they were lovers traveling through the streets in a horsedrawn carriage. All too soon Coop pulled the car onto the compound, and the duty guard checked the car before passing them through. She wasn't in a horsedrawn carriage and Duncan wasn't her lover. They were just two people who'd been caught up in someone's evil scheme.

And there was no getting out.

Aurora went on that afternoon. She did the taping with enough makeup to add another layer of skin to her face. It hid her bruises. Long sleeves covered the cuts on her arms. Duncan arranged the set so that she wouldn't have to move much. She was grateful for his thoughtfulness.

In the ensuing days nothing out of the ordinary

occurred. The show fell into a routine. She attacked the subject of deadbeat Dads, had fun with "Whatever Happened To . . ." stars from old television programs, and showcased some local talent trying to make it in today's entertainment world. She'd become used to the show—the cameras, the motion that went on around the set. Her injuries faded and she began to relax a little.

Cooper Dean had grilled her on possible enemies. Suppose the man pursuing her wasn't looking for Marsha, but really had his sights on her? Who could it be? She'd made enemies in Social Services—pulling women away from johns and pimps didn't always make her best friend material—but she had no reputation for being the master destroyer of the nightlife system. When she walked away no one missed her. Certainly no one had waited three years to begin a campaign to kill her.

She was sure that he was after Marsha, and she had unknowingly, stepped in the line of fire. As Aurora was the official Marsha look-alike, she had to do something about her position.

Aurora tried hard to make the mansion less of a prison. She became used to the guard patrolling day and night. She'd had food brought to stock the refrigerator and cupboards. Most days she cooked her own meals although the studio was prepared to supply them or hire a cook. Aurora was used to living alone and taking care of her own needs, and she didn't want another personality in the house.

Today's taping had proved long and it was well past dark when Aurora arrived at the mansion. Removing the stage makeup and changing into a knee-length, gold sweater and stirrup pants, she was about to sit down to eat when someone knocked on the kitchen door. Looking up she saw Duncan and her heart pounded.

"That's not your dinner, is it?" he said, coming into

the kitchen and seeing the tea and toast she'd set on the counter.

"Would you like to join me?" She didn't like heavy meals late at night. Duncan slipped out of his overcoat and jacket, then grabbed the loaf of bread from the counter and popped two slices in the toaster. Aurora sat down and watched him. They hadn't been alone since the accident. If he had any bruises, they were hidden. She had no physical problems, and had been allowed to resume all activities by the studio physician, Marvin Taylor. Aurora was glad of that. The taping the next day involved the national gymnastics team, and she was prepared to go through the motions with them—or at least try.

"How are you?" she asked, meaning his injuries. "Any lasting effects from the accident?"

He shook his head. "I saw Marv yesterday."

Aurora didn't need a doctor to tell her he was in good condition. He looked like a recruitment ad for the marines. Dress whites couldn't have made him look taller, leaner, or more delicious. Aurora took a sip of her tea and let the electrical impulses that seemed to jump from him to her skim over her skin. She'd thought she'd get used to the sensation. She hadn't. It grew more pleasurable each time they were together.

"Did you hear from Coop?"

"Not a word. I did hear from Marsha."

Just a small quirk flipped in her stomach. Aurora's eyebrows rose. Duncan took the seat before her and poured his own cup of tea.

"Is she coming back?"

"Not yet. She didn't even mention the show."

Aurora couldn't account for the elation that ran through her. "Isn't that a little unusual?"

He shook his head. "With Marsha, you never know."

As October blended into November, the trees in the landscaped yard had lost most of their leaves. A few of them dotted the walkway. The majority had been swept away by the groundskeeper.

"So I get to keep this gig for one more week," she tried to joke. Duncan looked at her over his mug. His face was serious.

"You're doing a wonderful job," he said.

She bowed her head. "Thank you, kind sir."

"I mean that. You're a natural out there, and you get involved. Audiences like that. Tomorrow the first show airs. I'm sure the public will find you just as lovable—" He stopped mid-sentence. She wondered what he was about to say. "You can probably expect calls to come in offering you a test, or your own show."

Aurora laughed.

"I mean it," he said. "I just thought I'd warn you."

She didn't know what to say. He had to be wrong.

She did like doing the show. She couldn't deny that. It was fun. The audience, the staff, and the guests—everyone made her job easy. Especially the man in front of her.

Aurora stood up. She didn't want him to see what was in her eyes. She didn't know what was there. She knew that whenever he looked at her she felt as if the world tilted a fraction.

Life had been simpler before she stopped reminding him of Marsha, Duncan thought. He couldn't remember when it had happened, maybe during one of the tapings, maybe when he felt her hurt and vulnerable in his arms as they came back from the hospital. He couldn't pinpoint the exact moment, but it had happened and there was nothing he could do about it.

Duncan couldn't pull his gaze away from her. Wherever she moved he followed her. When had this happened to him? She stopped in front of him. Did she say something? He couldn't hear. Blood rushed through his ears, making a hollow sound like a seashell.

He didn't know the moment when it registered in his brain that he was going to kiss her, but it was there involuntarily, as if he couldn't go on breathing if he didn't follow his instinct. He stood up. She stood facing the living room, her gaze not focused on anything. She was probably thinking about what he'd said.

Walking up behind her, he circled her waist and pulled her back against him. She didn't resist, didn't protest. She was soft to his touch, warm and sweet-smelling.

He turned her around. His left arm circled her waist and his right slipped under her hair and drew her toward him.

She resisted slightly. He continued to close the small distance until his lips hovered above hers. He smelled the scent of her, the rush going straight to his head, tasted her sweet tea-breath, getting dizzy as if it were a powerful drug.

Then his mouth touched hers and all his pleasure senses leapt into overdrive. He buried his hand in her hair, pulling her closer, leaning into her as passion's magnum force overtook him.

He felt the exact moment when Aurora's resistance evaporated. She arched her back, curving into him, her arms moving up his back. Her head fell back. His mouth touched hers. Her lips parted. His tongue rushed inside as if an abyss had been created and needed filling. He was there to fill it, and he could think of nothing other than the intoxicating aura that surrounded him, that drove him on, over the edge of sanity and into the region where individuals abandon the physical and defy gravity as they float toward another plane, another dimension.

Her body was boneless chocolate, warm and oozing against his heated skin. Duncan thought nothing could rival this moment. He wanted her and wanted her now. Lowering his hands to her hips, he pulled her hard against the agonizing juncture of his legs. He nearly shouted at the pleasure that drove through him. He had to stop. If he didn't he'd rip her clothes off in this kitchen and give new meaning to the term gourmet meal.

"Rory," he groaned, forcing himself to push back. She made a sound in her throat that nearly undid him. "Rory," he called again. It came so naturally to his lips, like a special name that only a lover could understand. He wanted to keep calling her that. In the dark hours of the morning he wanted to turn to her and call her Rory.

"I didn't come here for this," he said. Her eyes focused on him. A second later she stepped back out of his arms. He let her go.

"Why did you come?"

He couldn't answer. He couldn't remember. She looked too sexy for him to think of anything other than his hands mussing her hair, his mouth abusing hers. He wanted her body against his, keeping it warm, holding off the November cold and sending him into crazy delight.

Aurora took a step forward, abandoning everything except the fact that she wanted him. She reached for the suspenders. Today's were black, stretchy with gold clasps. She didn't know why they fascinated her. They did. She'd wanted to touch them, touch him, ever since they'd first met. Now she was going to.

Her eyes remained on his. Her hands opened the clasps. Keeping them from snapping upward, she slid her hands over his shoulders and let the suspenders fall down his back. Duncan grabbed her hands as they came up. His eyes seemed dark, a hot liquid that melted her in his gaze. She ran her hand over his chest and down to take both his hands. Hers were small inside his; long and slender matched with sure and confident. A soft smile curved her lips and she stepped back, tugging at him. He followed her up the curved staircase that led to the second floor and to the master suite with its huge bed. Anticipation made her mouth dry, sent a live wire dancing through her belly, and made her familiar with every nerve ending in her body. She could almost name them as they screamed at her.

Near the bed he stopped her and slid his arms around her small waist as slowly as clock hands moving toward the hour. As his arms met over the shock waves ricocheting inside her she leaned back. She heard his tortured groan. His mouth seared her neck until she was sure he'd branded her skin. She didn't want him to stop. Sensation washed over her like an oil fire—slick, fast, hot.

"Duncan," she called, her voice hoarse, lower than its normal pitch. "Duncan, this is driving me crazy."

"I've already passed crazy," he whispered, passion full-bodied in his sex-lined voice.

Quickly he turned her around, his mouth finding hers like a heat-seeking missile. The kiss burned her, sealing her mouth to his as his tongue swept inside, taking possession of her with a need that was deep with longing. Aurora had never felt so possessed, so willing to be possessed. Suddenly she wanted skin. She wanted to know the feel of his skin, merging, flowing, joining with hers. She wanted to see the color contrast, know the texture, learn her way around his body the way she'd learned the film, and the stage.

Groping for buttons, she loosened them, pushing each one through the holes until her fingers brushed the fire beneath the fabric. Could a man hold that much heat and not incinerate? Could she contain it, or would he liquify her?

Duncan's fingers gathered the sweater until they reached the hem. His hands slipped under it, speaking the sweet, passionate language of arousal as they found her, caressed her, massaged the pliant flesh that understood the tongue. The dialect was not foreign. She'd learned it the moment he looked at her. His eyes had spoken it and she'd understood.

Lifting the sweater away she felt the cool air. Gulping it in she tried to breathe, but took the male aroma of

Duncan into her nostrils. No aphrodisiac could be more potent than the smell of a man in full sexual arousal.

In seconds Aurora was clawing at his clothes and he was pushing her pants to the floor. Naked they stood. Her hands rested on his shoulders. A mere breath of air separated them. Her breasts, uplifted and pointy, stretched toward him. Light from the hall turned him into a golden god.

"Now," he said in a controlled voice. "I'm going to make love to you."

Her throat closed. No words had ever affected her so much as those just uttered. She felt each one touch her as if it were a precious stone he'd strung around her neck. Duncan didn't know it, but she felt as if it were the first time for her. Making love with him would be different from any experience she'd had in the past. She knew it. Her body knew it.

He laid her on the bed and joined her, hovering above her.

"Duncan, I want it to be slow."

"I'll try my best." He kissed her cheek, settling onto her, allowing her to take his weight as it pressed her into the mattress.

"I don't mean you."

His mouth didn't stop its motion. It worked its way down her throat to her breast. When he took her into his mouth she gasped, unable to stem the rapture that rushed through her like a wild fire. "I mean me," she finished when coherent thought made it possible for her to speak.

This was going fast, she tried to tell herself. She tried to let him know, but her legs spread and he filled the gap. A pleasure roared from inside her, threatening to overwhelm her. Unable to stop herself she rubbed against him. He groaned in reaction.

"It's been a long time, Duncan. I'm afraid."

He looked at her. His eyes were full of passion. "I won't hurt you."

"I'm not afraid of being hurt. I'm afraid it will come too fast."

Duncan silenced her with a kiss. His knee separated her legs. They were silky, smooth, and long. He slid his down hers, knowing she would move and brush against him, knowing the pleasure she generated with each movement. She was hot and he was burning off the scale. Her mouth tasted of love and sweet tea and he drank from it as a dying man drinks. She was driving him crazy. He wasn't sure he could survive this much longer. He wasn't even sure he could get the condom on before he exploded.

Raising himself, he entered her, easily filling her. She gasped into his mouth. Her legs wound around him and pulled him all the way into her. Together they made music, their own music. They joined and rejoined, swinging to the hot jazz rhythms of a New Orleans juke-joint, dancing to the down home sound of a blues guitar, and rising to the crescendo of a symphony orchestra.

Duncan knew his life was changing. He'd never really made love before. He'd told Aurora he was going to make love to her when he had no knowledge, no experience, of what he meant. Aurora had him wanting to shout, wanting to cry out for her to stop the pleasure, wanting her to continue it until he died from an overdose of her. He continued, drove himself into her as he'd never driven before. Over and over he pulled and pushed into the well that seemed to know him, want him, was made for him only. Then he felt it. He'd held it back as long as he could. It rose inside him, fighting to be released, fighting to burst through his control. The metamorphosis was fast, like a flash fire of nuclear proportions. His entire body changed, became a solid mass of need. It beat, throbbed, rushed blood through his system like a frenzied prisoner.

"Rory! Rory!" He shouted her name. The words came without volition. He could no more control them than he could the monster that drove him, the dragon that breathed fire into his loins and seemed to blow faster and harder, pushing him higher and higher until the two merged and he succumbed to the fiery-hot demon and exploded in blessed release.

Chapter 10

Aurora's eyelids drooped. Luckily she didn't have to go before the cameras today. The insistent little things were so unforgiving. They saw everything—every extra pound, every wrinkle, every shadow under the eyes. After making love with Duncan until the early morning she'd had to use extra makeup to hide the telltale results.

She felt wonderful. Duncan had said he'd make love to her, and he had. She smiled, checking the ceiling as if she could see him. She knew what he looked like—his golden body contrasting with the white sheet, disarrayed in a pattern that spoke of having sex and making love. She'd enjoyed both of them.

Fanning herself, she knew better than to let her thoughts go in that direction. She went back to making her cookies. Today she visited her mother and it was cookie time of the year. They celebrated the season, announced the coming of winter and the holidays. It was one of Aurora's favorite times of the year. Taking a moment to gulp down some coffee, she packed the car and left Duncan a note.

Smiling, she went out the door, waving at the guard as she passed him. November was one of her favorite months. The last of the leaves were gone and the holidays were in the air. The malls and stores had already been decorated and she could see a Santa everywhere she looked.

Somehow she felt today would be different. Maybe her mother would recognize her. Anyway, her spirits were high.

Aurora checked the mirror. She'd become used to Duncan doing it each time they went anywhere, and since the accident she'd wanted to make sure she wasn't being followed by a dark van. Behind her the street was clear except for two cars. One turned off at Washington Road and the other skimmed into a parking space on Nassau Street. She continued up Route 206 heading North.

Her visit was no different than those of the previous three years. Her mother talked, although her speech was beginning to slur. Aurora couldn't remember it being like that on her last visit. Cassandra Alexander hadn't lost any weight. Her frowns were more frequent, though.

Aurora shortened her visit to speak to her mother's doctor. He told her everything that was happening was to be expected. The man was compassionate and caring. Dr. Christian had been her mother's doctor from the time she'd moved into the facility. Aurora liked him and believed him. It didn't make her feel any better that her mother was folding inside herself, cutting off small pieces of reality.

When she left his office she returned to her mother. The need to be close to her kept Aurora there. For a while she just watched. Either Cass didn't notice she was in the room or had forgotten she'd left and come back. Aurora didn't know which was the case.

Then she went to her mother, sat next to her on the sofa, and pulled her into her arms. She held her like a small child and talked to her. Aurora knew she didn't understand, had no remembrance of her, her other children, or the husband she'd lived with for more than a quarter of a century. Aurora told her about her children, about the daughters she had who were married, about her grandchildren, her son in law school and her daughter studying in Hawaii.

She told her about her husband. Even when she knew her mother had fallen asleep she continued to explain. Continued to relive what she could remember of the relationship they'd had as a family. Even when the tears blurred her vision and spilled down her cheeks she went on. It was something she had to do, for herself as well as her mother. She needed to tell her mother everything. She needed to be forgiven. Why, she didn't understand. She needed to exorcize the guilt she felt for not being able to help, for not being able to stop this from happening. She understood, at least her mind did, that she did nothing to cause the condition and there was nothing she could do to stop it, but that didn't keep her heart from holding onto the guilt.

She wanted another chance—to make more memories, to take her mother to places she'd never seen, to sit and talk with her, tell her things that mothers and daughters understood. She wanted to take back her rebellious teenage years and replace them with glorious days of laughter and fun. Aurora wanted to hug her mother, and know that Cassandra Alexander understood the love that she'd always felt for her.

Aurora rocked her mother. Sitting on the sofa with Cass asleep, she rocked and rocked and rocked. She heard the door open and knew the nurses stood there. It was either time for medication or a meal. She didn't know which. She'd lost track of time, like her mother. Time didn't hold meaning. Only love had meaning. Hot tears spilled down her face. Her mother had said that to her long ago and somehow, from somewhere, she remembered it.

"I love you, Mama." She wiped away the tears with her fingertips. "I love you, Mama. I've always loved you."

Someone moved behind her, then came to stand in front of her. She didn't stop the rocking, didn't look up for the nurse. She just moved back and forth with a slow swinging movement, like a wind up cradle.

"Aurora."

Duncan stooped down and looked at her. Through her tears she saw it wasn't the nurse.

"She's fallen asleep," Aurora said. "She's isn't going to come back, Duncan." A huge sob made her sniff. "She's gone . . . lost to me. She'll never see me again. Never know me."

"Give her to me." He looked over her and signaled to someone. Then he took Cassandra Alexander in his arms. Aurora's hands released her. Two white coated orderlies lifted her mother and gently placed her on the bed.

"She's never coming back," Aurora whispered and the tears flooded through, falling from her eyes as if from a broken dam.

Duncan didn't speak on the way to his house. He didn't think he could. Being part of *The Marsha Chambers Show*, he'd been privy to emotional scenes that reached extremes. The worse moments happened when the cameras weren't rolling. Nothing in his experience compared with today's heart-wrenching episode, though. He wanted to help Aurora, wanted to take her pain away, and shoulder it as his own, but he could no more stem the flow of tears coming from her eyes than he could prevent the wind from blowing or the earth from turning.

She was alone, as alone as her mother, who was caught somewhere between this world and one of her own making. He thought Cassandra Alexander's was safe and painless, while her daughter struggled with demons.

He didn't want to take Aurora back to the studio compound until she'd had time to recover. He'd been furious when he woke to find her gone. The moment he smelled the sugar he knew where she was. Every nerve in his body was tense when he discovered the guards had let her pass through the gates alone. She was in his car. They'd assumed he was with her, when all she had was a seat full of boxes.

Arriving at the nursing home he had been ready to part with the few remaining brain cells he hadn't burned off worrying over her when he found her rocking her mother and crying. He never wanted to see her that unhappy again. He'd stood by the door, his heart lodged in his throat, his own eyes misty with emotion, until he could pull himself together enough to help her.

He pulled into his driveway and pushed the button for the garage door. He helped her from the car and into the house. He took her to the sofa in his living room.

"Lie down and I'll make you something to eat."

"I'm not hungry." Her voice was flat, as if she were in shock.

"Then rest and I'll make tea."

She sat staring. He didn't like it. She could make herself sick. After the night they'd spent together, how could she go off alone?

He'd reached for her, finding her space empty and cold. Disappointed, he'd gone in search, but opening the door he'd smelled the sweetness, tasted the sugar on the air—and knew. He didn't need the empty feel of the house or the sound of walls with no heart beating in them to tell him he was the only living person there.

He left her. Tea would make her feel better. He'd brew it, bring it to her, make her drink it. He spent his time in the kitchen efficiently, not dragging out time to enjoy the process, only following the functional and quick method of boiling water and gathering cups and saucers. When he returned to the living room she was no longer sitting up. He put the tray down. Her head lay on one arm, her feet still on the floor. He removed her shoes and pulled her feet up, then covered her with an afghan.

Pouring himself a cup, he sank in the armchair across from her and watched.

Bells woke her. Aurora heard them from a distance. She wondered where they could be. There weren't any bells in her house. Then the deep, resonant sound of the gongs beat out the hour. She opened her eyes. This wasn't home. Then she remembered. The morning's activities came back like the aftermath of a nightmare.

Duncan slouched in the armchair across from her. He'd fallen asleep. She smiled slightly at him. He'd come for her as if she were in danger and brought her here. The cold pot of tea sat on the table between them. He was a nice man, she thought. A good man. She admitted she was more than a little in love with him. In time she knew she could fall all the way. But she no longer had the right.

Alzheimer's Disease could be hereditary. She'd seen her future this morning. One day she would be in the same secret place her mother inhabited. In a land where no one could reach her, where there was no today nor tomorrow, no past nor future. The people she loved and who loved her would not even be memories. That was the worst part, Aurora thought. Tears formed in her eyes again. To think that the good times would go, that they would just slip away one night like the closing of a door, of never being able to open it again, or to even remember that there was a door to open.

This was her fate. She let the tears spill, hot and scalding, down her face. They collected in her ears and she didn't move to clear them. She cried for the lost

love she would never know, for the growing love she
had to forego. She cried for the children and grandchildren that wouldn't be hers. She cried for the past, the
memories she had which she'd lose, and for the future
ones she'd make and forget.

She'd been close, she thought, so close. Duncan was
the first man in years she'd wanted to know better. He
made love to her, incredible love. He'd taken her to
levels she didn't know existed and she wanted to go
there again and again with this man. She wanted to
savor her time with Duncan West, hold the memory of
him like a warm winter blanket when he left to pursue
his goals in California. Now she knew that no matter how
many times he made love to her, in time she wouldn't
remember it.

Split personality. That was the only term Duncan
could think of to describe what had become of Aurora
since the visit to her mother a week ago. During the
tapings she was the same—compassionate, warm, connecting with the audience and the guests. As soon as
the lights went out on the stage, she crawled behind
that protective wall she'd erected around herself. She
seemed determined she wouldn't let anybody get near
her. She wasn't unfriendly. If someone stopped her and
asked a question, she'd answer, engage in conversation,
but she'd soon excuse herself and slip off to the guest
house.

She spent hours there, seeing no one, talking to no
one. The only times she'd even let him near her were on
the set, or when discussing some aspect of the program.

She hadn't talked about her mother. Duncan recognized she was grieving for a woman alive but totally lost
to her. He wanted to help her through it but didn't
know how. He wanted to hold her, kiss her, make incredible love like they'd done before, but she barely spoke

to him. He felt she went out of her way to avoid him.
It was making him crazy.

Aurora came in then. He saw her from the window
in the control room. Wearing a red jumpsuit with a
short, blue, waist-length top and white sneakers, she
looked ravishing. The waist nipped in, and Duncan
clenched hands that itched to curve around it. She
stepped around equipment being readied for today's
taping, her movements as graceful as a tiger's. His loins
tightened in reaction.

Duncan watched in quiet fascination as the stage crew
and producers made final preparations before the audience filed in. They knew something was wrong. No one
said a word to her. They tiptoed around, not wanting
to be heard or to create harsh sounds. Duncan had to
talk to her today. This had to change. It was now affecting the show.

Moments later the audience began to come in and
the crew left the stage. Up today was the U.S. National
Gymnastics Team and then a segment on an up-and-
coming author. The usual stage had been replaced by
practice mats, four-inch beams, cheese mats, a trampo-
line, uneven and even parallel bars, a stationary horse,
and a few other pieces.

The music began signaling the start of the show, also
a signal for Aurora. Duncan witnessed the change in
her demeanor. The sadness defining her body language
changed to something resembling joy. The team filed
onto the stage and took up positions at various pieces
of equipment.

Duncan took his usual station, placing his microphone on his head. He tried to capture Aurora's attention. She didn't look at him. The show began.

"Explain this to the audience," Aurora asked a small
girl who couldn't have been more than fifteen. "What
is this called?" She stood in front of a small, carpet-
covered piece of wood with two industrial coil springs

raising it several inches off two slats that looked like runt skis.

"This is the springboard. It's placed before certain pieces of equipment like the horse or the beam to give us enough spring to mount the equipment, or to spring over it." Her voice was high and young, but she spoke with assurance.

"You're going to demonstrate what?"

Aurora held the microphone to the freckled, red-headed girl. "I'm going to do several exercises on the beam."

"The balance beam," Aurora explained for the benefit of the audience, "is this horizontal, four-inch, padded railing behind me." She turned to put her hand on it. "Look, it's only about as wide as my hand." The overhead camera immediately picked up the image. Images of her slender hands caressing him went through his mind.

The teenager backed away and Aurora said, "Let's watch."

The girl stood for a second, her feet flat on the floor, heels together, arms at her sides. Then she raised up on her toes and began to run forward. Three feet from the spring-board she leapt on the board, sprang into the air, turned a somersault, and landed with bent knees on the tiny platform four feet off the floor. The muscles of her legs were clearly defined as she held herself with not so much as a waver right or left.

The audience jerked in a breath and held it. She stood straight and went into a practiced routine that included splits in the air, cartwheels, back flips, and a final dismount that started as a run but ended with a front flip with a full twist in the air and a perfectly executed landing. When her arms went into the air to salute the audience the applause was deafening. Duncan let go of his breath, as did the rest of the staff.

Then it was Aurora's turn. She let the full demonstration go on, explaining the difference between women's and men's equipment and events. She asked about the ordinary person taking gymnastics classes, and she became the guinea pig for the first lesson.

"All right, now what do I have to do?" She laughed, and the audience went right along with her. Grabbing her hair she pulled it into a ponytail and secured it with a wide barrette.

"You're going to do a simple exercise."

"If this is simple, why are three of you standing around me?" Again she laughed. Duncan loved hearing that sound. When she was before the lights she was the woman he knew. Without them she crawled away into a shell that no one could penetrate.

"We're spotting you in case you fall. We do this for everyone until they become confident and proficient with the exercise."

She stood in front of the uneven parallel bars, wearing the hand grips that had been given to her.

"What you're going to do is stand in front of the bar with your hands facing you." The trainer took her hands and turned them around so she could see her palms before she closed them over the chalk-scored wooden bar. "Then you'll bring your feet up while your arms hold your weight, swing your legs over the bar, then hold yourself up, with straight arms right about here." The trainer tapped his own body at the hip.

He demonstrated the maneuver, smoothly and with ease. The audience appreciated the gesture. Then it was Aurora's turn. Her face became serious, and she concentrated. Then she swung her feet. Only one of them left the floor. She fell under the bar, coming up laughing. The audience laughed, too.

She looked at them. "You think this is easy," she accused, but she got up and tried again. Same result.

"I think," she said as she laughed again, "that I have too much behind to get over."

The trainer disagreed, but his protest was lost in the audience appreciation of her joke.

"All right. One more time." She pulled forward. Both feet came up and she swung over the bar, then supported her weight on her arms and the bar at the level the trainer had told her. She made it. The audience, even the crew and Duncan, poured out their feelings to her in their enthusiastic applause.

Aurora smiled from her perch, proud as a queen on a throne. Then she overbalanced and swung over the bar, face forward. The three spotters standing near her went forward, but she didn't fall. Her heels landed with a soft thud on the mat. For a moment she hung from the bar. Then she let go and sat on the floor, a wide smile curving her lips.

"And with that," she said, looking directly into the camera, "we'll be right back."

The applause light went on. The camera faded her image.

Duncan could only think that the show had been a success. After it aired, every mother in America who didn't already have a child in gymnastics would be calling schools to enroll them. Aurora disappeared directly after the audience began filing out. Duncan assumed she was changing clothes. He hadn't seen her before he'd returned to his office and things began settling down for the night. The equipment remained on the set. It would be removed before the next show. For tonight things were quiet. Duncan should be thinking of going home. Why was he still in the office?

Reaching for the desk lamp to turn it off, he heard something behind him. The control room door was open and he went inside. Aurora was on the studio floor. She still wore the jumpsuit. Standing where she'd been an hour earlier with a full audience in front of her and three spotters beside her, she performed the move that trainer had asked her to do. This time there was no falling, no hesitation, and no amateurish movements.

She swung easily under the bar, opening her legs in a perfect kip and swinging her lithe body up until both hands and feet were on the same bar. At the top she stood and reached for the higher bar. She took it with practiced ease, working back and forth between both bars.

Duncan stood in awe.

"What's she doing?"

"Shhh," Duncan whispered, tossing a glance over his shoulder.

"What's she doing?" Line producer Marty Shapiro stood next to him. "Why didn't she do that on the show?"

"I don't know." They watched until she finished her routine and began a series of stretching exercises.

"Duncan, I need to talk to you."

For the first time Duncan noticed Marty had a mass of papers in his hand.

"Sure."

Marty stepped back and Duncan took a final glance through the window before following him into the office.

"Joyce tells me you want to change the programming schedule for tomorrow's show."

"Yeah," Duncan confirmed.

"The guests are already here. They're checked into the hotel and ready to go on. One of them is very ill. We can't ask them to reschedule. What's wrong with doing the show?"

Duncan scanned the open door. He couldn't see Aurora. She was the reason. The program would bring a distraught mom on the show along with her dying child. The frame of mind Aurora was in, she couldn't handle the heavy emotional scenes the story was bound to elicit. He was trying to help her, save her from focusing on her own mother-daughter relationship.

He cleared his throat. "I thought it would be better if we saved the taping for another time."

"Why? We're ready for it. Personally, Duncan, I don't think this kid will make it if we postpone."

"Postpone what?"

Both men looked up to find Aurora standing in the doorway. She had a towel over her neck. Her face was clean of makeup and her hair, still in the barrette, swung loosely at her neck. Duncan thought she looked glorious.

"Duncan thinks we should cancel tomorrow's show."

"Why? What's tomorrow's show?"

Duncan wasn't surprised she didn't remember. The last few days she'd been pretty occupied with her own thoughts. He'd included her in regular meetings where they discussed the upcoming shows. This one had been mentioned more than once. Aurora didn't remember it.

"Children with rare diseases." Marty spoke before Duncan could think of an answer.

Duncan saw her swallow and nod before she asked, "Why are you postponing it?" She looked directly at him. Her eyes looked sad.

"I thought it would be better to tape it at a later date."

"Better for whom? Me or the children?" She didn't wait for him to answer. "I'm all right, Duncan. I can handle it."

He wasn't sure she was telling the truth, that she even knew the truth. When Duncan had initially interviewed the mother he'd been as close to tears as he'd ever come. With Aurora's state of mind, he wasn't sure she could manage the show without breaking down. That could be advantageous if he were filming a tearjerker. However, the show wasn't a tearjerker, and her breaking down would only show that the hostess had no control over her show.

"I'm fine," she said again.

"All right," Duncan agreed. "Marty, put them back on the schedule."

Marty nodded and left. When he closed the door Duncan turned to her. "What was that out there?" He hooked a thumb toward the studio.

"Nothing," she said, turning to leave.

"Aurora." His voice was sharper than he wanted it to be. He softened it. "Rory."

She didn't turn to face him. "Don't call me that."

He stood behind her, close enough to feel the heat from her body. He knew she could feel the heat from his. "What do you want me to call you?"

Duncan raised his hands to touch her, then dropped them. He knew she'd shake them away.

"When's Marsha coming back?"

The question came from nowhere. It was the last thing he expected her to say.

"I can't stay here much longer. I have to return to my home. I need to know what's happening there. Nothing happened here. It's safe to return."

Duncan didn't know how to answer, so he fell back on what he'd seen. "Tell me about the parallel bars. Where did you learn that?"

"College," she answered. "I took classes. When I got out I kept them up. It was my gym workout. Three years ago I quit."

Duncan didn't have to ask why. Her life had changed when she had to move her mother.

"Why are there cameras in here?"

Duncan knew she was fishing. "Sometimes I work from home. Most of this equipment is tied into my house. And stop trying to change the subject."

She knew how it worked. Duncan had explained the closed-circuit setup to her when she first came to work at the studio, when she was still in film editing. He'd told her how the cameras and equipment could be focused to let him view the studio from his house. If he was unable to come in or if he had to work late, he didn't have to actually be in the studio to monitor the proceedings.

"Rory, hold onto me."

For a moment she didn't move. He wasn't sure she'd heard him, heard the plea in his voice. Then, as stiff as her stance had been she softened and whirled about. Her arms went around his waist and she held onto him. She didn't cry. She just held on as if her life depended on her keeping her arms where they were.

Duncan folded her into his body as if protecting her. It was good to have her against him again. He buried his face in her hair, smelling the fragrant shampoo, kissing her forehead. He wanted to devour her mouth, bury himself inside her, make violent love to her until neither of them could think or even walk for a week. But that was not what she needed. She needed someone to lean on, someone to stand by and let her lead.

"Where's your coat?" Duncan asked. "I'll take you back to the guest house."

"I can go alone." She pushed back and stepped away from him. He didn't stop her.

"You can always do it alone, is that it?"

She stepped back as if he'd hit her. He wanted to shake her, shake some sense into her, let her know that he wanted to be part of her life.

"You're going to do everything by yourself. You don't need any help. You don't need another human being, the touch of a hand or the thought that someone else might understand what you're going through. Aurora, you've been on this show for a couple of weeks. Hasn't any of it sunk in? Can't you tell that life is people having the same experiences, helping each other get through them?"

Fierce hatred made her eyes dark as black ice. "You understand what I'm going through?" she spat at him. "You know that inside me is the same thing that's inside my mother? You understand that one day in my future I won't recognize another living soul? I won't remember this, or anything about it?'' She spread her arms, encompassing the building. Then she folded them around herself.

"I should understand that there are people just like me? I should understand that I'm not the only one? I *am* the only one!" she shouted. "I'm the only one who'll be in there." Her hand came up to point a finger at herself. "Alone, without anyone, confused and afraid. Can you imagine that?"

She took a step forward. "Well, let me tell you, Duncan West, I won't remember those people who are just like me. I won't remember them. They won't remember me. And I won't remember you."

Chapter 11

Rory. She could almost taste the way he said it. Aurora lay in bed wide awake. She hadn't been able to sleep after she'd walked out on Duncan. She'd said things she regretted but she could not pull the words back. He'd called her Rory, the word soft and loving, while she'd been catty and childish. Rory was her family name. It brought back memories of beach days, her first concert, and holiday celebrations.

In truth, she couldn't get past the fact that one day she'd be in the same position as her mother. She thought of her sisters and her brother. Were they all medical science experiments in waiting? Why had she taken it out on Duncan?

Because she was in love with him.

She knew they had no future. He had Hollywood on his mind and from the word around the set he was going to be moving on soon. She'd known all along that falling in love with him was the worst thing she could do, but somehow her heart hadn't found out until it was too late.

She wondered what he was doing now. Was he awake,

lying in the dark? Was he thinking of her, hating her
for what she'd said? She wanted to talk to him, apologize, make love.

Aurora threw back the covers and turned on the light,
squinting. Her eyes adjusted to the room. She looked
at the space on the bed where Duncan had slept. It was
neat, untouched, and lonely looking. She longed for
him. Reaching for the phone, she thought of calling
him. Before picking up the receiver she pulled her hand
back. What could she say?

Could she tell him she wanted him, wanted him to
hold her? He'd let her hold onto him. Could she tell
him she wanted to make love to him, wanted to find
that mindless place where they'd been a week ago,
before misery seeped into her pores like an invisible
gas?

Yes, she could. Galvanized into action, Aurora came
off the bed as if propelled. Slipping her feet into slip-
pers, she rushed down the stairs. Pulling on a coat, she
was in the car and out the guarded gates with a wave
of her hand. She saw the guards in the rearview mirror,
standing helplessly in the road as she went down the
curved driveway.

She'd call them when she got to Duncan's, let them
know she was safe. The drive was short and she was
standing on his porch, ringing the doorbell, before
she'd had time to think what she would say.

"I thought . . ." she began, when Duncan opened
the door. His eyes widened when he saw her. He wasn't
dressed. He wore the same paisley robe he'd worn when
she slept in his guest room that one night, only loosely
knotted at his waist. Her mind conjured up sexual
images that burned her ears and should most certainly
be reflected on her face.

Courage failed her, however. Her tongue grew too
thick for her to get words over it. She wasn't going to
be able to continue. "I wonder . . ." she started, but
stopped. She couldn't say it. She couldn't tell a man

outright she wanted him to make love to her. Women did it all the time. She'd met some of them, aggressive and sure of themselves. She'd also met the ones who couldn't verbalize any of their wants. Now she knew which category she fell into. Aurora had never done this before, and something like this would take practice. "Can I sleep in your guest room?" The question was weak and sounded that way.

Duncan took her arms, pulling her into the foyer and closing the door.

"No," he said with a shake of his head. "You can't sleep in my guest room. If you stay here, it's in my room. Take it or leave it."

She stared at him for any sign of humor, arrogance, or insincerity. What she saw was passion and something akin to concern, caring, even love—nothing hostile, only longing and need. She knew the same was reflected in her own eyes.

"I'll take it," she said.

Duncan let go of his breath. If she'd waited any longer to answer he'd have passed out from lack of oxygen.

His hands slipped down her arms, taking her hands. For the moment it was enough. She'd come to him. After she'd left his office he wasn't sure she would ever come back, but she was here. Elation seared through him. Then he slipped his arms around her, going inside her coat. Shocked, he stepped back. She wore only a thin, satin nightgown.

"You're not wearing any clothes."

Aurora smiled. "I didn't think I'd need any."

She let the coat fall from her shoulders. The light in the foyer was bright and she felt naked as Duncan stared at her. He'd seen her before, seen her with no clothes on. She felt more undressed now than she had then. His gaze rolled over her, settling on her breasts and her

thudding heart before moving lower to her stomach
and down to her slipper-covered feet.

Duncan turned but kept her hand in his. He walked
to the phone and dialed a number.

"Ms. Alexander is here," he said. "She's fine. I'll
bring her back in the morning." He hung up without
saying good-bye.

He turned to her. "I intended to call the guards,"
she said, leaving out the fact that when she'd seen him
every other thought had flown out of her head. "Duncan, I'm sorry about today."

"Forget it," he said. "You had a right."

"No right to take my feelings out on you." She
stepped forward and put her arms around his neck. Her
action was bold. Maybe she couldn't say the words, but
she could show him. His arms slid over the fabric of
her gown and she went into them. Pressing herself close
to him, she went up on her toes to touch his mouth.
She brushed her lips against his, moaning at the soft
texture of his skin. He was a big man, hard muscle over
bone, yet he could be gentle.

She continued her options with his mouth, running
the tip of her tongue over the contours of his lips while
her hips ground into his. She heard a low growl come
from his throat. The sound was heady, exhilarating, and
encouragement for her to continue. Aurora went higher
on her toes, moving up his frame to take his mouth
fully. She drove her tongue inside, sweeping it past his
teeth and mating it with his tongue.

Inside her she felt the pulling, a flow that seemed to
use the tides of the sea or the phases of the moon, she
wasn't sure. She knew it felt good, that it promised
pleasure, that it was a leading force and she wanted to
follow it. Her stomach coiled, pulling tighter and
tighter, building toward an explosion that could only
be wonderful when it came.

Then she was floating. Duncan lifted her off her feet.
She felt the cool air kiss her skin as he whirled about

and headed for the stairs. Laying her head on his shoulder, she settled close to him, breathing in the pure male scent that had her senses reeling. Duncan went into the warm darkness, setting her on her feet in his bedroom.

"I want to see you," she told him. Her hands went to the knot at his waist, pulling it free. She reached up, pushing the robe over his broad shoulders. He was naked beneath it. Boldly she looked at him. His body was magnificent—hard muscle, brilliantly defined, tight waist, shoulders to die for, legs strong and athletic. He was all male, made to pleasure a woman. Tonight she was that woman.

Her gown was long with wide straps and slits up the sides. She pushed the straps down and slid it to the floor, standing straight for Duncan to look at her as she'd looked at him. She felt no embarrassment. She'd stepped onto a bold new surface and she liked it.

His gaze took her in as it had downstairs. The burning inside her pulled at her center. She closed the distance between them, sliding her hands over his smooth skin as she stared into his eyes. She let her flat palms skim over his nipples. They extended into her hand, sending her signals that she was affecting him. In the valley between her hands she placed her open mouth, tasting him. She shuddered, his hands taking hold of her upper arms. Aurora went on, pushed forward by a need she didn't know she possessed. She slid her tongue over him, round his nipple and upward. She felt him tremble. It thrilled her, pushed her on.

Her hands circled his waist, caressing him as she let them learn his body. Like a blind woman she smoothed over his skin, feeling the quivering muscles play under the skin. Downward her hands traveled until she was holding him, erect and hard in her palms. She rubbed her palm over his tip. He grabbed for her. His jaws tightened.

"You've got to stop," he told her in a voice heavy with emotion.

She didn't stop, she pushed him further, massaging him more, using her hands as erotic weapons.

The hands on her arms tightened, communicating difficulty in maintaining control. Aurora relished it, smiled at his drive, pushing him further and further. She wanted him to snap. She pushed her hips into his, feeling his erection against her legs, glorifying in the shock of passion that fissured through her when his body connected with hers.

She found his mouth again and pulled herself up his body, wrapped her legs around him, and tried to climb inside him. Duncan backed her up to the bed and fell with her onto the covers. His hands took over touching her, tasting her, bringing to life any nerve ending that wasn't totally and fully alive and sending rapturous pleasure throughout her body.

He reached into the drawer of the nightstand just before she rolled him over, straddling him, looking down at the man whom she was bringing to the brink of insanity. She took the condom, flicking the silver foil aside, and covered him with it. Her own mind had left her. Instinct and need replaced it as she leveled herself over him and guided him inside her. Her head fell back as she initiated the primal rhythm and began her ride. Duncan's hands grabbed her hips and guided her, picking up the pace.

She watched his face. His eyes closed, his mouth slightly open as emotions warred for dominance. His hands took her breasts. Aurora's back arched as she went wild over him. Sounds she'd never heard formed deep in her throat and gushed forward like a foreign language. Duncan understood it, spoke it with her.

Aurora felt the sensation begin. She wanted to scream. She could feel it coming, building, like a giant wave she couldn't stop, a force that made her work harder, faster, burning her, consuming her with passion. She'd never known she had an elastic center. She was equally surprised when it snapped, freeing her voice.

She heard herself calling Duncan's name over and over. Another voice blended with hers from a long way off. She reached for it, listened, heard.

The rush caught her, pushed her forward like the mushroom effect of an atomic blast. Warmth passed through her, turning her into a fireball that raged and clawed for oxygen. Like a blazing inferno it gulped everything in its path as Aurora maintained the ride of a lifetime. It transformed them from living flesh and blood to rapturous light as she climbed into the stars. Without form they joined hearts, minds, bodies, in a beautiful spangle that flung itself to the heavens and created a galaxy.

Aurora collapsed. Her breathing was hard, open-mouthed, and audible. She lay on top of Duncan, hearing the combined thumping of their two hearts. Her hands moved over his skin, fast and frenzied. Like a starving animal she refused to relinquish touch. Her mouth took his in a violent kiss that ended in silent worship.

This was new ground. Aurora knew if she made love with Duncan for the rest of her life it would never be the same. It would always be new and fresh and like the first time.

Duncan stared at the ceiling. Aurora lay next to him. His arm cradled her to his side. He could say tonight was the first time he'd been ravished. Aurora had been shy when she came through the door. That had changed. Beneath the surface she was a tiger, and tonight the tiger was loose. Duncan glanced at her and smiled. Her breathing was slow and even. Moonlight played across her features. His blood drained to his loins just looking at her.

She satisfied him sexually. He'd never wanted a woman as much as he wanted Aurora. Yet he couldn't help but wonder what had driven her tonight. For days she'd been totally withdrawn, except for the time she spent on the stage. After the taping tonight she'd worked out on the gymnastics equipment. He thought she'd exorcised her demons. After the way she made love to him, he hoped *he* had done it.

"Ohhhh," Aurora groaned the minute she tried to move. Every muscle, every bone in her body ached. She remembered her stint on the gymnastics equipment yesterday. She hadn't worked through one of those routines in three years, and today she was going to pay for it. She could only imagine what tomorrow would feel like.

"Duncan," she called, opening her eyes and looking for him. His side of the bed was empty. She wondered what time it was, but turning over to see the clock would take too much effort. She closed her eyes and remained still until she remembered the show. She had to get back and ready for today's performance. Pushing her feet to the floor she sat on the edge of the bed, trying to muster enough strength to stand. She longed for her four-poster bed to have something to hold onto. Duncan's bed offered no such support.

Pushing herself up she hobbled to the bathroom and into the shower. Warm water poured over her. She let the pulsating heads beat on her arms, her back, her legs. When she stepped out and wrapped herself in a huge towel she felt only slightly better.

"Coffee?" Duncan offered her a cup from across the room. He'd prepared breakfast and set it on a small, round table in front of the window. Aurora attacked the coffee as if it could save her life. "Is this your usual morning demeanor?"

She eased herself into a chair, her muscles protesting as she sat down. Refilling her empty cup she looked at him. "I feel as if someone's killed me, and I just don't know it yet."

"Well, it wasn't me."

Aurora stopped her cup midway to her mouth. He looked at her smugly, his expression telling her he remembered every second of last night. She'd been the aggressor then and she knew it. She hadn't been able to help herself. She'd never had sex like that before. She couldn't call it anything else. They'd made *love* in the guest house, but last night was pure lust, raw sex. Aurora never knew it was possible and certainly hadn't thought she was capable of initiating it, leading it.

She hid behind sarcasm. "Do you have a complaint?"

Duncan stood up and came to her chair. He stooped to eye level and held a crisp slice of bacon out to her. "Not a one," he teased. "You can ravish me every night."

She snatched the bacon. It snapped in her hand. He turned away. She bit down on the bacon and smiled at his back. When he'd fixed her a breakfast plate and set it before her the smile was gone.

"I need some clothes," she said.

He took his seat, resting his chin on his elbow. "I have nothing that will fit you. I would be willing to lend you a towel."

She glanced down at the white terrycloth fabric as she broke a piece of buttered toast. "What do you think the guards will say if I come back wearing only a towel, a monogrammed one at that?"

"That I'd gotten lucky." He threw her that devastating smile. "They have no idea how right they'd be."

Aurora had no comeback. She ignored him and ate the delicious breakfast.

"I'll get your gown." Duncan left her alone then.

By the time she pushed her plate away she knew she had to leave him. Staying on would only make things worse. She wasn't just falling in love, she was already in love, and despite Duncan's plans to return to California she thought it was time to get out.

Last night had told her what life with Duncan could

be like, what sex with him was like, and what making love would be like. She also knew what hell would be like. It would be being without him. She'd defined it herself, and would have to live with it.

Duncan didn't return with her gown. She found a sweater in the armoire and slipped into it. It covered her to her knees. She pulled white socks up to cover her bare legs, then went in search of him.

She found him standing in front of the door with an envelope in his hand. On the floor, next to her nightgown, lay a Federal Express package. "What are you doing?" she asked.

He turned to her. For a moment she didn't think he saw her, didn't think he heard her. "Movies," he said. "I've got the backers. I'm going to Hollywood."

Stunned, Aurora grabbed the newel post and tried to smile. "This is what you wanted," she said. She'd known he was going, that it wouldn't be long, but now it felt as if she'd already lost him. *How can you lose something that was never yours?* she asked herself. "When do you go?"

"Not for weeks yet, but everything is falling into place. Things are working out so smoothly it's almost frightening."

Aurora stepped down from the last stair. "What is the movie about?"

"Come on." He grabbed her hand and took her into his office. Equipment looking identical to that in the studio filled the room. Books and scripts lay on shelves around the room and a desk crowded with papers sat in the corner. Duncan went directly to one and pulled it out. "This is the script." He handed it to her.

She read the title and author's name on the bound cover: *Hostage* by Duncan West.

"I didn't know you wrote."

"It's what I started out doing."

"May I read it?"

"You want to?" His eyebrows raised.

Aurora nodded. She took a seat in a comfortable chair before a laid out but unlit fireplace and opened the script. Duncan left her after a moment. For two hours she read, from beginning to end. Closing the last page, she knew this would make a great movie—an action adventure about a pilot who gets caught up in a relationship with a woman in a small town. On the surface everything looks fine, but beneath are secrets that plunge them into a life-and-death struggle.

He came in almost the moment she finished the last page. She felt he'd been pacing outside the door while she read. Dropping down on a chair in front her, he asked, "What did you think?"

She could tell her opinion made a difference to him. "It's going to make a wonderful movie," she said.

"Why?"

She pushed herself up in the chair and leaned forward. "First, it's not a buddy movie. It has great characters who try to protect each other. The action is riveting, and the developing relationship between the two main characters is natural. One doesn't overshadow the other."

"This is what you really think? You're not just saying that?"

Aurora wondered why he didn't believe her. He'd sold the script. "I'm not a critic," she told him. "There's only—"

"Go on."

"I can't quite see the karate scene," she said. "When the protagonist, Jane, tries to save her lover's life, I can't see her doing the things you've written."

He looked at her for a moment. Aurora had the feeling he was deciding something. "You don't think she'd do it, or you don't think it's something she would be able to do?"

"I don't think she'd be able to."

"Stand up." It was an order.

Aurora stood. "What are you going to do?"

"I'm going to act out the scene with you."

Aurora started to resume her seat. "I don't know any karate." Duncan took her hand and pulled her up.

"Good, because neither does Jane."

Aurora hadn't expected to get involved in a karate lesson, especially in her current state of dress. She wore nothing under the sweater and only socks on her feet.

"We start with him holding her like this." Duncan turned her around. He put one arm around her throat and the other around her waist. Aurora felt it impossible to move. His hand was just below her breasts and her nipples were hardening at his touch. "All right," Duncan said. "See if you can throw me."

"Throw you? My muscles won't let me sit down normally in a chair. How am I going to lift your weight?"

"It isn't so much that you lift my weight as using it against me." He demonstrated, but Aurora was still at a loss. "Try it now."

Aurora didn't have a clue as to what to do. Her arms ached and Duncan behind her didn't conjure up images of strength—that pulled at her weaknesses. Still she tried, but nothing worked. Soon she felt Duncan laughing at her. Anger came to her rescue. She stomped on his foot, ignoring the muscular pain, and jabbed her elbow into his ribs. The surprise threw him off guard. He released his hold on her neck. She slipped down, grabbed both his legs, and pulled. He went down.

"See, that's what I would have done. No karate needed." Turning, she saw him sprawled on the floor. His eyes were closed. She'd hurt him. He'd bumped his head. Hundreds of thoughts went through her mind, all of them horrible. She rushed to him, pulling his head onto her lap.

"Duncan," she cried. "Duncan, say something."

He didn't open his eyes. Quickly she turned and grabbed for the phone. It banged out a ring as it hit the floor. Nervous, she punched in 9-1-1. Then Duncan's hand came around her and pushed the switch hook down. "That wasn't karate," he said.

Aurora was both glad and angry at the same time. He was all right.

"Why did you do that?" She hit at him, but he grabbed her arms and wrestled with her on the floor. In her present state she was no viable adversary. Her sweater rode up and Duncan pressed his knees into her body and used his hands to pin her to the floor. She lay still, breathing in and out heavily.

"It looks like this is a much better way to handle that scene," Duncan said, laughing at her. "But look at the trouble it could get you into." Then he lowered his mouth and took hers in a kiss that curled her toes.

Chapter 12

Concentration had always been his strong suit. Duncan would tune out anything he didn't want to bother him. Growing up with a brother with whom he had nothing in common, he'd often tuned out his music, his constant conversation, and his noise. Duncan prided himself on being able to work under any kind of circumstances. But he'd never met anyone like Aurora before.

She not only crossed his mind constantly, she invaded him, wormed her way into every part of his functioning mind, and made herself at home. His body was not immune, either. He could still remember having her in his bed and on the floor of the library. With her he was like a madman, unable to control his actions, letting instinct drive him until he fell over the edge. One day he wouldn't come back. He'd simply burn up in her flames like an astronaut tasting the friction of reentry. Duncan smiled at the thought.

"A grin like that could only be caused by thoughts of a woman."

Cooper Dean's bulk hogged the doorway. Duncan was glad to see him. Coop came forward, taking the hand Duncan extended. He sat in one of the leather chairs in front of the desk as Duncan resumed his seat.

"What've you got?" Duncan asked.

"Not much." Coop let out a sigh. "Whoever this guy is, he's good. We haven't found anything. It's as if he disappears into thin air."

Duncan knew Coop's feelings on this. Only the movies could make people disappear. In life they were only temporarily out of sight.

"We'll find him. Its Aurora who's the mystery."

"How so?" Duncan leaned forward.

"I've interviewed her former employers, her friends and peers, even the people who hired her to pose as Marsha Chambers. For the most part no one has a bad word to say about her. I got the usual amount of professional jealousy. She was good at her job, sometimes too good."

"What does that mean?"

"She worked for Social Services in New York."

Duncan nodded. "I know that."

"She wasn't supposed to work the streets. She did."

"That sounds like her," Duncan said.

"Kids in trouble, young mothers, abused women, she'd jump in her car and go help them. More than once she came between a pimp and his girl. One tried to kill her, but she took him down and got away."

Duncan's heart jumped at someone trying to hurt her. Then he remembered her taking him down. He'd hit the floor hard. "What about this pimp? Do you think it's him, trying to hurt her now?"

Coop shook his head. "We checked on him. He's serving seven to ten for manslaughter. He killed one of his girls during a fight."

Duncan shuddered to think that Aurora had been part of that kind of world. "Any others?"

"Most have moved on. A couple of them are dead. One other can't be located. Disappeared about a year ago and no one's heard of him. He'd been tangled up with something big. My assumption is he's now part of a bridge or building project within the greater New York New Jersey area. All of them were petty criminals. None were into jewelry—definitely not of the quality of the pearls Aurora received."

Coop had good instincts. Duncan knew he could bank on them. "That leads us back to Marsha."

"Yeah. I'm seeing her later. I thought I'd come by and talk to you first."

"About Marsha?"

He nodded. "Does she have any known enemies?"

"You should ask if she has any friends. The list would be shorter."

Coop's jaws tightened. Duncan knew when Coop did that he was holding something back.

"Anybody hate her enough to want to harm her?"

"I don't know," he answered honestly. "Marsha is difficult to work with. People in this business are often that way. If we went around killing every one of them, there would be no one left."

"So you don't think it's anyone in the business? What about her personal life?"

"I don't know much about her personal life. In the beginning Marsha and I were friends. That died shortly after I became part of this show."

"Do you think she has something against you personally?"

Duncan shook his head. He remembered the first day he met Aurora, and her profile of Marsha's actions. "Marsha's very insecure and expresses it by trying to exert power over other people. It just doesn't work with me."

Coop nodded as if he understood. He reminded Duncan of Aurora. Both she and Coop dealt in individual personalities. They looked at the psyche one person at a time. It was why Aurora could zero in on Marsha's behavior so quickly. He looked at people as masses—

the audience, what the collective group would do and how they would act.

"I think you should talk to Aurora," Duncan suggested.

"Why?"

"She doesn't believe Marsha's kidnapping happened the way Marsha reported it."

"Where is she?" Coop didn't bother asking him questions he was only going to have to ask Aurora.

"Makeup. Come on."

They went across the stage to the back area, where Aurora's face and hair were done each day before they began taping. Her back was to them when they came in. She sat in a chair while a woman in a smock chatted and worked with Aurora's hair.

The room smelled of hair spray and chemicals, sweet yet pungent, with an odor that spoke of female ritual. Duncan stilled his heart and his face. He didn't want anyone to witness how much Aurora affected him. He wasn't used to these feelings.

"Hi, Coop." Aurora smiled when he walked around to face her. Her makeup was done and the final touches were being put on her hair. She looked beautiful. Duncan wondered if he'd ever get used to seeing her. It didn't matter whether she was perfectly coutured or had scrubbed her face free of makeup. It didn't matter if she were under moonlight or stage light. She drove him to distraction.

"Would you excuse us?" Coop looked at the makeup artist. She smiled without a word and left them.

"You look great," Coop told her as the door clicked closed. Aurora checked her reflection in the lighted mirror in front of her.

"One segment of today's show has to do with makeup and hair care for the black woman. The other was cancelled. Apparently the child we had scheduled with the rare disease was taken to the hospital last night and won't be able to make it." Aurora looked at Duncan, then back to Coop. "What's this all about?"

"Coop wants to ask you some questions about Marsha."

She moved her gaze to Coop. Duncan perched on the arm of a nearby chair.

"I don't know Marsha. How can I help you?"

"Duncan tells me you have some theories on Marsha and her previous kidnapping."

Aurora threw a glance Duncan's way. "I told him your interpretation of her reaction the day of the attempted kidnapping," he said.

"They're theories."

"Just tell me what you think. It could help me."

Aurora looked deep into Coop's eyes. She wondered if she should read more into the word than was there. He'd said she could *help him*—not that she might be able to help with the investigation. She knew Coop was interested in Marsha personally.

"I thought her reaction was a little too fearful for someone who hadn't really been kidnapped. I thought she was lying about it, and that something else happened, something unpleasant."

"Any idea what that could have been?"

"Nothing concrete. I never talked to her."

"Give me a professional personality profile, then."

Aurora slipped out of the chair. She stood in front of Coop. She took a while to begin speaking, collecting her thoughts. "She seems afraid. I suppose in this kind of industry and with her show being number one, fear is part of the territory, but it goes deeper than that. I don't know what it is and I doubt she'd tell me. I don't even think she admits it to herself."

Aurora looked at Duncan, then quickly moved away. He distracted her. Keeping her mind on Coop and Marsha, she continued. "I'd say she didn't have an easy time getting to the number one spot on television. She's made a lot of enemies along the way, but I don't think she intended to."

"Why do you say that?" Coop asked.

"Her on-screen personality. The way she can elicit deep feelings from her guests. You can't fake that. I know how the audience likes it and I've seen her connect with them, not control them, be one of them. Down inside her is a woman who wants to be liked and needs to be loved. She can show that to the camera because she assumes we think she's acting. In truth, that's the only time she isn't acting."

"Then why isn't she here?" Duncan spoke for the first time. "Why is she allowing you to take over her show?" He paused. "Aurora is good, very good." He glanced at Coop. "I wasn't kidding when I said you'd be getting offers to do your own show. Marsha has to see that, too. She's not blind."

"There must be something else she's afraid of," Coop answered, speaking more to himself than Duncan. "Something more frightening than losing her show."

Coop sat in the township-issue detective's car inside the garage of The Princeton Medical Center. He'd followed Marsha there. She headed toward the entrance. Coop quickly followed her. She had no appointment, no reason for being there. When he'd arrived at her house she'd come out of the driveway alone.

Coop circled around and followed. Now he tried to tail her through the hallways of the new hospital wing. At his height it was difficult to go undetected, but Marsha knew where she was going. She walked with a purpose, striding confidently, neither looking left or right. She stopped in front of a closed door and hesitated before going inside. Coop checked the number. Flashing his badge he asked for the name of the occupant. The nurse's answer meant nothing to him. She said the patient was a strong boy and that his crisis period was over.

A child? Coop wondered. What connection did Marsha have with this child? Coop took up position within viewing distance of the room. In fifteen minutes the door opened and two women came out—Marsha and, he assumed, the child's mother. Coop didn't recognize her.

"Thank you for coming," she said. "You've made Adam feel so much better. I'm sure he'll recover faster since you came to see him."

Marsha squeezed the woman's shoulder and smiled. "Call me if I can help."

Coop saw the tears in the mother's eyes as Marsha left her. He followed and fell into step with her before she reached the end of the hall.

She stopped, glared at him, then walked away. "What do you want?"

She would have tried to out-stride him, but Coop's height would have had her in a slow run. "I want to know why you're here."

"I can't see how that's any of your business." She skittered through the double doors and headed toward the exit.

"I'm investigating attempted murder." He grabbed her arm and turned her to face him. "Yours!" Anger replaced his usual calm.

She snatched her arm away and resumed walking. If she thought she was getting rid of him, she could think again. Coop let her get to the parking lot but put his hand on hers when she tried to open the car door.

She jerked it away and turned around. *Mistake,* he thought. He had her pinned between his body and the car. She opened her mouth to speak. Making a lightning quick decision, he buried his hands in her hair and sealed his mouth to hers.

*   *   *

Sighing, Aurora slipped down in the tub. She smiled, feeling good, relaxed. She took more baths since she'd met Duncan than she had since discovering as a child that the water in the shower wouldn't hit her in the face. That first day he'd suggested she take a bath, and Megan had come over to check on her. Now bubbles came up to her chin. She'd liberally poured the bath salts into the water and luxuriated as the hot water massaged her screaming muscles. The day had been long even without the second part of the show. Now she had relax time. She never planned to move again. Closing her eyes, she let the water take her away. She floated, thought of nothing but the smell of the salts and the feel of the water as she communed with it.

In the other room the phone began to ring. She groaned. It *would* happen when she took a bath. The phone never rang while she showered. Standing up, she wrapped herself in a towel and went to answer it. It could only be Duncan. If it had been anyone else she'd have ignored it.

"Duncan, couldn't you wait just a few more minutes?"

"So it's Duncan now," a strange voice said.

"Who is this?"

"I'm for you, Marsha," he said. "I watched you today."

Cold fear shivered down her spine. She knew who it was—the man who'd tried to kidnap her. The one she felt following her, the one she looked for over her shoulder, her stalker, her attempted killer.

"You don't think I believe that story, do you?"

She couldn't speak. Her voice was paralyzed in her throat.

"I know television, Marsha. You can use any name you want, *Rory.*" He said it as if it were distasteful. "You'll still be my pearl."

"What do you want?" she whispered, her voice climbing over her heart and coming out with a hoarseness that made it sound small and fearful.

"I want you."

"Why?"

"It's nothing personal. I'll just unravel you like the necklace. How'd you like the pearls? You looked good wearing them."

Aurora's hand went to her throat. Soap dried on her skin.

"I'll make sure they bury you with them."

The phone clicked in her ear. Aurora dropped the receiver and backed away from it as if it were a snake on the floor. No sound came out. She tried to scream but her voice was denied her. Her heart thudded against her chest like a stampede. Her knees buckled under her, had her falling to the floor. The screams came then, loud, horrifying, like those of a dying animal.

That's how Duncan found her when he burst through the door. The towel had slipped away and she lay naked on the floor. He quickly checked for any injuries or bleeding, then pulled her and the towel into his arms and tried to stem the terror that had her screaming.

"Aurora!" he shouted. "Aurora! Stop screaming! You're all right. You're fine." It got to her. Her screams died, turning into sobs. He was helpless against them. He put her on the bed and rocked her, waiting for them to subside. It was then that he saw the phone laying on the floor. He pulled it up and listened. A disembodied recording spoke in his ear. He dropped it in the cradle and continued to hold Aurora.

The sobs turned to shivers. Duncan pulled the bedcovers over her. She still shivered. What had happened? he wondered. What caused her to scream in such terror? He was ready to fight whoever had done this to her.

"He called," she said through shivers. Her hand tightened on his sleeves, but the shaking continued. "I was in the bathtub." She hiccupped.

"Don't talk yet," Duncan said. He wanted her to tell him what scared her, but he knew she had to wait. She had to be calm enough to go through it or she'd end up screaming again. "Take a few deep breaths."

She did as he advised.

"Don't try to stop the shivering. Just relax, let go, and it will stop."

Again he proved right. After a few moments she moved to sit up. He let her. She put her feet on the floor, but didn't stand. He kept his arm around her.

"He called. The man who tried to kidnap me, kill us. He said he was going to . . . kill me."

Chapter 13

Marsha Chambers blew into her living room like a whirlwind, throwing her coat aside and turning to give Cooper Dean a withering glare he was sure many people had been repulsed by. Coop let it roll off him. He'd kissed her and he knew secrets she hid from the world.

"You had no right to kiss me," she ranted.

"I didn't notice you fighting me off." Coop stood in one spot. He removed his coat and dropped it over a chair. She fascinated him as no woman had ever done.

"You're a big man."

"I wasn't forcing you." She was gracious enough to turn away but not before he saw the dark flood of emotion in her eyes. He crossed the room and stood behind her. He made no move to touch her. "Your problem is that you enjoyed it and you don't want to admit it, not even to yourself."

"Don't you have an investigation to conduct?"

Coop did. He should be asking her professional questions, finding out who had singled her out as a target and why. But he was busy controlling his breathing, trying to keep his heart inside his chest, and letting his mind fantasize over her.

She's afraid. Aurora's words came back to him. "Do I make you nervous?"

She swung around. "No." She had to look up at him. Then she tried to step back and tripped. Coop's hands automatically came out and took her arms. His intention was to prevent her from falling. Instead he pulled her against his chest.

"You make *me* nervous," he said, and lowered his head. He didn't touch her mouth. He let his breath mingle with hers. If she wanted to refuse him, turn her head, twist out of his arms, he gave her ample time. She didn't. Instead she melted against him.

"You don't want to be involved with me," she whispered, her voice dark and sweet as chocolate cherries.

"You're right," he said. "Unfortunately, it's too late for that." His mouth closed over hers. Coop was lost the moment he felt her hands sliding around him. He bent, fitting her into his body and crushed her there, crushed her mouth, dove into her as if she were a pool. *"Use restraint,"* his mind said, but he pushed the thought aside. The force driving him was nowhere near his mind. He didn't want to listen. She'd driven him crazy for too long, since the first time Duncan had introduced them. Now he had her in his arms and he was holding on. Her arms climbed, too, her body shifting against him, her leg wrapping around his.

Coop wanted to take her, here and now, on the floor, on the sofa, even on the window seat, but somehow his official role asserted itself and he pushed her back. He didn't let go, but separated enough to let air flow between them.

"I need to talk to you," Coop said when he could trust his voice. He led her to the sofa and they sat down. Marsha let her head rest on his shoulder. Coop found it hard to think with her touching him. "I want you to tell me about your kidnapping."

That got a reaction out of her. She sat up and moved away from him. Coop let his breath go and hoped his blood would return to the normal paths of his body.

"Something more happened than you reported. I want to know what it was."

"Why do you think that?"

"I had a talk with a psychologist. She told me a lot about people and how they react. You've got classic symptoms."

"Symptoms of what?"

Coop hesitated. He could see the fear in her eyes, the fear that Aurora told him she'd seen.

"Symptoms of a woman being blackmailed."

Marsha recoiled. A second later she laughed. Coop stared directly at her, not moving, not reacting to her. She had no way of knowing how often he'd seen people react to his comments. He'd read the lie in her voice and the lie in her laughter.

"You weren't kidnapped by a fan, but by someone you knew. Someone who knows something that can ruin your career. And you've been paying him ever since. It's why you didn't want the police called, why you asked Duncan to hire Aurora Alexander, and why you're hiding out here."

"I am not hiding out."

"Cut it, Marsha. I'm not stupid. Now tell me the truth." He stood up, towering over her.

She sat back, closed her mouth.

"Who's the kid?"

"What kid?"

"Is he yours?"

"No."

"Do you have any children?"

"No."

"Have you ever had any?"

"No."

"Ever been pregnant?"

"No."

"Ever killed anybody?"

Her head snapped up. "No."

At least he knew she was listening to him. "Then what does this man have on you?"

"There isn't anyone, and there's nothing to be had."

"Come on, Marsha, you're no child. Anyone over the age of puberty has something in their past they want to keep hidden, and you're a public figure. You've got more to lose than most."

"If I did have something to lose, what makes you think I'd tell a cop?"

That tone was back in her voice. The one that she used to protect herself. Coop pulled her up to face him. He'd fired questions at her. This time he changed his tactics. His voice was soft when he spoke. "I think you'll tell a cop because you want it to stop. You want someone to know. You've shouldered this burden alone for three years and you want it over and done with."

"Let me go."

She tugged on her arm. Coop kept it securely in his hand.

"You'll tell a cop because a cop is the best person. I'll keep your secret, Marsha, no matter what it is. And I'll collar the guy who's doing this to you."

Tears formed in her eyes. She was going to talk. He knew it. She opened her mouth. No sound came out. He waited, knowing he'd pushed her enough. She was going to tell him.

Then his beeper went off.

With lights flashing and sirens blaring, Coop arrived within minutes of Duncan's page. He came into the guest house like a racer heading toward the finish line. For the next hour he pried every bit of information about the phone call she could remember from Aurora.

"He said he wanted to kill me." Aurora sat quietly on the sofa dressed in jeans and a sweater, far more calm now than she'd been when Duncan found her on the bedroom floor.

"Are you sure there isn't anything else?"

She shook her head. I've told you everything I can remember. He said he wasn't fooled by the episode on television, that he knew television and it couldn't fool him. I could use any name I wanted, but he knew who I was and that he was going to bury me wearing those pearls."

"He gave you no reason."

"No, only that it wasn't personal. That he was going to unravel me like a necklace."

Duncan put his arm around her and she leaned into him.

"How'd he know where I was?" she asked. "I thought the number was unlisted."

"It is," Duncan said over her head. "We'll have it changed tomorrow."

"No," Coop said. "I want permission to have the line tapped."

"All right," Duncan agreed.

Aurora spoke up. "Then you'll have to have someone else answer it." She remembered raving into the receiver, falling naked to the floor. No way would she go through that again.

"Aurora, did you recognize anything about the voice?" Coop was back to asking her questions.

"No," she said. "I'd never heard it before. I don't think it was anyone I know, and I'm not sure I'd know it again." She answered questions she was sure he was going to ask. "Coop, can we stop going over and over the same ground? I've told you everything I can remember—everything. If there was anything else, I'd tell you. Now I'm tired."

"All right." He stood up and squeezed her shoulder, then headed for the door. Duncan got up and followed him. Aurora was too tired to try to hear what they said. She wanted to sleep, but she didn't think she could.

She didn't think she'd ever sleep again. She needed a drink. Getting up, she went to the bar and found a bottle of white wine in the refrigerator. Opening it, she poured two glasses. When Duncan joined her she handed him one.

"I thought it might help me sleep," she said.

Duncan accepted the glass and took her arm. He brought her around to the sofa and turned the lights down to a cozy glow. Then he sat on the sofa and pulled her next to him.

"Sleep if you want," he told her. "I'm going to be here all night."

Aurora settled against him. She sipped her wine and closed her eyes. "What did you and Coop talk about at the door?"

"Marsha. Coop said she was just about to tell him something when he got beeped."

"You know . . ." Aurora wanted to giggle. She started to, then quickly stopped. She was exhausted and her head ached. If she started laughing she'd be hysterical, and she'd already gone through one hysterical episode that night.

"What is it?"

Duncan removed the glass from her hand as she tried to find a more comfortable position. Her eyes drooped and her head fell in his lap.

"You know what would be really funny?"

"What?"

"Suppose he isn't after either of us." Her words slurred. She was almost asleep.

"What do you mean?"

"Suppose he's not our enemy." She chuckled. "Suppose we're just pawns, and he's really not after me and not after Marsha, at all." She gave a short, little sleepy laugh. "Wouldn't that be funny?"

"Go to sleep," Duncan said.

"Wouldn't that be funny, Duncan? All this time we've been trying to find the wrong man."

"Aurora, what are you saying?"

"Not my coin, Darling." Her words were slurred and pronounced slowly. "Not my. . . ."

It was the last thing she said before she fell asleep. Duncan drained his glass and stared at the dark fireplace. This was a twist he hadn't thought of. It read like a bad movie script. In this business everyone had enemies. He had his share. Suppose she'd caught onto something? Suppose it wasn't her coin, as she called it. Suppose the stalker wanted to destroy *him?* It made sense. What better way to get at him than by destroying the show? With Marsha out of the way the show would die. *He* wouldn't, however. He had other projects in the works. He already knew he'd be leaving for Hollywood and the movie he'd received backing for. Why would anyone want to destroy Marsha to get to him?

He doesn't know. Rumors about his connections had flourished only here, and probably in a small circle on the west coast. So far nothing had been announced. They were saving the announcement until he arrived in California at the end of November.

On the surface it appeared that this show was his only endeavor. Without it he wouldn't have to work another day in his life, if he chose. He had investments, stock in major corporations, and interests in some Hollywood production companies. With *The Marsha Chambers Show* he drew a tremendous salary. Someone in the business would know that one show could not destroy a career.

Aurora was only rambling. He watched her as she slept. She was tired, stressed, and didn't know what she was saying. Still, her comments gnawed at him. Suppose it was *his* coin?

Three names immediately came to mind. He wondered where they were. Would they stoop to getting to him by trying to kill Aurora or Marsha? He wasn't sure, but he'd have Coop check it all out in the morning.

He set the empty wineglass on the table. Easing from under Aurora, he lifted her. She stirred in his arms as he carried her up the stairs and put her to bed. As he climbed in next to her she rolled into his arms. He cradled her close and let the worries of the world be shouldered by someone else for the night. For the time being he was only a man in love.

"I love you, Aurora," he whispered, and kissed her forehead. "Nobody is going to hurt you."

The offstage sound system poured music into the studio. Duncan knew Aurora had become used to it signaling the beginning of the show. The announcer introduced her as Rory. His voice was strong, and louder than Duncan's whispered caresses. The audience applauded at the flash of the sign that told them to do so.

Aurora entered from stage left and waited for the chaotic rise in applause to die down. Her usual smile was missing. In its place was an earnest expression.

"Good afternoon." She held no microphone. The tiny clip in her blouse propelled her voice to the back of the gallery. Her hands hung at her sides, fingers reaching the hem of the dark green suit jacket she'd chosen. "Today's show is a serious one. In a moment I'll introduce you to an extraordinary young mother and her son. I met them only a short while ago, but I've come to believe that this woman is stronger than anyone I've ever met."

Duncan watched Aurora. *She* was the strongest woman *he'd* ever met. He stood in the darkness of the studio, out of sight but in communication with the control room through the headset that arced over his head.

Coop sat in the audience. Duncan was relieved he'd decided to patrol the audience. Duncan's duties were too close to the stage for him to take time to review suspicious characters. He knew it would be better to cancel today's filming. Aurora had refused. Even after the horrors of the past few days, she'd insisted on continuing as if nothing had happened. The child was out of the hospital, and Aurora knew it was important to them to broadcast their message. With his present rate of deterioration he might not get another chance.

Her face was straight. She turned slightly as one camera light went off and another came on. "In the United States we think we have the best of everything, and most often we do ... the best schools, best hospitals, best scientists and engineers." She paused. "For one family the best is not good enough." She lowered her voice. "We'll be right back."

The lights came up and the camera panned back to encompass the entire room. The audience applauded. Then the stage was reset. A commercial would be inserted at this point, after which the show would resume.

When the cameras came back Aurora was seated on the stage. Tightly the cameraman filled the screen with her image. Duncan checked it. He could see the strain around her eyes. The camera would undoubtedly see it. He couldn't speculate how the public would interpret it.

"Three days ago my guest was lying in a hospital fighting for his life." She turned to the two people sitting on her right. "Meet Noreen Moore and her son Adam."

Adam sat in a wheelchair between his mother and Aurora. The boy looked pale. He smiled into the camera. His face was covered with freckles, and the mop of "dirty blonde" hair that covered his head also hung into his eyes.

"Adam, why don't you tell the audience why you're here?"

"We want to find my sister," he answered clearly.

"Why?" Aurora asked.

"She can save my life."

Aurora looked from the boy to his mother. "Would you explain what happened?"

The woman sat dry-eyed but as tight as an overextended spring. Her purple suit seemed to almost disappear into the chair of the same color. She pressed her hands together over the balled up tissue she'd had before they started filming.

"My daughter . . . disappeared four years ago."

Her voice broke on the first sentence. She wasn't going to make it, Duncan thought. The audience was quiet. There was only the sound of breathing and the energy of hundreds of silent people in the cavernous studio.

He checked Aurora. She appeared calm, yet he wondered about her emotional state, too. There were too many time bombs in today's program. Mrs. Moore would never make it through the program without breaking down. When mothers cried, so did their children. So Adam was apt to begin crying, too. Aurora's emotional state was unpredictable. Duncan drew in a breath. There was nothing he could do but hope he could salvage part of the tape for at least a short segment.

"Her name is Gilda," Noreen Moore said. "We call her Gillie."

A photo of the girl appeared on the bottom of the screen.

"This is Gillie's picture," Aurora explained. "She was sixteen then. We've had a computer enhance the image of her to show what she might look like today."

Magically, the sixteen-year-old's photo was blown up to fill the entire screen. It sat there for three seconds before splitting into two exact photos side by side. While the image on the left remained unchanged the one on the right aged before the camera to show what the twenty-year-old should look like now. There wasn't much of a change, but with makeup and a different hairstyle she was an adult.

"Mrs. Moore, how can your daughter help Adam?"

"Adam . . ." The woman put her hand to her mouth. Tears rolled over her face. Duncan sighed. A lump rose in his throat and he pushed it down. This woman was obviously in pain, and that pain was being transferred. He felt it. He knew the audience must feel it, too. She would be great on a news program, but Duncan hadn't done the news in years and he'd never put this woman before the cameras in her state. He was afraid Noreen Moore wouldn't be able to complete the filming. She'd insisted she wanted to do it.

"Adam suffers from a rare form of kidney dysfunction." Aurora spoke to the camera, taking over for the mother. "He needs a transplant. His parents have been tested and neither of them are an exact enough match. They need Gillie to come forward and see if she can save her brother's life."

"We're running out of time," the mother got out before she was again swamped by tears. Duncan panned the audience. Open tears rolled down the faces of several women. Some of them held their hearts. The men in the audience looked stoically at the stage. He knew from his own elevated heartbeat they were effected but holding back any outward form of emotion.

"Gillie, if you're out there, please listen to me." The camera moved in tightly on Aurora.

"On the bottom of the screen are two phone numbers. Call either one of them and let some one know that you are all right. Your mother wants you to come home, and Adam needs you." She paused. "We'll be right back."

The audience took a collective breath, Duncan included, then applauded. For a moment Aurora consoled the mother, handing her a tissue from the box on the small table next to her and having the wadded up one in her hand taken away. Mrs. Moore took several deep breaths. Her tears dried and she indicated she could go on.

The camera light went on at his direction and Aurora began to speak, updating the television audience who might have just tuned in to what the subject of the day's program was. "Many people don't know how often kidney transplants are needed and done in this country. Our guest today, Adam Moore, is one child who needs a match in order to live. Most often matches come from someone with the same genetic makeup. Adam's only chance is his sister, who is missing."

She turned back to her guests. Duncan checked the monitor. The 800 numbers were still displayed. "Mrs. Moore, you've told us Gillie disappeared. You mean she ran away?"

"I don't know," her mother said. "You hear of children being abducted. It was the first thought that went through my mind when she didn't come home. We've had no word from her in the four years she's been missing. The police can't find her and . . ." She broke off, but regrouped quickly. "We've hired private detectives and checked the national runaway bureaus."

"If she ran away, do you think she had a reason to leave?" Duncan knew by the quietness of Aurora's voice she didn't want to put the mother through this. Yet the audience would want the answer to that question. What had driven the sixteen-year-old away?

"I don't think any mother understands, or any teenager knows either. Its such an unstable time in both people's lives. My ex-husband and I were going through a divorce. I can't say what deep effect it had on Gillie. I know she didn't want it. The day it became final, she dis—"

"Gillie left that day and no one has seen her since," Aurora said, immediately taking over when Noreen Moore's voice closed off. Her manner was quiet, unassuming. "If Gillie is out there, we need her." Duncan liked the way Aurora had made herself part of the story. Somehow she'd become the surrogate in this interview. "We're not asking you to come and stay if you don't want to. We're asking you to save your brother's life." The camera flashed on the child in the wheelchair. "We can get you here, Gillie. All we ask is that you call. Let you mother know you're well. The phone numbers are on the bottom of the screen.''

At that moment Aurora looked toward Duncan. The stage lights would have him in shadow. He knew she couldn't see him but he connected with her, nonetheless. "When we come back we'll talk with the president of the National Kidney Foundation and Adam's doctor. Stay with us."

Duncan had seen Marsha enthrall an audience. He'd seen actors on telethons and charity auctioneers making appeals. Aurora outdistanced them all in her genuine and sincere approach to saving this child. Duncan returned his attention to the audience as the house lights came up. If he didn't already know it he'd believe it now. Any one of them would be willing to give this child a kidney after the softly spoken but fervent plea by the show's substitute hostess.

The audience whispered to each other. They couldn't resist Aurora's sincerity. She'd taken the pressure off the mother, filled the teary void with her own charismatic magnetism.

Coop knew the moment she entered the studio. Flags stood up and waved in his bloodstream. Marsha Chambers stood alone in the dark well where the bright stage lights faded to darkness. Her disguise, if it could be called that—hair parted on the left and flipped to one side, laying flat against her head, a long coat over jeans—did nothing to prevent recognition.

Of course, Coop would have recognized her if she were wearing protective armor or a level four space suit. Her stare was riveted to the stage and the nervous boy who sat between Aurora and his mother.

Coop again wondered what association she had with this child. He'd made discreet inquiries, doing them himself so as not to arouse undue attention. He could hide his investigation under the guise of official justification and department sanction in an ongoing investigation, but the truth was *he* simply needed to know.

What he found wouldn't fill a thimble. She had no prior criminal record. He thanked God for that. He could find no medical anomalies such as pregnancies, either full or aborted. No long, unexplained absences, no drunk and disorderly's, loud parties, family quarrels, nor parking tickets.

She took few vacations, was considered difficult to work with, yet Hollywood clamored to sign her to multi-movie contracts. In the last three years she'd refused every one of them. Why? Coop wondered. What was it about New Jersey that kept her here?

He scanned the crowd, looking for anyone who might be suspicious. Had someone else noticed her standing there alone? Coop's heart went out to her. She was hiding something, and had been for a long time. He knew it. His instinct told him, his interrogation told him. If that damn beeper hadn't gone off he'd have discovered what it was. She wanted to tell someone. She was dying to get the weight off her shoulders. He'd seen it, probably more than anyone else had ever noticed. She screamed, made people dance to her tune, all so they wouldn't see the lonely woman inside—the one hiding a secret she went out of her way to protect.

Pulling his gaze away, Coop went back to checking faces. No one caught his eye. The audience's attention was as anchored to the stage as Marsha's was. His attention went back to Marsha. He stared at her rather than the action taking place before him, reviewing what he'd found out. Coop had discovered that her parents and a younger sister had died in an accident when she was nine. She'd been placed in foster care, where she was abused. She seemed to pull through the early part of her life, excelling in school. She was accepted at the college of her choice and went there on a full scholarship. She graduated in five years from the School of Fine Arts and went straight to Hollywood.

Only the foster care problem tainted her bio. Otherwise there was nothing shameful about it. Yet the story put out to the media about Marsha Chambers had little resemblance to this one. He wondered why. What was the anomaly there? *And college, too,* he thought. Fine Arts wasn't a five year program, at least not at Howard University, where she'd graduated. She was too good a student and too good an actress to have failed courses and not qualified for graduation. He made a mental note to order a transcript when he got back to the office. He made another note to find out more about Marsha Chambers. And that he'd do in person.

Then there was Aurora Alexander. He studied her from his darkened seat at the edge of the gallery. She'd grown up in Rocky Hill. Her mother had taught music at the local high school and her father had run the rat race in New York six days a week working as the chief financial officer for an architectural firm. Her parents divorced shortly after she graduated from college. When downsizing became a household word her father had taken the package and retired. He now lived in Japan and worked as a consultant. Coop hadn't suspected him of anything. However, he did have him checked out. He hadn't left Japan in the last six years. Aurora had visited him twice for a summer holiday.

After getting her master's degree Aurora had worked in social services, bouncing from area to area. The hope was to keep people from burning out. It didn't work, Coop knew. Social services was worse than police work. No one ever came in without a problem. At least in police work there was resolution. Not always what you wanted, but it did end. In the services there was always another battered wife, teenage runaway, abused child. It came to a point where the counselors couldn't survive the stress of other people's lives. Aurora had survived there for five years, two years longer than most people. She'd also taken to the streets, a process reserved for specifically trained people. She'd searched back alleys, poured through bars and flophouses looking for her kids.

Coop came back to the woman on the stage. This was a cleaner atmosphere—no drug addicts or pimps here—yet Aurora was doing the same thing. She was searching, saving, looking for a way to get help for a child in need.

She did have a record, however. She'd been arrested for assaulting an off-duty officer. The charges were dropped when it was discovered that the officer had abused his child. Aurora had been sent to take the child to a doctor. She'd been confronted with the officer and when he threatened her with bodily harm and raised his arm to hit her she'd blackened his eye.

Luckily, she wasn't alone. She'd been accompanied by a burly Social Services agent who subdued the officer and prevented him from doing anything. Still, he'd pressed charges against her for blackening his eye.

Three years ago she'd begun her Marsha Chambers impersonation and today she stood to lose her life over it.

By one o'clock the next afternoon Fred Loring finished the editing. Duncan viewed the final cut immediately and transmission to the affiliate station had ended an hour ago. The show would air today. If Gillie saw that program, she'd have to be a hardhearted veteran of the streets to not call one of those numbers. He remembered the kid, his mother, and Aurora's performance. When it was over the crew talked of her; how well she'd done, how they were bound to lose her to another talk show.

Duncan agreed with them. He'd known she'd be good at interviewing even before he knew she'd worked with people in trouble. Noreen and Adam Moore were in trouble. Aurora couldn't do anything *but* help. It was ingrained in her. She'd studied helping, knowing when to speak, when to listen, how much to push, and when to back off. Duncan had been on the receiving end of her interview techniques. He had the film of it to prove her power on camera. He'd seen the essence of her ability the day they visited her mother, too—the way she spoke to the nurses, remembering their families, asking about other patients, and the way she talked to her mother. She thought Noreen Moore was strong. She didn't understand her own strength or the influence she had over other people. She'd only been sitting in for Marsha for a short time. Her actual interviews had only been on the air for a few days. This one coming up would garner her an Emmy. Duncan had no doubt of it. It made people want to help, made them feel good about themselves.

They had a show scheduled on volunteering in local communities. He wondered what the percentage increase in volunteerism would be after that show aired. Right now he had an overwhelming need to call his parents and tell them he loved them.

Picking up the phone Duncan dialed a Chicago number.

"Mom, it's Duncan." Her voice was always the same. He thanked God she was there and she was whole, healthy. He didn't envy Aurora and her relationship with her mother. It affected him to the point that he closed his eyes and thanked heaven for his parents.

"Duncan!" He heard the excitement in her voice. Then the concern kicked in. "Are you all right?"

"Of course."

"We just watched your program."

"Already?" He knew they watched it every day, although he had only been on camera once.

"You know your father. He may be in his sixties, but he's still an eleven-year-old kid who has to have every new toy that comes along."

Duncan chuckled. His dad was interested in every new gadget that came along. "What's he bought now?"

"A big screen TV. Calls it high-definition, and on top of that he got a satellite dish."

Duncan had visions of a eight-foot diameter radar-type dish sitting in his family's backyard. He hoped he was wrong, and the dish was the eighteen-inch one.

". . . says it'll pull the signal right out of the sky," his mother was saying. "He's done nothing but watch it since."

"Hey, Duncan. Is that you?" His father got on the phone. He could see his dad wrenching the phone from his mother. He smiled at the image of loving banter created in his head. They had been that way his whole life, but up to now he hadn't realized how truly lucky he was.

"Yeah, Dad, it's me."

"You know that new gal . . . Rory? I like her a lot better. Not that I didn't like Marsha, but this Rory, now she even makes *me* cry."

Duncan leaned his head against his hands. She could make him cry, too.

"You know, Duncan, if she's anything like she is on the screen you ought to think about her." Duncan knew exactly what his father meant. Since his former marriage had broken up, his father had been the one pushing him to get married again.

"I do, Dad."

"What did you say?"

"You heard me."

"Is it serious?" He could hear his mother in the background asking what was serious.

"I don't know yet."

"Do you want to protect her, Duncan? Do you wake up thinking about her, wondering if she's all right, and finding yourself rushing to her to make sure?"

Duncan didn't want to admit he had these feelings, even to his dad. He'd been with Aurora when someone tried to hurt her and he'd been there when the pearls arrived, when she'd comforted her mother and her insides bled with the helplessness that he could not fill. It had torn him apart. Yes, he wanted to protect her.

"You don't have to answer," his father said seriously. "I can hear it in the phone line. It's serious."

Deadly serious, Duncan thought.

Chapter 14

Aurora wanted to walk, run, swim, do anything to get out of the house. The walls were closing in on her. She felt as if she were going to scream. She needed something to do, someplace to go. The phone hadn't stopped ringing since the show with Noreen Moore and her son aired. Producers, directors, and agents bombarded her with questions, offers, invitations to meetings or lunches.

Duncan had told her it would happen. Like everything about this business it came in bursts. You were a nobody today but tomorrow the world clamored for you. She couldn't think, decide.

She didn't know if she wanted to stay in this business. She admitted she like being a hostess. She liked the programs that had been aired. She got to meet all kinds of interesting people from mega-stars to people like Noreen Moore.

The phone rang again. She stared at it, afraid it would be the stalker. Often she turned on the answering machine and let it take the calls. She hadn't answered one directly since the night *he* had called. Now she was avoiding an array of strangers who invited her to become one of them. She couldn't distinguish a real producer from a killer over the phone. He might be smart enough to have seen the program and decided to call and have her set up an appointment with him.

Hadn't he said he knew television? What did that mean? Was he in television? Was he here, on the set? Had she passed him going to and from the studio?

Aurora stopped. She had to get out of here. She was making up ghosts, seeing killers in every face. She needed something to do. *Go shopping,* she thought, then doused the idea. She hated shopping.

Since the call she'd been jumpy. Why didn't whoever it was identify himself? At least she'd know what she was up against. This waiting and watching and having her heart pound each time the phone rang was too much. She looked at the instrument. In the bedroom the telephone was a standard white fixture, but now it seemed like an ominous snake ready to strike. She picked it up before it rang again and dialed Duncan's office.

"I've got to get out of here," she said when he answered.

"Anything wrong?"

"I'm going stir crazy. I haven't been off this compound in days and I can't stand it anymore."

She listened, waiting for him to sigh.

"Its the phone," she said. "It rings constantly. I thought this was an unlisted number. It appears that only the general public doesn't know it. Every producer, director, and agent in the business calls it directly."

She was ready for an argument, dying for one. At least if she couldn't leave, she could vent. If he tried to stave her off this course, she'd scream so loud whoever was after her would know exactly where she was.

"All right," he finally agreed. "Wear jeans. Get your coat and meet me in front of the studio."

Aurora's mouth hung open as she heard the phone

go dead in her ear. He was going to take her somewhere. She sprang into action, discarding the skirt and blouse she had on for a pair of jeans and a Howard University sweatshirt. Ten minutes later she came around the path leading to the studio and headed for the parking lot. Naturally suspicious, she checked the front of the building before stepping openly into the light.

Duncan backed his car out of the space and stopped as she approached.

"Where are we going?" she asked moments later as they sped out of Princeton heading toward Lawrenceville.

"Mercer County Airport."

Airport! "Sounds like someplace good," she said hopefully. She imagined them boarding one of the smaller planes and winging over to another part of the state to spend the day.

"You could say that."

"Mysterious, too."

Mercer County Airport sat off of Interstate 95 in West Trenton. Its runways were long enough to handle small jets, commuter planes, and an occasionally 727. Aurora's father used to take her there as a child to watch the planes take off and land. She wondered why seeing planes held such a fascination for children. Maybe because flight was so against gravity. Seeing the huge, silver machines defy nature made everything possible. If planes could fly, then was there anything she couldn't do?

"Its a flight to nowhere."

She turned to look at Duncan. "I don't understand. I'm familiar with the cruise to nowhere. It leaves from a New York port." She been on it several times playing the Marsha Chambers look-alike.

"Same principle." He glanced at her. "This one is over land . . . about ten thousand feet over land."

She let her mind mull that over. Ten thousand feet was below the cloud level. She checked the sky. Clear.

The air was warm, in the sixties. Colder weather was predicted by the end of the week. Maybe they were flying into Philadelphia and having lunch somewhere. She decided to wait and enjoy the ride. It was a joy just to be in the car and away from *The Marsha Chambers Show.* Turning onto the highway Duncan accelerated to the maximum speed, and quickly the powerful car ate up the miles.

"This is your idea of helping me get over someone threatening to kill me," she said moments later when it became apparent where they'd been heading. "I'm supposed to save the man the trouble and kill myself."

Duncan laughed at her. "You don't have to do this."

Aurora looked at the hangar with Skydiving Lessons painted in huge white letters on its side. "Come on, you'll love it." He took her arm and pulled her inside. Across from them was a man in a flight suit. Duncan called to him.

"Duncan." He came forward and they shook hands. "After yesterday I didn't think you'd be back until the next good weather day, but I expected that would be at least a week away."

Aurora looked from Duncan to the man. He had long, blonde hair and a cherubic face which didn't allow Aurora to guess his age. His teeth were straight, and even and under the flight suit she could see he was muscular.

"Aurora, meet Ennis Grey. We did a segment about skydiving a couple of years ago and used his school as the base."

Aurora offered her hand only to have it swallowed by the calloused palm of Ennis Grey.

"That segment brought me a lot of new students, Duncan included." Aurora's eyes widened and she glanced at Duncan. "He tells me you're going up for a tandem freefall."

"A what?"

Ennis laughed, a hearty sound that said the man

enjoyed what he did. "Come on in. You have a forty-five minute class before we fly."

He turned toward the door and she looked at Duncan. "You can back out any time before you actually go through the airplane door."

She followed Ennis inside and found a room looking much like a classroom. It had a blackboard and ten desks floating in the center of an expanse meant for small aircraft. An engine sat discarded in the corner and cans lined the floor under windows that couldn't have been any lower than thirty feet off the ground. It smelled slightly of chalk and machine oil.

Ennis offered her one of the desks. Apparently she was the only student today. He began teaching, telling her she would jump with Duncan—two people . . . one parachute. Duncan smiled when she looked at him. It was called tandem, because the two of them would be acting as if there were only one. It was the fastest way to go about skydiving. If she wanted to do more later she'd have to take a class that was at least five hours and do several jumps to be an expert.

"You sure you want to go on?" Duncan asked.

"You're sure he's safe?" she asked Ennis.

"I can show you my diploma," Duncan teased.

"All right." Aurora nodded. She'd been bitten by the wonder bug long before Duncan ever parked the car. When her father had brought her here there was no skydiving school. However, the thought of how airplanes work and how she'd seen skydivers performing air ballets made her want to try it. Aurora was a participant, not a spectator. She loved to try new ventures. It was how she'd ended up in classes in painting, auto mechanics, and flower arranging, why she'd attended the first interview for the Marsha Chambers look-alike. And now she was about to fall out of a plane, on purpose.

"There will be no air ballets," Ennis cautioned. "This is a straight jump. You'll exit the plane at ten thousand feet. In forty-five seconds you'll freefall five thousand feet. The remaining five will be spent releasing the parachute and gliding to earth.''

When he finished he'd answered most of her questions, but she still had a few. ''Where will we land?''

''Right here. Behind the airport is a field we use.''

''How come the wind won't throw us off course and send us to Flemington, or into the Delaware River?''

He laughed and she knew she'd asked a ''whuffo'' or—as he'd already explained—a non-skydiver question. ''You're remembering World War Two movies of sky jumpers.''

She had thought of that but refused to acknowledge it.

''They had parachutes that looked like big umbrellas. The ones we'll be using are square parachutes. I say square, but they're really rectangular. These have hand controls so we can steer, and pretty much land where we want to. Another thing from the World War Two films—people landed like a sack of flour. That doesn't happen anymore. In those films, a jumper would roll, and could break a leg or some other body part.''

''Since I'll be controlling the landing,'' Duncan interjected, ''It'll be soft enough for us to remain standing and complete it.''

Ennis took over again, completing his instruction, telling her how to breathe while falling and then pointing her in the direction of the women's locker room. She suited up in the flight suit left for her and joined both Ennis and Duncan, who were dressed exactly as she was, in the classroom. Duncan, however, was fastening a parachute to his back.

Ennis flew the plane as Aurora sat nervously on one of the benches. Did she really want to do this? She had wanted to get out of the house, but jumping from a plane, from 10,000 feet had never crossed her mind. Did she still *have* a mind, or had she lost it along with her heart? She looked at Duncan.

He took her hand. ''You'll be fine,'' he said.

Aurora gave him a crooked smile. Duncan stood up and pulled on gloves.

"It's time."

She mimicked the action, pulling her own gloves over her hands until they connected with the flight suit. Duncan pulled the door open. Air rushed inside, taking her breath away. She turned away from it. She was really going to do this, she told herself. She was going to jump from a plane in flight.

Duncan handed her a helmet and she pulled it over her head. He snapped his strap under his chin and took a step toward her.

"You'll love it," he said, then kissed his finger and pressed it against her mouth. "Turn around."

She did and he attached the two of them together with the parachute.

"Remember everything Ennis told you," he shouted above the wind. Then he walked her toward the door. Aurora took a deep breath. "Ready?"

She wasn't sure. Looking through the door she could see the ground in the distance. Once she'd thought of the rolling green hills as a patchwork quilt. Now she looked at them as sturdy, immovable objects that would come into contact with her when she hit them.

Duncan pushed her a step closer. She resisted, straining her neck to look at him.

"I'm with you," he assured her.

She turned back. The wind whipped at the small amount of hair that poked out from her helmet. Duncan held her hands. They took another step together. *Closer to oblivion,* she thought. Suddenly she was falling. Duncan was holding her. His arms were strong about her. The tendency to close her eyes was enormous. She forced herself to keep them open. Her jaws were tightly clenched. The wind forced her body to contour to Duncan's. Her knees were bent and she held her arms out like extended wings.

In seconds she relaxed. Duncan removed his hands

and extended his arms. She was flying. Like a bird she glided on the air currents, feeling them pressing her body, holding it in the air and letting her float.

The ground bolted upward, toward her but not as fast as she expected. She liked it. She wanted to do things in the air, turn over, swim, see what would happen if she rocked. She felt free, uninhibited, exhilarated. This was thrilling, she thought, almost like her first dive off the high diving board in college. She remembered the coarse air against her face before she hit the water. This was like jumping from a 10,000 foot board.

She took in the scenery below. All too soon Duncan pulled the ripcord. Aurora felt a powerful tug as the red and white chute opened and she was pulled back against Duncan. The chute reduced the falling sensation. In a moment they were floating on the air. Aurora hung in the air, dropping slowly. Half the fall had been done in forty-five seconds. The last half would take five minutes to reach the ground.

Aurora let Duncan control the chute while she enjoyed the ground below. She couldn't explain why she loved the falling, the excitement of having nothing between her and the ground but air.

"We have to do this again," she shouted excitedly when he softly set them on the ground, right on target.

"I take it you liked it." He pressed the release that tethered them together.

Aurora was completely out of breath. She turned to him, excitement coloring her cheeks. "I loved it. It was wonderful. I want to do it again."

Duncan gathered the nylon fabric, pulling it toward himself and rolling it into a huge ball. He hadn't seen her look happy in days. Now she glowed with new life. Enthusiasm made her talk incessantly and he loved hearing it. She described every aspect of the fall as if she were telling it to someone who had never jumped. While he didn't consider skydiving living on the edge, a lot of people did. Most people thought he'd lost his mind when he made his first jump. None of them would consider diving for themselves, but Aurora took to it with the same style and perseverance that had her doing gymnastic routines with the show's guests.

As they fell into step on their way back to the hangar, Ennis landed the plane.

"How'd you like it?" he asked when he joined them.

"It was wonderful." Aurora's eyes were huge like those of a child with a new Christmas toy, and her smile covered the bottom half of her face.

"Duncan, you should bring her by when we have the air show in the spring."

"I don't want to wait that long," Aurora stated. "I'd like to go up again today."

"Not today." Duncan dropped the parachute and looked at his watch. We have a show to do."

She'd forgotten about the show, forgotten about everything except the astonishing exhilaration of sailing through nothing but air. Now memory came flooding back. The stalker's phone call. The threat of being killed. The inescapable fear that surrounded her heart, forcing it to beat faster until she thought it would burst. The uncanny logic that whoever was after her sat in the audience and watched her film the show.

Silent.

Lurking.

Deadly.

Hopewell Township backed into Princeton on the north side. Established a hundred years before the American Revolution, it was quaint, small, and quiet. Duncan parked in Coop's driveway and rang the doorbell of the modest house on a street where the oak trees had witnessed the French and Indian Wars.

Coop opened the door and Duncan smelled onions, the smothered kind. His mouth watered as he realized Coop had made pork chops smothered in onions and gravy. He hadn't eaten that in a long while, and it was all the more mouthwatering for its rarity.

"God, does that smell good."

"Just like you to cut to the chase." Coop smiled. He stepped back and Duncan came inside.

The big man didn't look out of place in his kitchen, an airy room with light yellow walls and large windows. Duncan and Coop had spent many hours in kitchens, both cooking and eating. The table was set and Duncan dumped his coat and took a seat. Coop shoveled a healthy helping of the meat and onions onto his plate. He complemented it with mashed potatoes dripping in gravy and green peas, which they both hated as children but had grown to love as adults. From the oven he removed fresh corn muffins, and Duncan was in heaven.

While they ate neither of them mentioned Marsha, Aurora, the show, or any of the problems that plagued them. Duncan related his call to his parents, leaving out the statement his father made about his association with Aurora, but telling Coop they sent their love.

After dinner, and over glasses of brandy in the living room, Coop asked him the reason he was really here.

"As I remember it, you invited me," Duncan said. He took a drink of his brandy. It was smooth going down his throat, and warmed his chest. Coop looked steadily at him. Duncan tried to ignore it. Eventually he began to speak. "Aurora said something to me last week that I can't stop thinking about." While he didn't think it was true he couldn't get it out of his mind. "She was rambling, almost asleep when she said it, but it's been with me since."

"What was it?"

"She mentioned that the man stalking her might not be anyone she knows or anyone Marsha knows. That it isn't her coin he wants."

Coop set his drink aside. Every instinct for police work he possessed went into action. His body tensed, his senses went into sharp attention, and his eyes noticed every nuance of movement from the man talking to him. It was a visible change to Duncan.

"Then whose coin is he after?"

"Mine."

"Yours?"

"I thought about it, Coop. Three people come to mind. I don't know where they are or what they're doing. I made a few calls but no one could tell me much about any of them." He felt absurd. Aurora hadn't known what she was saying. He didn't even think she remembered it. She hadn't mentioned it again.

"What would be the motive?"

"Revenge mostly. Disgruntled employees. One went to jail on my testimony."

Coop grabbed a pencil and paper. They were never far from his fingers. "Give me the information."

"I don't really think it's any of them." Duncan could take care of himself. He didn't need to give Coop details on his thoughts. He was sorry he'd mentioned it. "My money is on Marsha and something that happened in her past. Aurora is only a pawn who looks like her and this man, whoever he is, is fixated on the wrong woman."

Duncan saw Coop's reaction to his comment. He was sorry for it the moment he said it. He knew Coop was falling for Marsha, although he couldn't imagine them having anything in common.

"Aurora was rambling when she said it," he went on, hoping to cover his earlier comment. "I'm sure there's nothing to her comments. She was tired. It was the night she got the phone call. I've already looked into the three people I had in mind and there's nothing to what she said."

"It's not going to hurt for me to check on them. Let's have it."

Duncan sighed. Coop was poised to write. Duncan gave him the information. Instead of feeling foolish, he felt relieved. Coop was a good cop. He'd do what he could. He also had access to information sources that Duncan didn't. If they could be found, Coop could do it and he would keep it quiet.

"The focus is still on Marsha and Aurora," he stated.

Coop nodded. "Got any idea why either of these men would want to harm Aurora or Marsha, if they really are your enemies?"

Duncan shook his head. "None of them know Aurora. Two of them know Marsha. They worked with her on previous projects. I don't think any of them would have a reason to harm her. When she knew them, there was no *Marsha Chambers Show* and she wasn't as difficult to work with."

"What about the sketch? Do either of them look like the sketch or an older version of the men you remember?"

Duncan thought a moment, then shook his head. "The man would have to be a fool to come without a disguise if he planned to get in and out of the compound. The sketch is probably no good if he wore makeup."

"It would have had to be good makeup, stage makeup. Hadn't Aurora said he understood television? Were either of these men part of the makeup team?"

Duncan shook his head. "That doesn't mean they didn't learn it. Any actor sitting in a chair sees what's being done to his face. It's nothing to buy the materials. Women spend a fortune on makeup every year."

"You think it's someone who's coming from Marsha's past?"

"It's the only explanation that makes any sense to me. She has the most to lose."

"Tell me about her, then?" Coop asked. His question was harmless, but Duncan heard the restraint behind it, as if he didn't want his friend to know his interest in Marsha wasn't purely professional. That was the thing about friends—they could read you even when you didn't want them to.

Duncan told him. They spent the better part of the night talking about Marsha, what she'd been like before she started the show, how she'd changed afterward. Coop said very little. However, Duncan knew Coop didn't miss anything. There was something growing between Cooper Dean and Marsha Chambers, just as there was something growing between him and Aurora. He'd never felt this way before, thinking of her first thing, wanting to know where she was and that she was safe, wanting to spend his nights buried inside her and his days holding her close, wanting to go where she made him feel things he'd never felt before, soaring to heights he didn't know a man could live through, let alone enjoy.

He closed his eyes, letting his head fall back against the upholstery as he remembered Aurora.

The first snow of winter fell two weeks before Thanksgiving. Aurora woke to find the world blanketed in white. It looked as if a designer had gone out and set the scene. Each tree branch was covered on the windward side, every leaf straining to hold the snow. Rhododendron bushes hung low from the weight. The ground was undisturbed by footprints or animal tracks. No snapshot could reflect a more perfect picture. Aurora's spirits rose. She felt like a young girl again, waking up and finding winter had joined them. No school, just a day to play.

She thought of Duncan sleeping upstairs. Lifting her cup she drank the coffee and sank onto the window seat. Pulling the folds of her gown around her, she hugged her knees and watched the outside.

"You look like you know a secret."

Duncan leaned on the newel post. He wore jeans, zipped but unsnapped, and nothing else. She swallowed, thinking he couldn't get any sexier. If they ever did a show on sexy men she'd have to convince him to be

guest number one. He came toward her, sitting in front
of her. He took her cup and drank her coffee.

"I thought you were still asleep."

"How could I sleep with all that noise?"

"What noise?" she smiled.

"The noise of all that falling snow." He turned to
gaze out the window before bringing his attention back
to her. He leaned forward and kissed her mouth. "You
taste good," he told her. "Like morning and coffee and
winter snow." Then he moved in for more.

Aurora wondered if her attraction to Duncan would
always be this strong and this instantaneous. When she
was fifty and his image flowed unbidden into her mind,
would her nipples tighten the way they were now? At
sixty, would the pull of need flow through her like a
raging river? She didn't know, wouldn't go that far.
Their relationship was short-term; here today, no tomorrow. Aurora slipped one foot to the floor. Duncan's
arms went around her and she slid toward him. His
mouth was tender, brushing over hers with the softness
of velvet. His teeth teased her bottom lip and his hands
got lost in the folds of her nightgown, seeking, searching
for her under the voluminous fabric.

One hand skimmed fire along the leg still on the
window seat. She trembled, then jerked at the arrows
of heat that flashed between her legs when his hands
found her breasts. Her back arched, seeking continu-
ance of the agony that had her clinging to him,
devouring his mouth, pulling him closer to her, and
wrapping her leg around him.

She didn't know when the beast invaded her, didn't
understand that there was one dormant inside her, until
it came to sudden and uncontrollable life. Her other
leg circled him. She pulled herself onto his lap until
she was sitting on him, feeling his arousal through his
jeans. His body thrilled her, sending strings of electricity
singing through her blood.

She pressed him back, straddling him on the narrow

bench. "I want you," she said. She didn't recognize herself. She was tigerish, her nails raking over his skin as if she owned it. Every nerve pulsed to life. She felt his breathing, knew the pounding of his heart.

Aurora stretched out atop him. Her mouth connected with his, devoured his, delved inside. Her tongue danced in unison with his while her hips rolled over him. He opened his legs, letting her settle between them. Her breath accelerated, forcing itself through her mouth. He kneaded her buttocks, pressing her into the strength of him. She would have screamed if she'd had enough air but he took it away, sucked it like a vacuum, and left her reeling.

Aurora didn't remember him lowering her to the floor. She lay under him. He peeled the gown over her head and lay her naked before him. She let him look, glorying in his gaze. She felt beautiful. He made her feel beautiful.

Reaching for his zipper she pulled it down.

"You make me crazy," he rasped.

"Good," she purred. "Come here." Aurora's hand went inside his pants at the point of the open zipper. Duncan groaned. The sound spoke of the passion ripping through her. She pulled him forward, working the jeans over his slim hips, taking him into her hands, listening to the guttural sounds that seemed forced from his body.

Duncan discarded the jeans after taking a tiny silver packet from his pocket. Aurora took it, snapped it open, and sheathed him with the latex. He gritted his teeth, squeezed his eyes shut, and held his head back as he tried to control the raging emotions Aurora's hands created on his most erotic spot. She moved slowly, driving him further and further to the point of insanity.

He couldn't stand it. Duncan grabbed her hands and pulled them away, falling forward and holding them on either side of her head. His body covered hers. She smiled at him as her eyes roamed about his face. Her

eyes were deep pools of dark rapture. He kissed her
nose, then took a slow trip around her cheeks to her
lips. She moaned, a sound that sent blood pouring to
his loins. As his tongue filled her mouth he drove himself into her. Her body shuddered. He loved that sudden
catch of elation that escaped from her when they joined.

Duncan was inside her. Her hips rotated beneath
him. He tried to hold back. He wanted to take it slow,
savor their time together, but didn't know if he could.
This was morning. They'd made love all night. Where
he got the energy to continue, he didn't know. His only
thought was that Aurora drove him. She pulled her
hands free. They smoothed over his shoulders, trailing
streams of lava down his back and over his exposed
flanks. Her hands worked magic, igniting him, turning
him into a four-alarm fire.

She consumed him. He drove himself deeper into
her, no longer trying to be gentle. Her body accepted
him, pulled him in. She bent her knees and he filled
her to the hilt. Each time he was with her, control totally
abandoned him. He couldn't hold back, didn't want to.
He wanted to go where she led, to take her places
neither of them had imagined, places they could find
together.

He'd made love before, made love to her before, but
this was the first time he'd ever been fully and totally
under the control of someone else. He usually had the
upper hand. Aurora held it now. Her body contoured
to his, fit, drove, asked, and took. He gave, without
volition, without thought. He wanted to give, wanted to
make her feel good, wanted nothing more than to die
in the throes of this powerful exchange.

He looked at her face. It changed, relaxed, tensed,
as he moved inside her. He was a crazy man, driven by
instinct, pushed by a raw, uncompromising need. He
rode her, rode high and wild. The wind whipped at him
on his imagined ranch. He rode harder and harder,
climbing toward the sky, a big Montana sky, one in

which there was no limit and only two people. He consumed her, like an insatiable fire that fascinated him with its flames, licked at his control, searing it layer by layer until the string holding him together was only the thickness of a single thread. The thread snapped, launching him over the edge, inflaming him. He pushed deeper, grabbing for the bright sun, reaching until it burst, exploded, catapulting them to a level longed for, reached for, and found only by lovers.

Aurora breathed hard. Duncan covered her like a blanket. She couldn't remember feeling like this, relaxed, loved as if she were precious. She didn't want to move, never wanted to move again. Duncan was a great lover. It made her weak to think about him. She hated to think of him leaving for California, but it would come.

She kissed his neck, listening to his heart beating wildly. He rolled off of her but kept her close to his side, his arm around her, his hand fondling her breast. Aurora closed her eyes and let the feeling wash over her.

Duncan made her feel so good. She was going to miss him when all this was over. She'd thought she could come out of it unscathed, but she knew better now. She'd known better the first time they made love. Now, after this bonding, this communion, her heart was involved. She closed her mind, trying to force the image of loneliness away, but it persisted. She wondered how much longer they had together now that his movie project in California had come through. Although no announcement had been made at the studio, rumors flew every day. It was only a matter of time before he told the crew.

Aurora ran her hand over his stomach, savoring the feel of him, the smell of love in the air. "God, I'm going to miss you terribly." Aurora hadn't realized she'd spoken aloud until Duncan's hand stilled hers. He pushed himself up and stared at her. "When?" She asked the question, but knew the answer already.

"Soon," he said. "Right after Thanksgiving."

Her stomach muscles clenched. She hadn't expected to feel as if he'd kicked her. She knew this was coming, had known for a while. She tried to keep her face still. She looked down in case the pain showed in her eyes.

"We'll have to celebrate," she told him, hoping she appeared happy for him. "We'll order a big cake and have a huge party on the set."

"Aurora." He took her chin and lifted it until her eyes met his. "I don't want a cake." His voice hitched.

She knew what he meant. She wanted him, too, wanted to spend every minute of the next two and a half weeks with him. Aurora lifted her hand and rubbed it over his cheek. Yesterday's stubble grazed her hand. Her eyes clouded with tears. Her arm went around his neck and she brought her mouth to his. *I love you*, she thought as she kissed him.

Aurora realized that when Duncan left he'd take part of her heart with him. She'd be left with a hole where their love had been. Right now she wouldn't think about that. She pulled him closer, deepening the kiss. Right now she would think of nothing except this moment, the snow outside, and the frozen point in time where they lived. All the future moments were pushed away.

Duncan's hand raked over her skin, heating it. His fingers brushed against her breast. Her mind went blank and only the dreamy, crystalline, fragile feeling of first love was left.

Twenty-four hours later, while Duncan stood in front of the full crew to announce his departure from *The Marsha Chambers Show*, Aurora accepted a telephone call from a tearful Gillie Moore, who was willing to fly in and save her brother, Cooper Dean picked up the report he'd dropped on his desk.

Leaning back in the chair he read through it for the third time. *Nothing,* he thought as he pushed it away. Duncan had given him three names—Kevin Baldwin, Freddie Turner, and Melvin Master. Each one of them had reason to exact revenge from Duncan, but it didn't appear they had. Opening the folder again, Coop read. Baldwin had been a producer-writer. Six years ago he'd been sent to jail for placing subliminal messages in his films and TV programs. Apparently Duncan had discovered this and been the principle witness against him at his California trial. He was released from prison a year ago and apparently had picked up his connections. He had two programs ready for scheduling now. There was no indication that he was back to his old tricks.

Freddie Turner lived in New York. Only a short drive and a river separated him from Duncan. He could come and go with no one knowing if he wished. Freddie had worked at the same studio as Duncan in Hollywood. His show had run its rating-course and production money had been pulled and put into Duncan's show. Eventually Freddie left Hollywood, and now he ran a men's clothing outlet in Brooklyn. According to the report he had no idea where Duncan was today. Also, he commented he'd never seen *The Marsha Chambers Show,* since it came on during his hours at the store.

Melvin Master had hated working in television. He'd been a sound engineer. When Duncan fired him he'd gone to work for a recording company. Later he'd taken a job managing a music and video store in downtown Los Angeles. On the surface was the appearance of legality, but Master's life style was much too rich for the salary he commanded. No arrest had been made but he was currently being investigated for operating a bootleg cassette business.

Coop went over each of the three folders again and

again. There wasn't enough here. He needed more. He'd make some calls before he talked to Duncan. And he needed to see Aurora again. With the knowledge he had now he wanted to make sure the message she'd gotten over the phone couldn't narrow the list down. Of course, there was always the chance he was following a tangent. In his mind Marsha was the primary target. He needed her to tell him the truth. He needed her to trust him. More important, he *wanted* her to trust him.

Chapter 15

The phone remained under Aurora's hand long after she'd hung up. She smiled widely, even as tears blurred her eyes. She'd wished, hoped, and prayed that Gillie would see the program, but until she took the call she hadn't believed that she could actually reach out and do something.

Her heart was in her throat. If anyone had asked her to speak she couldn't have saved her life by doing it. Luckily she was alone in her dressing room. She needed to call Mrs. Moore. She needed to let the distraught mother know her daughter was alive, well, and on her way home. She'd take another moment. There was no need for them both to cry over the phone.

She did cry. Noreen went silent on the phone when Aurora spoke to her. Aurora could sense the tears through the quiet air of the phone. Hers started, and she could do nothing to stem them. When she hung up she brushed her eyes with her fingertips. At that moment the door opened. Glancing into the mirror she came face-to-face with Marsha Chambers.

Her breath caught as the door slammed shut. She

didn't have to ask if something was wrong. Marsha stood with her feet apart, her hands on her hips, and a face as set as concrete.

"I'm back," she said.

Aurora stood up. "I can see that."

"I want you out of here. This is my show and I can do it."

"No problem there," Aurora agreed.

"You think you're good, don't you?" Marsha took a step forward. Stubbornly, Aurora refused to be intimidated. "Well, I'm here to tell you, you're nothing. Your interviews stink. A trained seal could ask better questions."

Aurora knew better than to fight with a person who couldn't be reasoned with. She knew Marsha was too angry to listen to anything she had to say. It wouldn't matter if she agreed or disagreed. The woman was on a mission, and at the moment *she* was the mission. Knowing all this didn't stop her, however, from hitting back.

"My interviews were the best I could do, and I didn't get any complaints from any of the crew or the guests."

"Well they don't count, and I do." She pointed a finger toward herself.

"Then why weren't you here to conduct them? You've been off hiding somewhere while I've stood out there making a target of myself to save your—" She cut herself off, not wanting to say something she could never retract.

"Save my what?" Marsha glared at her. Her eyes were as angry as her red nail polish.

"Save your show." Aurora paused. Anger got the better of her. "You opted out. You hid in a house with guards and watched safely from the sidelines. You would have nothing to do with reruns. Don't look at me as if you don't like what you got."

"I don't like it. I don't like you making yourself comfortable here." She looked about her dressing room.

Aurora had used it since she took over Marsha's role. "I don't like you coming in and taking over."

"You needn't let it bother your little head any longer." Aurora went to the closet and got her coat. Punching her arm into the sleeve, she turned back to the hostess. "You want your show back. You can have it." Aurora grabbed her purse from the shelf and slammed the closet door.

She pushed past Marsha and reached for the door. It opened before she could stop it. Stepping back to avoid collision she saw Joyce come in.

"What's going on in here?" she asked.

"Nothing," Aurora answered. "Anything that was going on is finished."

She passed her and left the room. She didn't stop at the studio but went straight to the house, threw everything in her suitcase and then into her car, and left the grounds. Her breath came in hard gasps.

She was glad to be rid of them, she told herself. Marsha could resume her show. She could be the target. Duncan would be gone by the end of the month. There was nothing to stay for. She had a life of her own and it was time she resumed it.

Aurora drove fast. She whipped the little car around curves and over road bumps in an effort to put as much distance between herself and the loonies who did television. The lot of them should be gathered together and dropped on a desert island.

The small car roared into her driveway. *No guards,* she thought. Duncan had told her he'd posted guards on the property. Just like him to be absentminded. She didn't care, she told herself. Didn't care that Duncan was leaving, that she'd never see him again, except maybe accepting an Academy Award on television.

"No!" she shouted as she hit the button for the garage door. She wouldn't watch him on television. She wouldn't even own a television. She'd throw the thing out her next trash day.

Getting out of the car she took a deep breath and tried to control the anger. It was over now. She was home. Safe. She didn't have to worry about Duncan or Marsha again. They had their lives, and she had hers.

Grabbing the suitcase, she went into the house. The garage door led into the kitchen. Her own kitchen, she thought. God, it was great to be home. She flipped on the light.

Her heart stopped. Sitting at the table was a man dressed in black. A ski mask lay in front of him. Aurora recognized the mask. Memory of her previous association with it took her voice away.

"Hello, Marsha." He stood, pointing a large black gun at her heart. "It's good to finally meet you. You look better in person than you do on the screen, but then television will change you. You should have gone into feature films."

"Mr. West, this is Finch at the front gate. Is Ms. Chambers still there?"

"Ms. Chambers? I haven't seen Ms. Chambers." A cold fear fissured down Duncan's spine. He knew he wasn't going to like what the guard had to tell him.

"She arrived about an hour ago."

"She didn't come into the studio."

"I saw her go in, sir. Then a few minutes ago I believe Ms. Alexander left. I know the woman who left wasn't wearing the same clothes as the one who arrived. I just wanted to be sure everything was all right."

Duncan sighed heavily into the receiver.

"I'm sorry, Mr. West. I can't tell them apart. This is why I called. I thought—"

Duncan cut him off. "Have you checked the guest house?"

"Sir, we've called but get no answer. I'm awful sorry, Mr. West."

Duncan's hand gripped the phone so tightly he could

feel the tension up his arm. He relaxed it. "It's not your fault." He knew Aurora. If she got it into her head to leave the compound, she would. Something had to have driven her away.

Marsha!

Duncan hung up the phone. He'd go to the guest house himself. Maybe Marsha had left the compound and Aurora was preparing for bed. Snatching the phone up he dialed the guest house. The phone rang four times before the answering machine clicked on. He heard Joyce's voice asking whoever it was to leave a message. Duncan remembered the phone call she'd received before. More than likely she wouldn't answer without hearing who was calling.

"Aurora, it's Duncan. Pick up the phone." He waited a second. "Aurora, if you're there, please pick up the phone." Still nothing. He dropped the receiver in its cradle. Fear crept up his spine like a silent enemy.

Duncan left his office at a fast walk. He didn't want to panic. He was sure Aurora was fine. He just needed to make sure. On his way to the outside he swung by her dressing room. The door was open and he saw someone inside. Pushing the door open further, he called her name.

"She's gone." Marsha's voice was strong and confrontational. She stared at him like a satisfied cat.

"What do you mean she's gone?"

"I sent her packing. It's my show and I'm back."

Duncan reigned in his temper. He tried to remind himself that Marsha did not know the things that had gone on. That she was just a frightened artist who thought she was losing control of her program.

"Where did she go?"

"I don't know and I don't care." Marsha sat down on the sofa and put her feet up. She looked relaxed, as if there were nothing important in the world except the comfort of Marsha Chambers.

Something inside him snapped. He grabbed her arm and hauled her up. Her face was extremely close to his.

"What did you say to her?" Duncan shouted. He saw fear enter Marsha's eyes. He wanted to choke her. He was as close as he'd ever come to wanting to hurt a woman.

"I merely told her I was back."

"I can just hear how you said it too, Marsha. You never think of anyone but yourself." Duncan released his hold on her and swung away. He didn't even want to look at Marsha. He knew if he continued he might put to action the thoughts that were going through his mind. "She's not in the guest house. She's left the compound."

"She's a big girl, Duncan. She doesn't need you escorting her everywhere she goes."

Duncan rounded on her. He must have looked menacing, because Marsha took a step back.

"You don't know what's been going on here. You've been safely hiding out while Aurora stood in for you. She's been harassed by phone calls and frightened that whoever is looking to harm *you* will get her instead. Her home has been broken into and her life turned around. All because she had the misfortune to be on the set the day someone mistook her for you."

"You don't know that," Marsha shouted. Duncan knew her, knew she'd attack. "The man who attacked her could have been looking for *her.* There's no evidence that he was looking for me."

She was hiding something. "They came to your show in broad daylight. If they were looking for Aurora, she lives alone in an old house that's big enough to fit a circus in it. A man could easily wait there and grab her without anyone knowing. No, he came here. He was looking for you. Why, Marsha? Who is it?"

She turned away, but Duncan grabbed her arm and pulled her back. "Who is it?"

She snatched her arm away and Duncan let it go. He

didn't want to touch her. "I have no idea what you're talking about. There is no one."

"What really happened when they kidnapped you, Marsha?"

The swift change in subject threw her off guard. He saw the change in her. The quick intake of breath. The fear in her expression. Emotion played over her face as if she were a veteran actress in an Academy Award winning scene. This was no scene. Duncan saw the raw fear.

"I told you what happened. I've told Coop what happened."

"You can stick to that story if you want to. Sooner or later one of us is bound to find out the truth." There was a threat in Duncan's voice and he hoped she heard it.

Blue uniforms and badges were intimidating enough. Even a person identifying himself as a cop had clout over the average American citizen. With Coop, size was a major factor. Coop knew this and it played a part in his cutting through the red tape of channels that let him cross the river into New York City to personally talk to Freddie Turner.

The city was decked out for Christmas shoppers. Lamp-posts and store windows sported colored lights, Christmas trees, garlands, and sale signs. Coop liked the city. It reminded him of Chicago, with horns blaring, hundreds of taxi cabs, and constant road construction. He liked the Christmas lights, too. Annually, he made the trip to Radio City Music Hall to see the Rockettes, and a couple of times a year he went there for a play and dinner. A few times he had been here on business, like tonight.

Mike Kelly, a six-foot, red-faced Irishman, met him at the corner of the fashionable neighborhood in the West Twenties. Kelly came with all of Coop's requirements. He was a uniformed officer with big hands and big feet, and he drove a patrol car. He commanded attention when he walked up to someone. With Kelly, he'd get what he wanted. Kelly had jurisdiction here, but before entering the men's clothing store, they established that Coop would ask the questions.

Inside the space was well lighted. Suits hung against one wall. Sport jackets and pants took up the other. The floor had shirts and ties on various round tables. The dark mahogany furnishings were upscale and expensive. The room was spacious and uncluttered, with sofas and tables, giving the appearance of a place to relax while picking out next season's wardrobe.

"Mr. Turner?" Coop asked the man who came forward.

"No," he shook his head. "I'll get him for you."

The man looked relieved and scared at the same time. He went to the back of the store and disappeared through a curtain. Moments later he returned with another man. He was short and a little too round about the middle. He wore a white shirt with the sleeves rolled up and dark pants that looked as if they'd been made for his unsymmetric body.

"I'm Freddie Turner."

"Cooper Dean." He extended his hand and the man took it. "This is Officer Kelly." They both flashed badges. "We'd like to ask you some questions."

"What's this about?" Coop glanced at the salesclerk hovering close by. Turner saw him. "My office is this way."

They followed him to a backroom filled with a drafting table, bolts of fabric, a cluttered desk, and a stand with awards on it.

"You design clothes, too." Coop noticed the paper on the drafting table, a woman's evening gown.

"I try," he smiled.

Coop looked about the room. He was good at reading people from the space they chose to occupy. Freddie

Turner's office held none of his former life. There wasn't even a television here, no memento of his short-lived series. A bookcase held books on fashion design and use of accessories, nothing on film or television. On the floor were jars of buttons, a rack of various colored threads on huge spools, an isolated pair of worn shoes, and fabric, all kinds, everywhere.

There was nothing personal—no pictures of a wife or child, no children's drawings from kindergarten—only awards from various fashion events. The case holding them was dusty and neglected. Only a coffeemaker sitting next to his desk gave Coop any insight into his personality. At arm's reach, it probably supplied Turner with several pots during the day. Dregs filled the room with a burnt odor. A jar of Vanilla Cream non-dairy creamer, gave away a Hollywood memory that had Coop smiling.

Freddie Turner's life revolved around the industry of making and selling clothes. The only out of place item was the design of the evening gown.

"What's going on?" Turner asked.

"We're here about an old friend of yours." Coop paused. "Duncan West."

Turner smiled.

"When was the last time you saw him?"

Turner inched over to his chair and sat down. He leaned back in it and looked at the ceiling. "I haven't seen Duncan since the day he usurped my show." He laughed as if sharing a private joke with the absent Duncan. "It was the best thing that ever happened to me."

Coop kept his eyes on the man. He had the urge to look at Kelly, but years of training had him looking directly at Turner.

"He took over your show?"

Turner was already shaking his head before Coop finished the questions. "I had a television show out in Hollywood about eight years ago. Duncan had one, too.

His was on the way up, mine down. The old 'a-star-is-born' thing." He waved his hands like a producer, short on time and in a hurry. "My show was pulled and Duncan's went on in its place. God, I hated him. Hated him for years."

"Have you had any contact with him since?"

"No." He held onto the word. "What's he doing now? Is he in some kind of trouble?"

Coop shook his head. "No trouble. He's producing *The Marsha Chambers Show.*"

"Television?"

"Yeah."

"I don't watch it. Don't even own one."

"Thank you, Mr. Turner. You've been a lot of help."

Coop and Kelly left then. Outside, Coop asked the cop to check out where Mr. Turner had been on the day Aurora had been attacked and the night the phone call came. Coop thought the man was telling the truth. Still, it wouldn't hurt to check every angle. Turner could probably afford the pearls that had been sent to Aurora. Yet his profile didn't call for women.

The gown on the drafting board intrigued him. The office had been purely masculine, almost sterile, then that gown. If he had a gown, maybe he'd have pearls, too.

And maybe he'd be up on the use of makeup.

Not a single light shone in Aurora's house when Duncan got there. The fear that gripped him earlier had taken up permanent residence in his body. His heart raced, his hands were cold and clammy, and he felt the need to shout her name. His internal radar told him something was wrong. Where were the guards he'd posted? Where were the police cars that regularly patrolled the area?

Duncan parked across from the house and got out of the car. He saw nothing. Crossing carefully, he went up the drive. Old news reports of snipers snapped into his mind. The darkness of the place was disconcerting. If Aurora had come here, wouldn't she have turned on a light? The guards would have called the studio. Where were they? Why were they nowhere to be seen?

Duncan peered through the front window. He saw nothing. He should have called Coop, but his phone was back in the car now. Going around the house he found nothing out of place. Then he saw the car in the garage. She had to be here.

Forgetting his fear, Duncan rushed to the door, rang the bell, and pounded on the heavy wood. He squinted through the glass ovals trying to see inside, hoping to see Aurora coming toward him, but nothing happened. No one came. Duncan called her name. His voice got louder and louder, more frantic, almost insistent. She had to be here.

"She's not there."

He turned. Standing at the edge of the property was Aurora's neighbor. Duncan remembered her. She probably didn't remember him. She stood far enough away to make a run for it if he were a criminal. *Her name?* he asked himself. *What is her name? Megan.*

"Megan, she's been here." He remained where he was, not wanting to frighten her. "It's Duncan West from *The Marsha Chambers Show.*"

She searched his face in the dark. Then he saw recognition change her body language. She smiled. "I remember you."

"Aurora's car is here. Did you see her?"

She shook her head. "I haven't seen her for weeks, since she went to do the show."

"She left tonight. She was angry." Duncan went toward the woman. "I want to talk to her." His voice was low, persuasive. If Aurora was at Megan's he wanted to convince her to let him talk to her. "I just want to make sure she's all right."

"I haven't seen her. She's not at my house." Megan

glanced over her shoulder, then back at Duncan. She'd picked up a signal that he thought Aurora might be hiding.

"Did you see anyone else about the house? There should be some guards."

"I thought it was strange that they weren't there today when I got home from work. I thought they had been called away. They've been there a couple of weeks and nothing has ever happened."

"They were sent by the studio, and we didn't release them."

"Do you think something happened to them?"

Duncan didn't want his mind to go there. He didn't want to know that anything could have happened to the guards. Unfortunately he couldn't stop the thought.

"I have a key," Megan said. "Maybe we should look inside."

Duncan could have hugged her. "Would you get it?"

She nodded and turned to leave. He stopped her. "Megan. Call the police."

Aurora resisted but the stranger pushed her into the dark little shack in the middle of nowhere. He'd taped her mouth, hands, and legs and hauled her into the van. Everything hurt now. The drive to wherever they were took at least half an hour. She'd lain in an unnatural position and her back, neck, legs, and arms ached.

Sitting her in a chair, he re-wrapped her legs with duct tape. She tried to talk. Her voice was muffled. He ripped it off her mouth.

"Who are you? What do you want?" Aurora asked as soon as she could talk. She didn't want the terror to be in her voice, but it was there. She didn't care that her mouth was swollen, that the tape left a burning sensation on her face.

"Simple. I want Duncan West."

"Then why did you take me?" As soon as she said the words, she felt guilty. She wouldn't want Duncan to be kidnapped. She loved him.

"It's nothing personal."

"What!"

"I mean, I'm sorry. You're just a diversion."

"What are you going to do to me?"

"I told you on the phone."

Aurora's heart slammed into her chest. Sweat popped out on her brow. The phone call came back with vivid clarity.

"Why? We don't even know each other."

"Like I said, it's nothing personal. Just payback. Duncan West is going to lose his star, and I'm going to ruin him like he ruined me."

His star. He thought she was Marsha.

"How did you get into my house?"

"This isn't Twenty Questions."

She ignored his statement. "Did you happen to look at my mailbox, see any of my mail."

"I'm not a fool!" he shouted. "You can tell the world you're Rory, even have mail sent to yourself in that name, but I know better. You're Marsha Chambers, the bread and butter of the show. Duncan is deep into this production and I'm going to take him out." He pronounced each of the last three words as if they were single sentences.

"Why? What did he do to you?" Aurora had to keep him talking. It was the first rule of self-defense. Keep the person talking and perhaps you can keep them from killing you, or you can delay them long enough for help to come. There would be no help tonight. No one knew where she was. The guards saw her leave. They probably thought she was Marsha. No one had seen her go into her garage. Even if they found her car there, she'd left no clue that she'd been there. Duncan and Coop would have no place to look.

She'd been alone with people who wanted to kill her

before. Then she'd had backup, but barely got away with her skin. She'd been in a city where she could scream and people would hear her. Out here she was alone.

Chapter 16

Coop's fingers flew across the keys of the computer on his desk. He'd searched for everything he could find on Freddie Turner, Kevin Baldwin, and Melvin Master. He'd gone through police records, airline information, even high school and college transcripts, and come up against the two drawbacks the machine had. It couldn't get through a brick wall, and it couldn't answer questions that weren't asked.

Turner's financial records were without reproach. He'd had trouble with the IRS once, gone to court, and won. That alone reinforced Coop's assessment of the man. He was driven to succeed, worked at it, excelled, and fought for his rights. Did he think that Duncan had done him wrong, and was he determined to make him pay for it? It didn't appear so. The officer in New York, Kelly, verified Turner's whereabouts on the nights in question. He couldn't be in two places at one time. But he could mastermind a kidnapping if he chose.

Baldwin had a prison record. Duncan testified against him for slipping subliminal messages into the film. He'd gotten a light sentence because he'd only focused on personal greed by suggesting that people view his next film. He hadn't perpetrated any mind control games.

Coop had placed a call to the prison and spoken to the warden. Often there was information not contained in the files. He learned Baldwin was suspected in the death of another inmate, but no one could prove it. According to the prison report Baldwin had been a model prisoner, being released early for good behavior. But then practically everyone who went to the "Country Club," a white-collar crime facility, had lived in luxury and was furloughed early. Most returned to their former professions, as did Baldwin. He was back to making movies. Apparently, he had a huge project in the works. It was expected to do well and there were rumors in all the trade publications that it would be the blockbuster of the summer. Baldwin needed it to flourish. What money he had was tied up in his production and he was heavily in debt. If he had a pearl necklace at his disposal, Coop was sure he'd have used it to finance his work. Baldwin was also in California. On the surface, that precluded him. Coop had someone checking airline flights just the same.

Lastly, Melvin Master, the sound engineer. Reports of him were shrouded in shady and underhanded deals. The Los Angeles Police Department knew he was bootlegging cassettes and videotapes but they hadn't been able to catch him at it. He blamed Duncan for firing him and had vowed to get even. Although he wasn't living hand-to-mouth he certainly couldn't afford a million dollar necklace. He was also three time zones away from any personal contact on this coast.

Coop was up against a wall. None of these people appeared to be involved. They also had Duncan as their focal point, not Marsha and not Aurora. What would the connection be? Revenge against one by using the other? It wasn't out of the question. It had been tried before. One of them might want to ruin Duncan by destroying his livelihood, giving him a taste of his own medicine, so to speak. He could even go so far as to frame Duncan for a crime *he* commits. Coop didn't want to think of that. It meant he could hurt Marsha or Aurora for no reason.

That was the kind of criminal he hated; the one who killed without remorse and with no reason. To achieve an expected end he could just kill another human being.

Coop pushed himself back from the machine. Maybe coffee would help clear his mind and give him energy to find another avenue to approach. He stood up.

Marsha Chambers walked through the door. She stopped the moment her eyes locked on his. All the haughtiness she usually showed to the world was gone. This was a different Marsha Chambers. This one was the woman bending over that child in the hospital; the one standing in the shadows as the child's mother made an appeal for her lost daughter to return home. Coop's heart reached for her. He wanted to cradle her in his arms and absolve her hurt, take it away and leave her with only happiness and joy.

"I need to talk to you." Her voice was small and her eyes looked sad and confused.

He came around the desk. He was going to go to her, touch her, but that would give him the opportunity to crush her against him and he didn't think he could stop himself if he got that close. He couldn't do it. He was still a cop, and he'd always be. Marsha Chambers had a secret that affected this case. He needed her to tell him what it was and he needed his mind sharp when she did. If he touched her he couldn't account for his actions.

Coop stopped when he reached the chair in front of his desk. Crooks and robbers had sat there. He held it out for Marsha. "Sit down."

Marsha took a seat. "I *am* being blackmailed," she said.

Coop closed the office door and resumed his own chair. "Is this an official visit?"

Marsha hesitated. "I don't know."

"Do you want to make a report? Swear out a warrant against the blackmailer?" He sounded like an unfeeling cop, there only to fill out forms and pass along reports which would be filed and forgotten.

"I only want to tell you about it." She paused. "I know it won't be long before the news people find out. I need you to know first."

Coop swallowed the lump in his throat. She'd said she needed him. She trusted him. "Go on."

"Aurora Alexander is missing."

Coop leaned forward. "When?"

"She left the studio last night after the taping and no one has seen her since. Duncan is in a panic. It's all my fault." She broke down in tears. Coop kept himself from jumping out of his chair and going to her. He grabbed a box of tissues from the credenza and set them on the end of the desk. He waited until the tears subsided and his voice could be trusted.

"Tell me what happened." He had no reports of a kidnapping. Duncan hadn't called. There were no messages on his machine, just a couple of hang ups.

"I don't know what happened." She got up and paced the room. "One moment I was watching that show on the missing child and the next I was sailing through the gates and demanding that she leave my show." She turned back to him then. Her gaze was steady but troubled. "She was so calm, so under control. I felt like an idiot, and the more she agreed with me the worse I felt and the louder I screamed. Finally, she grabbed her belongings and left. I didn't know anything would happen to her, Coop. I swear I didn't." She pleaded for him to believe her.

He did. He knew how deeply she could be touched. The scene of her standing in the darkened studio came back to him. He'd held her in his arms, made love to her. He knew she could feel deeply. She hid that as if it would make her weak in the eyes of the world. The truth was, it would make her seem more human.

"You've got to believe me!" she shouted at him.

"I do," he told her. "Tell me about the blackmailer."

She didn't sit down but walked to the window and looked out. "I was in college. We did some pretty crazy things being away from home, no parents, no rules."

"All college students do that."

"I know." She sighed. Then she turned and faced him.

Coop sat down. He didn't want her to see how much control she actually had over him.

"It was my senior year. Graduation was only a couple of weeks away. Exams were over and we were celebrating. We'd go out every night and party. One good time after another." Her eyes rolled to the ceiling and her tone told him the opposite of her words. "The aunt and uncle who raised me gave me a car for graduation. I got it the day after grades were posted. My uncle thought it would be good to get used to it since I'd be driving it a long distance."

Coop glanced toward the door as someone stopped outside. Through the glass partition he saw Duncan. Marsha saw him and reacted.

"I'll get rid of him." Coop started for the door.

"No," she said taking a step toward him. "He should know this, too."

Coop opened the door. Duncan stepped inside and closed it. He looked like a man in need of sleep—red eyes, tired expression, rumpled clothes. Seeing Marsha he stopped, his face tightened. The tension in the room increased to slicing thickness.

"Marsha told me Aurora's missing."

His friend nodded. "I haven't been able to find a trace of her."

"Duncan, I'm sorry," Marsha apologized. She took a step. His expression backed her up. "I didn't mean for anything to happen to her."

"You never mean it, do you, Marsha? You walk over people as if they're ants, and never think of consequences."

"Duncan," Coop said with warning in his voice.

"I'm sorry," Marsha said. Her eyes were full of tears. "I didn't mean it."

"You don't know anything's happened to her."

"No, I don't."

"Sit down, Duncan. You too, Marsha."

After a moment Duncan removed his coat and slung it over a chair, then took a seat in front of Coop's desk. Marsha took the other one and Coop resumed his own seat.

"Marsha has something she wants to tell us."

Marsha swallowed and hazarded a glance toward Duncan. "I was telling Coop about the blackmailer."

Duncan's head came round to look at her.

"I've been being blackmailed for three years, since the show became a success."

"Why didn't you say something?"

"I didn't want anyone to know that I'd murdered someone."

Aurora didn't think her shoulders would ever be the same. With her hands behind her she'd spent an uncomfortable night on the smelly cot. She was hungry and in pain, and her legs were going numb.

"What's your name?" she asked, sitting up.

"Trying to get familiar with me? It won't work."

"Where is this place?"

"Timbuktu," he snapped.

"You haven't told me why you want to hurt Duncan."

"You ask a lot of questions." He grunted. "I suppose it comes from that show. You're always asking questions."

"It doesn't come from the show. I'm not really Marsha Chambers. I am Rory, Aurora Alexander. I was on the

show as a look-alike the day you tried to kidnap me.
You made a mistake. I'm not Marsha Chambers."

He laughed at her. "Good try."

Aurora knew this wasn't working. She had to use
another form of persuasion. Another method to get
him to move her away from this house. No one knew
she was here and there was no way she could get help
unless she got back to a place where there were other
people.

"What is the plan you have for Duncan to come here?
He doesn't know where we are."

"He doesn't need to know. When they find you,
they'll blame him. He'll be ruined."

"No, he won't," she told him. "You left no clues, no
note. Duncan will have an alibi. He's probably with his
friend, a cop. He'll have a police officer swearing he
was no-where near this place."

She had his attention. He wasn't looking at her, but
she recognized the taut features telling her he understood. She knew when she reached a person, when her
words touched them. Years of training had taught her
what to look for, to see stillness in eyes, arms, shoulders.
Even when the change was small, almost imperceptible,
she could see it.

"You'll have killed me for nothing. And they'll find
you. The police have all kinds of equipment. They can
probably track you by smell alone."

He snapped, raising his hand to strike her. Aurora
instinctively moved back and closed her eyes, bracing
herself for the blow to come. It didn't. She opened her
eyes. He hovered over her, anger evident in his stance.
She'd touched the truth. He believed her. Now he had
to do something. She hoped he wouldn't kill her first,
then try to move her.

"All right." He spoke softly—like an actor during a
big scene played quietly to make the audience teeter
on the edge of their seats, knowing the quietness was

only a prelude to something more sinister. "We'll go to the studio. Right to Mr. Duncan's West's office."

Aurora shook inside but kept her gaze steady. He pulled the roll of duct tape out. She tried to get away from him.

"I don't need the tape," she said. "I won't cry out. I promise."

"Liar," he snarled, then pinned her to the small cot as he taped her mouth.

Duncan couldn't move when Marsha made her revelation. He stared at her as if he'd never seen her before. Seconds passed and no one spoke. The only sound in the office came from something going on outside the door.

"I don't believe you," he finally said. She was hard to work with, always thought she knew the best way to do things, but this woman was no murderer.

"We'd had a lot to drink. The car was full, four of us. I was driving. We'd been in Georgetown and decided to run over to Virginia and go to one of the clubs there. I missed the turn for Key Bridge and ended up on a road that only had trees and nowhere to turn around. I was driving too fast. The music was too loud. And everyone was talking, giving me directions, telling me what to do. I only took my eyes off the road for a second. Suddenly there was a man in front of me. He was carrying something. I couldn't stop. I hit him."

Tears ran down her face. She reached for a tissue from the box on Coop's desk, checked them, and continued. "It was another student. I only knew him slightly. We'd had some classes together. I didn't even know his name. Then suddenly he was dead."

Coop placed his elbows on the desk and folded his arms. "What happened then?"

"There was a lot of screaming from the other girl in the car. The guys pushed us back and made us stay in the car. We couldn't get the other girl to stop crying. Finally, one of the guys told me to take her back. When I protested that I should stay there until the police arrived, they said no police. They would handle it."

"You left the scene of an accident? One in which someone had died?"

"Don't glare at me," Marsha told Coop. "I was twenty years old. I was scared. I didn't know what to do. I figured they would handle it and I would be called to the police station. Every day I waited in fear for the police to knock on my door. I was frantic, jumpy. The longer nothing happened the more afraid I became.

"After graduation I left for California. By the time I got there I'd changed my name and started a new life. The four of us never saw each other again."

"One of them is blackmailing you?" Coop asked the question.

"Charles Hagan. He was my date that night. Three years ago when the show went national and I was suddenly in the limelight, I got a program in the mail. It was our graduation program. A yellow marker had been used to highlight one name, the student I'd killed."

"You've been paying blackmail for three years?" Duncan asked.

She nodded. Her face was dry now, but drawn. Duncan felt he understood a lot more about Marsha Chambers. She'd been going through hell while maintaining an on screen persona, keeping people employed and having her life hanging under a sword.

"It stops now, Marsha," Coop told her.

"How? If I don't pay him I lose everything."

She isn't the only one, Coop thought. He was a law officer. His life was the law. He was in love with a woman who just admitted she'd killed someone, then driven away from the accident. She challenged all his convictions. He didn't like it. In fact, he hated it. He couldn't let it be true. There had to be something else. He wanted to marry Marsha Chambers. He couldn't marry her and be who he was.

"What was the name of the student who died?"

"Jeff Sherman." She looked at her hands, then across the desk at him. "He was from Michigan and majored in Chemistry."

"Where does the child in the hospital fit into this?" Her eyes stared accusingly at him. "I followed you. I saw you there and at the studio."

Embarrassment flooded her face as if he'd caught her naked feelings, as he had. "The child has nothing to do with any of this. I set that interview up from the mother's appealing letter. Her story reminded me of myself." She paused, moving her gaze from Coop to Duncan and back. Both of them waited for her to explain.

"The accident that killed my parents also took my sister. My parents died immediately. My younger sister didn't. She hung on for hours. I'd run away that day and they were looking for me." She tried to swallow the sob in her voice. "If they had only found me. If I'd known, I could have gone to the hospital, given her my blood or my kidney or my arm . . . I don't know. Maybe she would still be alive." She stopped fighting tears that threatened to fall. "I didn't want that to happen to Gillie."

"I never knew you had a sister," Duncan said.

"You don't know my name isn't Marsha Chambers, either. I legally changed it and thought I could hide."

When she stopped speaking the room was quiet, too quiet. Coop's throat was dry. He knew he should speak. It was his office, his investigation, his evidence. He hated it. He hated what she'd told him.

"You know I can't ignore what you've told me," Coop stated.

Marsha stood up. Coop envisioned a condemned prisoner standing before her judge, being sentenced to life in prison.

"I know," she whispered.

Chapter 17

The lights, the cameras, the set. He turned around, taking it all in. Even in the dark he could see. He knew where everything was, where it should be. It was different sitting onstage from being a member of the audience.

He breathed in deeply. Show business had a smell to it—body heat, makeup, nervous energy. Each stage was different, personalized by the people who worked there. This one had Marsha Chambers at its core. He looked at her sitting across from him. This was her domain. It had her signature on it. Even with tape across her mouth and fear in her eyes, this was still her home.

Hers and Duncan West's. His eyes swept the studio. It was dark. Everyone had left for the night. The guards never came into the studio. There was no need. The perimeter hadn't been breached. There was no need to check the inside. He could wait here for Duncan to arrive, but he didn't have to. He had other plans. Plans that would send Duncan West exactly where he'd sent *him*, into oblivion.

Pulling a knife from his inside pocket he went toward Marsha Chambers.

* * *

Duncan thought he should have gone into songwriting instead of producing. All the old clichés in songs were correct. All the lyrics about love and longing were true. Who would have thought he and Coop would end up like this? Both in love and both in jeopardy of losing the women who'd captured their hearts.

Coop had sent Marsha home with a policewoman. Duncan refused to leave. Aurora would try him here or call the police. He'd forwarded his phones—the office, his home, and his cellular—to Coop's office. Who could have taken her? And where would they take her? Why was there no message, no note, no indication of what they wanted? The guards had been found tied up in one of the bedrooms. They'd been knocked out separately and had not seen anything that could help.

The police had spent the better part of the night going over everything, asking questions and then asking them again and again, but so far nothing had happened. Megan stayed until everyone left. Then Duncan sent her home to sleep. He'd tried to do the same but only fitfully tossed and turned, imagining he heard the phone ringing. Finally he'd ended up here in time for Marsha's confession.

Cooper Dean was in love but he couldn't let the admission of murder, even by the woman he loved, go unresolved. It was unbelievable. Coop refused to believe it. Duncan couldn't imagine it, either. Marsha's stage presence had too much compassion, even if her off-screen personality didn't. He understood why now.

She'd fought to allow the appeal show against his wishes. *The Marsha Chambers Show* didn't do appeals. It wasn't a fund-raiser, telethon, or tearjerker. Their format included soft news items, human interest, celebrities, and nostalgia pieces. They could tackle the subject of teenage runaways, catastrophic illness, or mothers wanting reunions with their children, but they did not do appeals. Marsha had fought hard for this one child, and finally Duncan had given in.

Now he prowled. While Coop showed all the signs of an angry bear, punching keys and barking orders into the phone and at the officers who ran interference for him, Duncan paced the room, trying to think of something he could do. He needed to feel useful. He needed to find her, help her, save her.

"I'm leaving," he said abruptly.

"Where are you going?"

"To see Aurora's mother. She might be of some help."

He headed for the door. The phone rang. Duncan stopped.

Coop snatched it from its cradle with such force he wondered that it didn't break in two. Duncan's stomach clenched. He could feel the acid churning. Was it Aurora?

"What?" Coop asked.

Duncan listened.

"You're sure?" Coop's face split into a smile as he listened. "There's no mistake? You're sure? Positive?" Coop scribbled something on a pad. Duncan tried to read upside down. "Get a warrant. I want that bastard in custody within the hour."

He hung up. "What's happened?" Duncan asked.

"He's not dead. He's alive."

Coop stood up and like a quarterback about to be sacked, he rushed from the room. Duncan had no idea where he was going. He grabbed the paper. "Michigan Home for the Blind" was written on it in Coop's slanted handwriting.

He caught up with Coop just as he got into his car. "Who was that?"

"An officer I'd asked to check on Sherman. The kid was never reported dead in D.C. Never even appeared in a hospital during the entire four years he spent in college."

"Then what did Marsha—"

"She hit him all right. He saw the car in time and jumped out of the way. She hit his backpack. It ricocheted into him and knocked him cold, but he wasn't hurt. He didn't go to graduation because he had a headache and some bruises."

"All this time the other kid knew this?"

"Yeah, two of them, Charles Hagan and Alfred Lloyd, an insulin diabetic. Three years ago when Marsha's show topped the scales, Lloyd suddenly died of insulin shock. No one could determine why he hadn't taken his shots."

"Leaving Hagan as the only living person who knew Sherman was alive."

"It was an opportunity he couldn't pass up, and for three years he's been banking on Marsha's fear that he'd expose something which never happened."

"You're going to see her?"

Coop nodded. "I have to tell her she didn't kill anyone. The man is alive and well, working in Michigan teaching the blind and visually impaired."

Duncan smiled and stuck his hand out. "Congratulations," he said.

As Coop's tires squealed against the pavement Duncan turned to his own car. He'd been on his way to see Cassandra Alexander. He'd go on. He didn't hold out any definite hope that she could help him, but it made him feel that he was doing something.

The nurses at the home hadn't seen Aurora when he inquired. Her mother stared into space, alone with her thoughts, her memory, and her own world. He was glad Aurora wasn't here. Seeing her mother like this made him sad, and he had no relational connection. For Aurora it was devastating.

Duncan tried, anyway. "Mrs. Alexander, I'm looking for Rory. Your daughter, Aurora."

She didn't move, didn't respond. Neither name seemed to have any connection with her.

"She brings you the cookies and bread."

Mrs. Alexander continued to look through the window into the darkness. The only indication that she understood anything he'd said was a gentle rocking. Duncan had seen Aurora holding her and rocking this same way.

A light rain splashed against the car window as Duncan drove back to Princeton. He'd gotten nowhere with Aurora's mother. Calling the police station from the car proved a waste of time. Nothing further had been discovered. Wherever she was, she was on her own. Duncan didn't like the tightness that squeezed his heart at the thought.

He pulled into his yard and waited for the garage door to lift. Then he drove inside. Mechanically, he walked about the house turning on lights, starting the coffeemaker, looking in the refrigerator. Something grated at him, but he couldn't figure what it was. He poured himself a glass of wine and made a sandwich. Taking the glass he went into his office. Without thinking he turned on the cameras and his computer. It was an automatic reaction to entering the room. He didn't think anything of it, didn't even know he'd done it until the soft hum of the equipment began.

Remembering he'd left the sandwich in the kitchen, he returned there. *Why?* he wondered. *Why would someone who was blackmailing Marsha want to hurt her?* The question irritated him. Half an hour later he was still trying to find an answer. No scenario he worked out made any sense.

"It can't be him," Duncan said. It had to be someone else. It had to be someone with something to gain by getting rid of Marsha. Hagan would be cutting off his money supply.

He grabbed the phone and dialed Marsha's number. It went to the fourth ring before the answering machine clicked in. He waited impatiently for Joyce's voice to complete the message.

"Coop, if you're there, pick up. I need to talk to you."

"This better be good," Coop said, obviously irritated.

"Coop, it's not Hagan. He wouldn't jeopardize Marsha's ability to support him. It's got to be someone else."

"What are you talking about?"

"About Aurora, and whoever has her. It can't be Hagan. Think about it, Coop. Hagan wants to keep Marsha working. She's his meal ticket, his livelihood. He waited for her to get to the top to begin his scam. No way will he drown his goose now."

Coop didn't say anything, but Duncan heard him sigh heavily into the phone. "Where are you?"

"Home."

"I'll be right there."

"Don't get any fancy ideas about screaming or trying to run away," he told her.

Aurora had no voice. Her heart beat so fast. When he'd drawn the knife she'd known her life was over. She'd thought of her mother and who would care for her. She thought of Duncan, and that she'd never told him she loved him. She'd thought of her brother in law school, and her father in Japan.

Then he'd cut the tape at her hands and feet. She tore the tape from her mouth but said nothing. She couldn't speak. She was so glad to be alive for a few more minutes that speech failed her.

She had to find a way of signaling someone. The guard was at the gate. He'd been on rounds when they arrived. Aurora thought this man had studied the studio as well as any medical student studying the internal organs of the human body. He knew about everything and everyone. He had the frequency for the automatic fence. It had opened and closed, silently passing them through. He'd hidden the van inside the huge doors used by tractor trailers to deliver everything from elephants to baby diapers. They were effectively encased inside the building.

"You've got time," he told her. "Duncan was always an early riser. He'll be the first to arrive in the morning." The laugh he delivered was malicious. "I don't think it will be one of his best days. Then he'll never have a good day again."

"You haven't told me who you are, or why you're doing this." Her toes had tingled since he'd cut the tape bonding her legs together. She stood up anyway. Her life was hanging here. He had no reason to remain. He'd gotten in. He could kill her and leave. He could frame Duncan for it. But he wanted to make sure. Otherwise, he'd have already killed her. He wanted to make sure Duncan knew.

She felt he was using her. He'd cut her loose like some character in a movie would. He wanted to taunt her, like a cat with a mouse. He'd let her move around while he kept her in sight.

She moved tentatively.

"What are you doing?" He pointed the gun at her.

"Testing my legs. The tape cut the circulation." She completed a small circle. Then a wider one. He stood up, letting her know he had control. He had the gun.

"Know anything about these cameras?"

"Yeah," he said. "I know how they work."

"Mind if I turn one on? I've never worked with them. I've been in front of them, never behind."

He shrugged and she went to find the buttons. Looking all around, she found nothing. He came over and pressed a button on the side. The viewfinder came on. She could see the dark set before her. The room was a huge, warehouse-like place. She moved the camera to take in the area where he sat. The lack of light limited what she could see. Going to another camera, she found the on switch and turned it on.

"That's enough," he said. "Come out where I can see you."

Aurora moved back into his view. "You're not going to get away with this," she told him.

He laughed at her. "I've planned this for a very long time."

"You might have gotten away with it before we came here." She looked at his shoes. "Now you've got fibers on your shoes, carpet cleaner, any number of microscopic things the police can use to determine that you were inside this building."

"Shut up!" he shouted.

"I don't understand," she shouted back, ignoring the fact that he had a gun. "What did Duncan do to you that makes you hate him enough to do this to him?"

He came forward. Every instinct she had screamed for her to run, yet her feet were rooted to the floor. He grabbed her arm and pushed his face into hers. "He sent me to jail."

Duncan swung the door open before Coop got out of the car. "It's Baldwin," he said, stepping onto the porch.

"He's in Los Angeles," Duncan said.

"That's what I thought." Coop came inside and followed Duncan to the living room. When they were seated he continued. "On the way here I got a call from the officer who'd checked the airline files. There was no record of him on any commercial flight or any charter into the major airports. There was also nothing about him in any of the local private airports. He covers himself well."

"Then what did you find?"

"The origin of one flight matched the dates in question and the flight came from Los Angeles."

"He chartered a plane."

"No, he borrowed it. From a producer friend of his."

Coop sat back in his chair. "It landed in a private airport in Pennsylvania. He then rented a van and drove to New Jersey. It amazes me how people who have been convicted of a crime can manage to pick up the threads of their lives, then even go one better and get more money, more support, and more friends than they had before going to jail. There's something wrong with this country."

"Any idea where he is now?"

"No. He's filming a movie. Nothing was scheduled for today."

"That's unusual. Filming is expensive. Once it begins there aren't any scheduled breaks, barring religious holidays, until it's in the can. Production companies are independent these days. They have too little money and too little resources to take days off. The industry moves fast. They begin advertising before the film is actually done. It has a schedule, a distribution date. They can't delay it for scheduled breaks."

"He could be here."

Duncan's heart constricted again. "I'm afraid he already has Aurora."

"According to the officer who took the report, the plane came in yesterday. It's still at the airfield. The pilot thought Baldwin was going to visit his sick mother. He's waiting for him to return. I've alerted the Pennsylvania authorities to keep it on the ground. If he shows up we've got him."

"What do we do in the meantime?" *He could be hurting Aurora*. Duncan thought it, but he didn't say it. He didn't want the words to be true.

"We pray she's all right until she can get word to us." Duncan looked at his lifelong friend. "She'll do it."

Aurora had been in tight situations before. He recalled her telling him how she'd faced down pimps and drug dealers in New York. Somehow the image wasn't comforting.

* * *

He remembered Kevin Baldwin. The man had been going places. He had vision, was a master at his craft. The trades tapped him as one of the leaders of film's future. Duncan had discovered he was unwilling to wait for the future. He wanted it now, and he took steps to ensure it happening. He'd laced his films with subliminal messages, and Duncan had caught him doing it.

"What is that noise?" Coop asked.

Duncan listened. He heard the faint beeping. It came every fifteen seconds. "The camera. I guess I forgot to plug it in. It's been running on the battery."

Turning the coffeepot on came along with memory of switching the cameras on.

"I made coffee. Do you want a cup?" Duncan stood up.

"I want a beer."

Both of them headed for the kitchen. Passing the office, Duncan heard the beeping again. "I'll turn that off. Beer is in the refrigerator."

He went into the office. Light beamed from the computer on the desk. He could see the menu screen reflected in the French doors behind the desk. The camera's red battery light blinked incessantly. He bent over and reached for the plug. Pushing it into the wall, he straightened. The beeping stopped as the light indicating battery charging went on. Duncan was reaching for the off switch when he saw the view screen.

He froze as Aurora's miniature image walked before him. It was too dark, he told himself. There was nothing on the screen. His breathing stopped, his throat closed. He grabbed the camera support and stared at the screen. She walked past again. God, he wished there were more light. She said something. He couldn't hear it. Kevin Baldwin. She must be talking to him.

Somehow he found himself moving, running, sprinting toward the kitchen.

"Coop!" Duncan slammed the refrigerator closed. Coop jumped back, turning his hands back and forth as if making sure they were still there and not bedded inside the refrigerator. "You'd better come see this," Duncan said, ignoring his friend's actions. He towed Coop back to the office and forced him to look at the screen.

"Where is this?"

"Good girl," he whispered to himself. "They're at the studio."

"Let's go," Coop ordered.

Duncan prayed they'd be on time. Kevin Baldwin had tried more than once to harm Aurora. Would he make good on his promise before they arrived? Duncan's blood pumped through his system.

With lights flashing and sirens blaring Coop drove through the streets in route to the studio. He barked instructions into a CB radio while he drove at a speed that could tip the car over on a sharp turn.

Duncan pulled out the cellular phone he hadn't been without since Aurora went missing and dialed the studio.

"What are you doing?" Coop asked.

"I'm calling them. He might kill her before we get there. It's me he wants, not her."

"Be careful. You don't want to force his hand."

"Turn off the siren. I don't want him knowing I'm with a cop."

The phone in the studio began to ring. Aurora stopped her pacing and looked toward the control booth. The man with her followed her gaze. She hoped it was Duncan, hoped he's seen her incessant walking back and forth in front of the camera. She hoped he had his camera on. She hoped he was on his way, and that they would get out of this alive.

"We should answer it," she said.

Why? No one knows we're here.

"But you want them to, don't you? Isn't that why we're

here? You want Duncan to pay for what you perceive he's done to you."

"There's no perception involved. He tried to ruin me and I'm going to ruin him."

"Then we'd better answer the phone."

He gestured with the gun for her to precede him. The small control room was filled with equipment, mainly a switchboard and a wall of videotapes. The phone sat next to the switchboard. Aurora depressed the speaker switch.

"It's on," she said.

"Hello, Kevin." Duncan's voice came mechanically into the room. Tears rushed to Aurora's eyes, but she blinked them aside. She needed to remain calm. She couldn't fall apart at the sound of his voice. "It's been a long time since we last spoke."

"Ah, Duncan," he said as if they'd talked just the other day. "I knew you'd find me."

"What do you want?"

"I want you to pay, and you will. I'm going to kill Marsha Chambers and you're going to go to jail for it."

Aurora pressed herself into the darkness.

"You're wrong, Kevin. You don't have Marsha Chambers. The woman you have only looks like Marsha. Her real name is Aurora Alexander. Killing her won't accomplish anything."

"You don't worry about that. Just come on over here. And come alone. I even smell a cop, and she's dead where she stands."

To emphasize his point he turned the gun point blank at her head. Aurora moved back, unable to speak. Fear turned her arms and legs into dead weights. She could hardly remain standing. Then Duncan's voice saved her.

"Aurora, are you all right?"

Yes, she said, or thought she said. She could hear nothing but the roar of blood in her ears.

"She's fine."

"I want to hear her say it."

"Fi . . . fine. Duncan, I'm all right." She sounded afraid.

"I'm coming," he told her.

Kevin hit the button, disconnecting the line. Aurora feared he had no reason to keep her alive any longer. He knew Duncan was coming. Duncan knew who he was. If he killed her now and called the police, both of them would arrive at approximately the same time. They would certainly think he was involved. She had to keep him here and keep him talking until Duncan and Coop arrived. She prayed he was coming with the police. He couldn't handle this man alone. She knew that. Duncan didn't.

He was bent on revenge, an emotion which killed rationality. It attached itself to the soul and grew like a cancer. He said Duncan had sent him to jail. If that was true, he would have had plenty of time to let the cancer fester inside him until nothing could stop him from the course he'd set.

"Kevin," she said. "He called you Kevin."

"Kevin Baldwin. Maybe you've heard of me."

Aurora hadn't. She shook her head. "What do you do?"

"I produce movies."

Aurora understood now how he knew about the equipment. He worked with it.

"What did Duncan do to send you to prison?"

He looked directly at her. "He testified against me. He refused to believe I wasn't hurting anyone. Now he's going to go to jail." He paused. "My films had messages in them."

"Message films aren't illegal. Every film has a message." She hesitated, shaking her head. "Yours, your messages couldn't be seen with the naked eye, could they? They were hidden so the brain could read them." Mind control went through her mind.

"Hey!" he shouted. "I didn't hurt anybody. I didn't say anything that would hurt anyone."

"It's mind control. It takes away freedom of choice."

"Now that's where you're wrong," he debated. "The freedom of choice is still there."

"But it's been clouded, directed, heavily weighted against free will."

She glanced at the door. Where was Duncan? How much longer could she keep him talking?

"I agree. It was wrong." He lowered his voice. "Did he have to ruin my life? I was on the verge. I was going to be a great producer. But Duncan West couldn't stand that. He wanted what I had. I promised him I wouldn't do it again. I begged him!" Aurora jumped at the force of his voice. "He would listen to nothing. Now it's his turn to beg."

Chapter 18

Police cars from the three neighboring municipalities lined up in front of and behind Coop and Duncan. The blue and red lights whirled, lighting up the dark, but no sirens blared. At the gate Coop stopped and the lights ceased, plunging the foliage outside the facility into eerie shadows.

Coop got out and formed a command center with the guard and the other officers. When he came back he drove slowly around the studio. The other cars formed a complete circle around the building. As soon as he stopped, Duncan bolted from the car. He was halfway to the door when Coop tackled him. They went down like two football players.

"We do this my way," Coop stated, flipping him over.

"He doesn't want you. He wants me. And we're running out of time."

"So let's not waste any of it."

Coop got up and offered Duncan his hand. He took it and they stood.

"Coop, I have to go in there. I have a better chance

of getting him to listen to reason than anyone else. Remember what he said about cops.''

Coop led him back to the car and opened the trunk. ''You're going in,'' he said. ''But you're going in with a bulletproof vest and microphone.'' Pulling the needed items from the car, Duncan quickly slipped into them.

''Aurora doesn't have a vest.''

Coop looked straight at him. ''I know that. You make sure he doesn't do anything to her.''

Duncan waited a moment, then slapped his hand on Coop's shoulder and headed for the door. It was open. He stepped inside.

''Come right in,'' a voice said. Duncan looked around, up at the security camera. ''We're in the studio. I hope you haven't done anything stupid.''

Duncan walked straight. He passed the receptionist's desk and headed around back toward the studio. ''I'm heading for the studio,'' he whispered to Coop. ''The security cameras are on. He can see me.''

There were no lights on in the cavernous room when Duncan entered it. He knew every inch of the place. He'd worked there for the past three years and could have negotiated the room blindfolded. He didn't see Aurora or Kevin Baldwin. His eyes adjusted to the darkness and he could make out the raised stage. Two cameras were on. He prayed a *thank you* for Aurora's insight in getting them turned on.

Looking around, he saw no movement. They could be anywhere, together or separated. He could be lined up in the site of an automatic rifle and Aurora could already be dead.

''Aurora,'' he called. ''Where are you?''

He heard a sound. Turning toward it, he faced the dark control room.

''Aurora, are you all right?''

Kevin Baldwin's voice came through the control room microphone. ''She's fine. For the moment.''

"Turn the lights up, Kevin. You and I never worked in the dark."

"Have them removed, Duncan."

"Who?"

"I'll waste her here and now."

"Kevin, I don't know—"

"Get rid of the cops or her blood will be all over this set."

Duncan heard the unmistakeable cocking of a gun.

"Kevin, wait! I'll get rid of them. Let me get to a phone."

"Use the mike you're wearing." He grunted. "I picked it up."

Duncan remembered Kevin well. He had been eager, wanted to learn every aspect of filming. He'd spend hours with anyone in any department until he'd mastered what they did. He'd especially liked makeup and the sound department. Why hadn't Duncan thought of that when they were sure the man in the sketch had been disguised? If he said he knew Duncan was wearing a mike, then he knew it.

"Coop, get them out of here!" he shouted. "He'll kill her, Coop. Get all of them in the cars and leave." Duncan could transmit but he had no receiver. He didn't know if Coop was following his instructions or not. From where he stood he couldn't hear anything going on outside. The stage had been made so that there was no outside interference. They didn't have time to do retakes when the program was filmed in front of a live audience.

"Ten came in, ten went out," Kevin said. Duncan let his breath out. He hadn't realized he was holding it.

"I want to talk to Aurora."

There was silence. Then he heard a small, scared voice. "I'm here, Duncan."

"Are you all right?"

"Yes . . . yes, I'm fine."

"Kevin, we're alone now. Come out so I can see you."

Again, silence. He didn't think he would get an answer. Then the house lights came up slowly, like in some horror film where they didn't want to reveal the monster too quickly. Soon Duncan was standing in bright, white light. The empty chairs screamed at him. He squinted against the harshness.

Aurora stepped through the control room door. Kevin Baldwin came in behind her.

"Stop," he told her when she started for Duncan.

He had changed a lot. His hair was shorter and grayer. His face had deep grooves in it, and a scar across his forehead told of at least one fight where he didn't emerge the victor. He'd been handsome. Women had fallen all over him. His face no longer looked handsome. It looked evil.

"Like what you see?"

Duncan shrugged.

"You put it there, this scar and the others. You sent me to jail and ruined my life."

"A judge and jury convicted you. I was only asked to tell the truth and I did that."

"You told the truth, all right, and with every word you changed my future. Stole it. Sent me away to places you can't imagine. Film does nothing to depict the real thing. No one could write the horror of what happens there inside a jail."

Duncan let him talk. He tried to communicate with Aurora. She looked at him. He saw fear in her body. He wanted her to concentrate. He couldn't run across the room and tackle Kevin. One of them would surely be shot. Twenty feet separated them.

"Now it's your turn, Duncan. You've got a number one show on television. In Hollywood you have connections. Big deals are falling into place. You're on the verge of the greatest success of your life. Exactly where I was."

"There's a difference, Kevin. I didn't manipulate it. I worked for it. I tried and failed and tried again until

I got all the irons in the right order. And I didn't have to fool people into thinking I'd done it when I hadn't."

"You don't think I had it?" He stepped forward, pushing Aurora ahead of him. Duncan took a step, too. He wanted the distance decreased. "I had everything. I could have done it without the sublims."

"Then why didn't you?" Duncan took two more steps. "Why did you force-feed the public, brainwash them into returning time and again to see your films and to see your future films? You *did* have it, Kevin. Your name was used in all the right circles. Producers were rushing to you to invest in your projects. It wasn't enough, was it? You wanted to be the best. You wanted to outdo all the other filmmakers. You wanted to be the best of all time."

"What's wrong with that?" he shouted. "This country was built by people who wanted to do better."

"Those people waited, Kevin. They went out each day and they worked at their craft. They didn't try to trick people into thinking something that wasn't true."

"It *was* true."

"It wasn't true then." Duncan took a deep breath. "It could have been. You were the best I'd ever seen. I admired you. I wanted to emulate you, learn the way you did. You had a natural ability far better than my own to see things."

Kevin smiled. "It won't work, Duncan. Too much water has fallen for me to ever think that your kind of praise could be anything more than getting me to release this woman." He jerked Aurora's arm. She screamed and Duncan started for her. The gun came up. Kevin placed a shot at his feet. Duncan stopped.

"Duncan!" Aurora called. She knew he'd been hurt. She reached for him. Kevin restrained her.

"I'm all right," he said.

"It's not him I'm after," he said coldly. "I want him alive. I want him to feel the pain, to experience every minute of his future. I want him to know what it's like to be confined to a tiny cell with the stink of urine and nothing to do but count your lifetime away.''

"Don't you see this isn't going to work?" Aurora questioned. ''They know who you are. They know *where* you are. If anything happens here tonight, Duncan isn't the one they're going to go looking for. It'll be you.''

He looked at her as if he wanted to kill her. She glanced at Duncan, knowing he'd lunge for him if he made a move. She was in no position to do anything. If she tried anything he'd have time to shoot one of them. She needed to wait for an opportunity. Since Duncan arrived he'd had another person to concentrate on. It was harder for him to keep them both in line.

She knew Duncan was thinking of her. She wouldn't do anything to harm him and she didn't want Kevin to shoot her. At the moment the best thing to do was wait and keep him talking.

"Don't you worry about that," he sneered. ''Soon all your worries will be over.''

Duncan put his hands out in front of him. ''Don't do anything stupid, Kevin. We can still walk away from this.''

"Drop the gun, Baldwin.'' She heard Coop's voice from somewhere in the audience. It startled them all, but Kevin reacted first. He grabbed her from behind. His arm circled her neck and pulled her against him. The gun pressed against her temple. Aurora wondered if she would hear the bullet when it ripped through her brain. What was dying like? she wondered. What was it like to kill someone from this close range?

"I told you no cops! I told you I'd kill her.''

"Don't do it, Baldwin. Nobody needs to die here today,'' Coop reminded him.

"Die! I'm already dead, and it's his fault.'' He nodded at Duncan. ''If it weren't for him, I'd be on top. Hollywood would be considering *my* work, not his. He doesn't have the vision, the skill, the downright nerve to do what I could do.''

Kevin got passionate about his abilities. He screamed at Duncan and Coop. The gun pressed closer to her head, but every now and then he relaxed his hold.

Aurora studied Duncan. She wondered if he remembered teaching her the karate move that night in his office. She wondered if she remembered it well enough to execute it now. It was the only one she'd ever learned. Kevin was taller than she, heavier. Could she use his weight against him, could she throw him over without giving him time to get a shot off? She didn't know, but she was going to have to try. She'd wait until the time was right, when neither man was in the line of fire. Unless he decided to kill her first.

Aurora worked with him, like learning to ride a horse. She felt his rhythms, read them. She knew how long it took between his moving the gun and bringing it back again.

Duncan was giving her signals. She tried to read them but she couldn't concentrate on him and Kevin at the same time. She watched Duncan's eyes for a moment, then signaled him. Imperceptibly, he shook his head. She signaled again, and again he told her to hold. She had to go back to what Kevin was doing. He had the gun, and Coop wasn't getting anywhere with him in conversation. She only hoped both men would be ready when she made her move.

"I want you out of here," Kevin was saying. "I warned you, Duncan. I warned you."

"Stop," Duncan pleaded. "Think, Kevin. There's a cop standing here. If there's one there's more. Do you think you can get out of here alive if you kill her?"

Aurora felt the indecision in his body. The gun pressed against into her flesh. She squeezed her eyes shut. She wasn't sure he was rational any longer. His losing his hold on reality would be the worst thing. She had to keep him believing they both could survive.

"Kevin, it's all right," she soothed him, using her hands to tell Coop and Duncan the situation was too volatile and needed to be defused. "We need to talk it out. We need to—"

"I want him out of here!" he shouted at Coop. When he did that he used the gun and his free hand to point at Coop. Aurora made her decision. As she screamed Coop's name, she grabbed the arm with the gun in it and pulled it down. Using her foot she stomped the heel of her shoe on his foot and jabbed the elbow of her other arm into his ribs. Then she stooped and using ever ounce of her hundred and twenty pounds pulled his feet out from under him.

Duncan lunged toward Coop, pushing him out of the way as the bullet discharged from the gun. Aurora rolled away from Kevin. In the split second before Kevin regained control Duncan rushed the stage and kicked the hand holding the gun. Kevin screamed in pain.

Kevin turned over and reached for the gun he'd lost.

"I wouldn't do that," Coop said, pointing his own gun toward the man on the floor.

Aurora lay curled in a ball against the chair she usually occupied when she did the show. Duncan rushed to her, pulling her into his arms. She clung to him, calling his name, running her hands over him, up and down his arms, making sure he was there, unhurt, that no blood came from any part of his body.

"That was a bold move, Lady. He could have killed you." They both looked at Coop.

"He could have killed us all. I had to do something."

"I'm never teaching you any more moves," Duncan said. "I thought I was going to die of heart failure when you signaled. I knew what you had in mind."

"I was betting my life you did," she told him.

Suddenly the room was full of policemen. Aurora didn't know where they came from. Duncan helped her up as Kevin was being led past her.

"Wait." The uniformed policeman stopped. "The pearls," she said. "Why did you give me the pearls?"

Kevin moved his gaze from her to Duncan. "Dripping with Pearls," he said, then laughed and walked away.

She twisted around to look at Duncan. Coop came up behind her.

"What did he mean?"

"It was part of the message he embedded in his film. It urged people to see *Dripping with Pearls* when it was released in theaters."

Aurora laid her head on his chest. Duncan's arms tightened around her. "I'm glad it's over," she whispered.

"Me too," Duncan told her. "My heart can't stand your heroics."

By the time they finished with police procedure and Duncan drove Aurora home, dawn's cracked-gold fingers streaked the sky. Aurora looked up as she got out of the car. Duncan took her hand and said nothing. He led her to the door and they went inside. Aurora was exhausted. Her insides still quaked from the past few hours.

He turned her into his arms. "You should take a bath and go to bed," he said.

She smiled. "You told me that the first time you brought me home." She laid her head on his chest.

"It was good advice."

He looked at her. His eyes were tired, too. She reached up and smoothed his forehead. She liked touching him.

"Come on, I'll help you." He took her hand and turned her toward the stairs.

"Are you going to take one with me?" she asked.

Duncan stopped and stared into her eyes. His face softened. He planted a kiss on her mouth and went the rest of the distance up the stairs.

In her room Aurora sat on the bed, her arms wrapped around one of the four posters. She heard water running in the bathroom. Duncan came to her. His jacket and tie were missing and his shirt was gone. She raised her head, letting her eyes move slowly up his torso. When she reached his face her mouth was as dry as a desert.

He offered a hand. Her arm felt heavy as it raised to meet his. She put her hand inside his and he pulled her to her feet. Walking backward, he took her into the bathroom. She smelled the sweet air tinged with her bath salts. Duncan didn't move to touch her or kiss her. He slid the zipper of her dress to its base and let his hand fall away. The dress slipped from her shoulders. She watched it pool at her feet like a dark green puddle.

Desire flooded his eyes. She stood straight, allowing him to look at her. Her body was aroused. She ached for his touch. He reached behind her, unhooking the bra. Her breasts felt heavy as the confining fabric was released. She let her head fall on his shoulder and she kissed his heated skin. A shudder went through him.

Then he was sliding her stockings down her legs one at a time. Her panties were last, then he assisted her into the hot water. It felt good against her skin. She stood, waiting. Duncan removed his clothes and got in behind her. They sat. He cradled her in front of him in the huge tub.

Her body had no resistance, no will of its own. She closed her eyes. He used the sponge, dripping water over her, brushing it down her arms and over her breasts. Then he washed her hair, his strong hands gentle against her scalp. Aurora felt no more able to help herself than a piece of pliable clay.

When he finished he pulled her back and wrapped his arms around her. They lay that way in the hot water, body against body, artist and sculpture, friend and lover. She closed her eyes and refused to think, to remember. This was the only moment in time she would allow in her mind. His hands moving gently, the lapping of the water, the smell of bath salts, and his solid body holding her.

The water cooled all too soon. Aurora was content to lie like that forever. Duncan stood and pulled her up. Water shimmered down their bodies as they stepped from the tub. He wrapped her in a huge, thick towel and dried her like a baby. Looking at herself in the mirror, she saw that her hair fell like spikes against her shoulders. Her skin shone like smooth chocolate. His more yellowy tones contrasted with hers in a blend that she knew could produce fire—gold and red and hot flames that burned, consumed, ate at the air as explosions racked them.

After skimming the towel over himself he took her to the bed and lifted the covers. She slid between the smooth sheets, making room for him to join her. The bed took his weight and his warms wrapped her in a safe cocoon.

"Sleep," he told her.

And she did.

The sun was high when Aurora opened her eyes. The room was still dark, but light fought to get in through the edges of the shades. She lay with her back to Duncan, his arms holding her. Warmth washed through her at the thought that the man she loved lay with her, that they'd spent the night in each other's arms as if they couldn't be parted.

She turned to him, a smile on her lips. He shifted, unconsciously smoothing his hands over her skin, settling them possessively around her. He was comfortable with her, even in sleep. The thought aroused her more.

Using her fingernail she drew a small circle on his arm. She grinned when he moved. Still he remained asleep. Gathering boldness she moved to his nipple, circling it with her nail. It puckered. She felt her own breasts peak and her body begin to flow. Moving her hand slowly over him she ran it from his shoulder down. Strong fingers grasped hers and her head came up.

Duncan's eyes smiled at her. An electrical bolt went through her she couldn't control. He had to feel it. One hand held hers. The other worked its way into her hair. He brought his mouth to hers and she took it like a starving person takes food. Her mouth burned his. She climbed over him, her hand sliding quickly through his hair, over his head as her mouth devoured the taste of him. She'd never wanted anything more, desired anything more. She wanted to absorb him, be part of him, make him part of her.

Duncan's hands seared her naked skin. She moaned as they skimmed over her, kneading her body, turning her into a volcano. She felt eruptive, explosive, knew she was building, knew he was pushing her upward to a place where she could gorge him like the queen bee.

With lightning speed Duncan reversed their positions. She was forced into the mattress by the comely weight of him. Her arms went around him, her legs twined with his like vines grown together. She heard his throaty growl, bathed in the feel of him, drank in the scent of his. With open mouth she kissed his skin. Muscles quivered beneath her touch. Her hips moved, gyrated, pulsed beneath him. She had no will, no way of preventing the passion that gripped her, took her forward, made her run with him. He entered her easily. She screamed, then whimpered at the indescribable pleasure that bulleted through her body. Like a cat, she arched her back. His mouth took her nipple, tugged and pulled it. His tongue danced over it.

She moaned dryly. Her voice called to him. She opened to him, taking him further inside her, giving up the struggle for control, for reason, letting feeling, sensation, and rapture lead her.

Duncan dug into her like a beast. He'd held back as long as he could. She pushed him, touching him with hands that felt like gloved velvet, moving against him creating fire. The heat built. Burned. Zoomed through his system like a four-alarmer. He snapped, grasped her buttocks, lifted her to him. He plunged into her, rode her like a wild stallion given his head. Her hands raked over his skin, shredding his arms as she met him, stroke for stroke. The wildness was in her. The street-smart woman from New York's underworld ground under him. The one-movement karate expert twined her legs around him, completing the circle that bound them together in a forever and unending climax.

Time, Aurora thought as she placed bacon in the frying pan. She didn't usually cook bacon this way. When she indulged in bacon she often put it in the microwave. This morning she needed something else to do. Time wasn't really what she needed. It wouldn't make things better. It would make them worse.

Duncan had already announced he was leaving. In less that two weeks he'd be gone and she'd be lost, heartbroken, alone. She'd known this would happen. Since the day he'd first kissed her, she'd known this moment would come. She turned the bacon over. It sizzled in its own grease, spattering itself over the clean stove.

Taking a wet cloth, she mopped it up. Then she popped the tray of rolls in the oven and heated water for grits. This would be a southern breakfast like her grandmother used to make. Too bad she didn't have any chicken livers. She could make gravy and biscuits. The coffee was already brewed.

Lifting the bacon out of the pan she laid the crispy strips on paper towels. She'd never learned to measure when cooking. She used handfuls instead of cups, pinches, or sprinklings instead of teaspoons and table-spoons. Pouring two hands of grits into the boiling water she stirred it to keep it from clumping, then covered it with a glass lid. She buttered toast, poured coffee and drank, all to keep her mind off the man upstairs in her bed.

It wasn't working. She could think of nothing else.

She could see his body as she'd left him. Sprawled over the white covers, his golden skin called to her from a distance. She forced herself to keep her attention on the food.

"Good morning." Duncan's voice sounded like music. It wrapped around her heart more warmly than the baking bread in the oven could ever do. Her back was to him and she didn't move. He came up behind her and slipped his arms around her waist. She smelled the soap from the shower on his skin. Closing her eyes, she leaned back, breathing in deeply. She should resist. She should end it now, not drag it out.

Somehow she steeled herself. Her back straightened as if she had an iron bar instead of a spine inside her. Duncan turned her around.

"What's wrong?"

She didn't want to look at him. She knew that if she looked she wouldn't be able to say what needed to be said. Pushing back, she opened the oven. The bread was browning, but it wasn't ready yet.

"Aurora, what is it?"

"I want you to leave," she said, straightening.

"What?"

She turned about the kitchen, looking for something to do. She moved the plate of draining bacon, got eggs from the refrigerator, closed it. Then she opened it again for cheese and closed it. The space, which she'd always considered extensive, seemed close and confining.

"Stop," he demanded, taking her arms and turning her to face him. She kept her gaze fixed, but it fell on his sensuous lips. "Tell me what's wrong."

She tried to disengage herself, but Duncan's grip tightened.

"Nothing is wrong. Please let me go. The food will burn."

He released her and went to the stove. He removed the bread from the oven, turned off all the burners, and set each pot and pan onto trivets. Then he turned back to her.

"I want an answer."

"There isn't anything wrong. You'll be leaving in a few weeks. I'm out of a job. I was just thinking of what I could do now." The lie sounded weak even to her.

"Rory," he whispered, taking her in his arms. She was too weak to resist. She wanted to be there. *Just one more time*, she thought. *Let him hold me for a few moments.* "I want you to come *with* me. I want to marry you."

A slap couldn't have hurt her more. Pushing out of his arms she put the distance of the kitchen between them. "I can't marry you!" she screamed. "I have to stay here." She pointed to the floor, wanting to childishly stamp her foot. "I can't move my mother."

Chapter 19

Christmas cookies: silver bells, Christmas bells, ginger-bread men. Aurora iced the last one with the face of one of the nurses. She smiled, thinking how like her the caricature looked. She loaded the car as she'd done for the past three years before driving the short distance to the nursing home.

The snows from before Thanksgiving had long since gone. Today there was no snow, only the dark winter trees against a cold blue sky. She smiled, trying to forget that her mood reflected that of the day.

Christmas decorations greeted her at the door of the facility. As usual the nurses rushed to help her inside with her burden of freshly baked cookies. There was the usual flurry of activity before she went to sit with her mother. Today there seemed to be an increase of that activity. She thought people whispered behind her back. When she turned people stopped speaking.

"Has anything happened to my mother?" she asked the head nurse.

"Oh, no. Mrs. Alexander is the same."

"I'll go see her now." Aurora took the box of cookies

she'd reserved for her mother and started down the hall. She looked over her shoulder at the nurses. Something was wrong, she thought.

She found out what it was the moment she opened the door to her mother's room. Marsha Chambers stood up. Impeccably dressed in a winter white suit, she had a Christmas tree pin on her lapel. Aurora looked at her mother, then at the woman standing over her. All three women looked incredibly as if they'd been cast from identical molds.

"I've been waiting for you," Marsha said.

"Why?" She went to the bed tray and placed the box on it. Removing her coat she placed it over the bed and stooped in front of her mother. "Hello, Mom." As usual, her mother said nothing, did not acknowledge her presence. "I brought you some cookies. They're your favorite Christmas cookies."

"Your mother and I have been having a nice visit."

Aurora scrutinized Marsha's face. What did she want? She came here for a reason.

"You haven't told me why you're here." Aurora removed her coat and laid it on the bed.

"I know we haven't been friends." Marsha glanced at the floor, then back at Aurora. She looked nervous, and Aurora had never seen her nervous before. "It's been my fault, not yours."

Aurora said nothing. She waited for her look-alike to explain further. "I suppose Duncan told you about Charles Hagan."

"No," Aurora said. "Neither of them mentioned him."

She laughed. "I guess they wouldn't. It was my secret." She stopped, took a deep breath, and went on. She related the story of the blackmailing. "I thought he was trying to kill me because I'd refused to increase the payments I was making."

Aurora stared at her over her mother. Cass sat there, lost to them. She heard nothing, understood nothing.

"I apologize for putting your life in jeopardy. When I saw the appeal program and how well you did, I knew I'd lost my show, and I had no one to blame but myself." She laughed again. "Coop says I never blame myself so I placed it on you and came to the studio spoiling for a fight. You were the unlucky recipient."

"Is that what you came to say?"

"Not everything. Charles Hagan has been arrested and will probably spend a lot of time in jail. I'm going to have to testify against him and the press will have a field day with the story."

"What do you want me to do?"

"Be my friend. Coop says you're a wonderful person and that while everyone else believed me to be 'difficult' you were the only one giving reasons why I acted the way I did." She paused. "I know it might take some time, but I'm willing to try it. Will you help me?"

Aurora couldn't refuse. She knew about Marsha, the things that had happened to her, why she protected herself from the world. She wanted to be her friend. She'd been trained to help people. How could she refuse someone openly asking for it?

Aurora nodded and Marsha impulsively hugged her. Tears sprang to Aurora's eyes.

"Now, I want you to see something," she said. She went to the television, which wasn't a new item in her mother's room. The VCR that sat there was. Marsha turned the television on and pressed the PLAY button on the VCR. Both women took seats on opposite sides of Aurora's mother. Aurora held her mother's hand. In seconds the tape came on and she heard the music of *The Marsha Chambers Show*.

"We filmed this yesterday," Marsha whispered.

Aurora watched. The show was about Alzheimer's Disease. First Marsha interviewed people living with relatives who had the disease. Children, sisters, fathers, husbands, and spouses each told how they coped with the loved one who was no longer there. Tears gathered in

Aurora's eyes. She understood the guests' feelings. They mirrored her own.

"Turn it off," Aurora said. "I don't want to see that."

Marsha immediately stopped the tape. "I know this is hard, Aurora. I understand that you live with the same problems as the people on the tape, but I want you to see it all the way through."

"Why? What will it change? When it's done my mother will still have Alzheimer's. She still won't recognize me and I won't be able to do anything about it."

"It can change your attitude, Aurora. I hope it will make you better able to cope with your own life."

"What do you know about my life?"

"Very little," she said. "I'd like to know more, and I'd like for you to have more. Please sit down."

Aurora resumed her seat and the tape picked up where it had stopped.

Marsha went on to interview an authority on the subject. Aurora knew the facts of the disease. She understood that little by little Alzheimer's ate the brain away, stealing memories and leaving the patients unable to care for themselves.

Finally a psychologist came on, giving advice to the individuals on how they should go on with their lives. There was nothing they could do, nothing medical science could do, at this time. There was no need to take the guilt onto their shoulders, trying to make something happen, to change what they had no control over. They should live their lives. Aurora couldn't help taking her mother's hand as she watched with interest.

"You can't live your life through them," the woman on the screen said. "They wouldn't want you to give up your ambitions, your dreams, to watch them slowly die." Tears spilled down her cheeks. Aurora listened. She heard what Duncan had tried to tell her two weeks ago.

Then one of the guests asked about heredity. Fear bolted through Aurora. She felt she was a time bomb and that sooner or later the same fate that had befallen her mother would he hers.

"You can't live like that," the psychologist explained. "You have a life. It's a precious gift. You can't waste it thinking about something that might not happen."

Then Marsha went into the audience, but she didn't take questions. Turning, she asked a question of one of the guests on the stage. "Amy, you have a mother who has Alzheimer's and you have a fiancée in the audience."

Aurora recognized the researcher she'd met her first day on the show, when she was leaving and Amy mistook her for Marsha. A man next to Marsha stood up. "This is Galin North. Galin, how do you feel about the possibility that Amy might one day not remember you?"

"I love her," he said. "I think any time we have together is better than not having time." Marsha started to remove the microphone, but he continued to talk and she pushed it back toward him. "There isn't any real proof that Alzheimer's is hereditary," he went on. "I'm hoping she'll carry the memories we make into old age."

He sat down and the audience applauded. When they finished Marsha spoke again. "We have another member in our audience who feels like Galin."

Aurora drew breath in when Duncan stood up. "This is Duncan West," Marsha introduced. "His situation is similar to Galin and Amy's."

"I don't have a fiancée," he said. "I'm in love with a woman you all know. She was Marsha's replacement for a few weeks. We called her Rory. Her mother has Alzheimer's. Rory, I love you. I want to marry you, for better or worse."

Tears rolled down her face. Hot, scalding tears poured from her eyes. She couldn't hear anything else Duncan said. Marsha pushed a handkerchief into her hand and turned the machine off. Aurora cried her eyes dry. She heard Marsha leave the room.

She stood then and again stooped in front of her mother. The eyes that looked back at her were blank. While Aurora had been moved by the program, her mother viewed it as noise in the room. "I have to go, Mom. I might not come to see you for a while, but I will come." She kissed her mother. Duncan loved her and she loved him. He wanted her to marry him, and she wanted nothing more than to spend whatever time she had with him. If it was only a day, she wanted to be with him.

"I'm going to get married," she said.

Her spirit lifted as she had always wanted it to when she came here. She turned and picked up her coat. As she passed her mother she squeezed her shoulder. She hoped that touch meant something, since her words could no longer reach her.

Leaving the room she closed the door silently. She took a step, then stopped abruptly. Duncan stood a few feet from her. For a moment she couldn't talk. He said nothing. She went numb. She'd just seen him on the screen in miniature. Life-size, he scared her. She hadn't prepared what she intended to say. Had he meant what he'd said on camera?

"Say something." she said.

"Marry me."

Aurora's feet found movement and she flew down the hall. Duncan's waiting arms closed around her, squeezed her, lifted her off the floor. She kissed him hard, clinging to him, planting kisses on his mouth, over his face, his eyes, his chin, then back to his mouth. She was holding on. Nothing would take her away. Nothing would keep them apart. From now until the end she was his, and he was hers.

"I require an answer," he said, setting her on the floor.

"I'll marry you, Duncan."

"And California?"

"California." She smiled and nodded.

She kissed him again. This time softly, rubbing her lips over his. He held her tenderly, caressing her like a rare gem. Then she put her whole heart into it. When she pulled back she lay her head on his shoulder. He held her for a precious moment. She leaned back and looked at him.

"California or anywhere," she whispered, and kissed him with a force so soft and loving it told him their love could not be limited by time and circumstance.

Dear Reader,

Characters are the elements of reading that we remember most. We love the people. As a writer I, too, fall in love with the people. Aurora and Duncan work in the exciting and fast-paced world of television. Like all television programs most of the work goes on behind the scenes. What we see on the screen may only be a *Mirror Image* of what really happens. Their lives and the culmination of the love between Duncan and Aurora had me crying the same hot, scalding tears as Aurora did over her mother.

Mrs. Alexander also touched my heart, along with the information I learned about Alzheimer's Disease and its victims. Not only does the patient suffer, but the families, also. Now that you've completed this novel, I suggest you take Duncan West's advice and call your parent or loved one just to say "I love you."

I receive many letters from the women and men who read my books. Thank you for your generous comments and words of encouragement. I love reading your letters as much as I enjoy writing the books.

If you'd like to hear more about *Mirror Image,* other books I've written, or upcoming releases, send a business size, self-addressed, stamped envelope to me at the following address:

Shirley Hailstock
P.O. Box 513
Plainsboro, NJ 08536

Sincerely yours,

Shirley Hailstock
Shirley Hailstock

ABOUT THE AUTHOR

Shirley Hailstock, a short-story writer and award winning novelist, has been writing for more than ten years. Holding a bachelor's degree in Chemistry from Howard University and an MBA in Chemical Marketing from Fairleigh Dickinson University, she works for a pharmaceutical company as a systems manager. She is a past President of the New Jersey Romance Writers and is a member of Women Writers of Color and the International Women's Writers Guild among others. She lives in New Jersey with her family.

COMING IN JULY ...

HEAVEN SENT   (0-7860-0530-0, $4.99/$6.50)
by Rochelle Alers
When Serena Morris-Vega returned to Costa Rica, corporate CEO David Cole showed up on the Vega estate, close to death. Serena soon discovers secrets about his true identity. David's gratitude towards Serena for saving his life turns into an all-consuming passion, and Serena finds him to be a dangerously seductive challenge.

LYRICS OF LOVE   (0-7860-0531-9, $4.99/$6.50)
by Francine Craft
Gina Campbell was a famous singer married to police officer Joe Dauterive. When her brother turns up dead and Joe's name was ruined by the scandal, he asked for a divorce. Gina runs off to Lyric, her Pacific island hideaway ... and when Joe followed her, he was set on rekindling their love and determined that nothing would keep them apart.

HEART'S DESIRE   (0-7860-0532-7, $4.99/$6.50)
by Monica Jackson
Kara Kincaid has discovered that Senator Eastman is her father and that he abandoned her and her mother years ago to pursue his political ambitions. Now she wants revenge. Using everything in her power to get to the senator, she targets his right hand man, Brent Stevens. Their attraction to each other is sure to make a mess of her plans. It is not long before her scheme leads them both into a dangerous game and an uncontrollable passion.

EVERLASTING LOVE   (0-7860-0533-5, $4.99/$6.50)
by Kayla Perrin
Two years ago, Whitney Jordan ran away from her husband, Javar, when a freak accident took the life of her small stepson. Guilt-ridden, she was returning to end the marriage when another accident leaves her in the hospital. When she finds Javar at her side they rekindle their love. Together, they fight to save their marriage ... and Whitney's life from danger.

Available wherever paperbacks are sold, or order direct from the Publisher. Send cover price plus 50¢ per copy for mailing and handling to Kensington Publishing Corp., Consumer Orders, or call (toll free) 888-345-BOOK, to place your order using Mastercard or Visa. Residents of New York and Tennessee must include sales tax. DO NOT SEND CASH.

LOOK FOR THESE ARABESQUE ROMANCES

ENJOY THESE ARABESQUE FAVORITES!

FOREVER AFTER   (0-7860-0211-5, $4.99)
by Bette Ford

BODY AND SOUL   (0-7860-0160-7, $4.99)
by Felicia Mason

BETWEEN THE LINES   (0-7860-0267-0, $4.99)
by Angela Benson